D0250860

THE
WORLD'S
ONE HUNDRED
BEST SHORT STORIES

VOLUME SEVEN
WOMEN

THE
WORLD'S
ONE HUNDRED
BEST SHORT STORIES

[IN TEN VOLUMES]

GRANT OVERTON
EDITOR - IN - CHIEF

VOLUME SEVEN
WOMEN

FUNK & WAGNALLS COMPANY
NEW YORK AND LONDON

CONTENTS

THE WORLD'S 100 BEST SHORT STORIES

SHE WALKS IN BEAUTY

By Fannie Hurst

By the same mausolean instinct that was Artimesia's when she mourned her dear departed in marble and hieroglyphics; by that same architectural gesture of grief which caused Jehan at Agra to erect the Taj Mahal in memory of a dead wife and a cold hearth-stone, so the Bon Ton Hotel, even to the pillars with red-freckled monoliths and peacock-backed lobby chairs, making the analogy rather absurdly complete, reared its fourteen stories of "Elegantly furnished suites, all the comforts and none of the discomforts of home."

A mausoleum to the hearth. And as true to form as any that ever mourned the dynastic bones of an Augustus or a Hadrian.

It is doubtful if in all its hothouse garden of women the Hotel Bon Ton boasted a broken finger-nail or that little brash place along the forefinger that tattles so of potato peeling or asparagus scraping.

The fourteenth story, Manicure, Steam-bath, and Beauty Parlors, saw to all that. In spite of long, bridge-table, lobby-divan and *table d'hote* séances, "tea" where the coffee was served with whipped cream and the tarts built in four tiers and mortared in mocha filling, the Bon Ton Hotel was scarcely more than an average of fourteen pounds over-weight.

Forty's silhouette, except for that cruel and ir-refutable place where the throat will wattle, was al-most interchangeable with eighteen's. Indeed, Bon Ton grandmothers with backs and French heels that were twenty years younger than their throats and bunions, vied with twenty's profile.

Whistler's kind of mother, full of sweet years that were richer because she had dwelt in them, but whose eyelids were a little weary, had no place there.

Mrs. Gronauer, who occupied an outside, southern-exposure suite of five rooms and three baths, jazz-danced on the same cabaret floor with her grand-daughters.

Fads for the latest personal accouterments gripped the Bon Ton in seasonal epidemics.

The permanent wave swept it like a tidal one.

The beaded bag, cunningly contrived, needleful by needleful, from little colored strands of grass caviar, glittered its hour.

Filet lace came then, sheerly, whole yokes of it for *crepe de chine* nightgowns and dainty scalloped edges for camisoles.

Mrs. Samstag made six of the nightgowns that win-ter, three for herself and three for her daughter. Peach-blowy pink ones with lace yokes that were scarcely more to the skin than the print of a wave edge running up sand, and then little frills of pink satin ribbon, caught up here and there with the most de-lightful and unconvincing little blue satin rosebuds.

It was bad for her neuralgic eye, the meanderings
of the *filet* pattern, but she liked the delicate threadi-
ness of the handiwork, and Mr. Latz liked watching
her.

There you have it! Straight through the lacy mesh
of the *filet* to the heart interest!

Mr. Louis Latz, who was too short, slightly too
stout, and too shy of likely length of swimming arm
ever to have figured in any woman's inevitable visualization of her ultimate Leander, liked, fascinatedly, to
watch Mrs. Samstag's nicely manicured fingers at
work. He liked them passive, too. Best of all, he
would have preferred to feel them between his own,
but that had never been.

Nevertheless, that desire was capable of catching
him unawares. That very morning as he had stood, in
his sumptuous bachelor's apartment, strumming on one
of the windows that overlooked an expensive tree and
lake vista of Central Park, he had wanted very suddenly and very badly to feel those fingers in his and to
kiss down on them. He liked their taper and the rosy
pointedness, those fingers, and the dry, neat way they
had of slipping in between the threads.

On this, one of a hundred such typical evenings in
the Bon Ton lobby, Mr. Latz, sighing out a satisfaction of his inner man, sat himself down on a red velvet chair opposite Mrs. Samstag. His knees wide-
spread, taxed his knife-pressed gray trousers to their
very last capacity, but he sat back in none the less evident comfort, building his fingers up into a little
chapel.

"Well, how's Mr. Latz this evening?" asked Mrs.
Samstag, her smile encompassing the question.

"If I was any better I couldn't stand it"—relishing her smile and his reply.

The Bon Ton had just dined, too well, from fruit-flip *à la* Bon Ton, mulligatawny soup, *filet* of sole, *sauté*, choice of, or both, Polette *émincé* and spring lamb *grignon* and on through to fresh strawberry ice-cream in fluted paper boxes, *petit fours* and *demi-tasse*. Groups of carefully corseted women stood now beside the invitational plush divans and peacock chairs, paying twenty minutes after-dinner standing penance. Men with Wall Street eyes and blood pressure, slid surreptitious celluloid toothpicks, and gathered around the cigar stand. Orchestra music flickered. Young girls, the traditions of demure sixteen hanging by one inch shoulder-straps and who could not walk across a hardwood floor without sliding the last three steps, teetered in bare arm-in-arm groups, swapping persiflage with pimply, patent-leather haired young men who were full of nervous excitement and eager to excel in return badinage.

Bell hops scurried with folding tables. Bridge games formed.

The theater group got off, so to speak. Showy women and show-off men. Mrs. Gronauer, in a full length mink coat that enveloped her like a squaw, a titillation of diamond aigrettes in her Titianed hair and an aftermath of scent as tangible as the trail of a wounded shark, emerged from the elevator with her son and daughter-in-law.

"Foi!" said Mr. Latz, by way of—somewhat unduly perhaps—expressing his own kind of cognizance of the scented trail.

"Fleur de printemps," said Mrs. Samstag in quick olfactory analysis. "Eight ninety-eight an ounce." Her

nose crawling up to what he thought the cunning perfection of a sniff.

"Used to it from home—not? She is not. Believe
me, I knew Max Gronauer when he first started in the
produce business in Jersey City and the only perfume
he had was seventeen cents a pound, not always fresh
killed at that. Cold storage *de printemps*."

"Max Gronauer died just two months after my husband," said Mrs. Samstag, tucking away into her
beaded hand-bag her *filet* lace handkerchief, itself
guilty of a not inexpensive attar.

"Thu-thu," clucked Mr. Latz for want of a fitting
retort.

"Heigh-ho! I always say we have so little in common, me and Mrs. Gronauer. She revokes so in
bridge, and I think it's terrible for a grandmother to
blondine so red; but we've both been widows for almost eight years. Eight years," repeated Mrs. Samstag on a small accented sigh.

He was inordinately sensitive to these allusions, red-
dening and wanting to seem appropriate.

"Poor, poor little woman!"

"Heigh-ho," she said, and again, "Heigh-ho."

It was about the eyes that Mrs. Samstag showed
most plainly whatever inroads into her clay the years
might have gained. There were little dark areas beneath them like smeared charcoal and two unrelenting
sacs that threatened to become pouchy.

Their effect was not so much of years, but they
gave Mrs. Samstag, in spite of the only slightly plump
and really passable figure, the look of one out of
health.

What ailed her was hardly organic. She was the
victim of periodic and raging neuralgic fires that could

sweep the right side of her head and down into her
shoulder blade with a great crackling and blazing of
nerves. It was not unusual for her daughter Alma to
sit up the one or two nights that it could endure, un-
failing, through the wee hours, with hot applications.

For a week sometimes, these attacks heralded their
comings with little jabs, like the pricks of an explor-
ing needle. Then the under-eyes began to look their
muddiest. They were darkening now and she put up
two fingers with a little pressing movement to her
temple.

"You're a great little woman," reiterated Mr. Latz,
rather riveting even Mrs. Samstag's suspicion that
here was no great stickler for variety of expression.

"And a great sufferer, too," he said, noting the pressing fingers.

She colored under this delightful impeachment.

"I wouldn't wish any of my neuralgia spells to my
worst enemy, Mr. Latz."

"If you were mine—I mean—if—the—say—was
mine, I wouldn't stop until I had you to every specialist in Europe. I know a thing or two about those
fellows over there. Some of them are wonders."

Mrs. Samstag looked off, her profile inclined to lift
and fall as if by little pulleys of emotion.

"That's easier said than done, Mr. Latz, by a—a
widow who wants to do right by her grown daughter
and living so—high since the war."

"I—I—" said Mr. Latz, leaping impulsively forward
on the chair that was as tightly upholstered in effect
as he in his modish suit, then clutching himself there
as if he had caught the impulse on the fly—"I just
wish I could help."

"Oh!" she said, and threw up a swift, brown look from the lace making.

He laughed, but from nervousness.

"My little mother was an ailer too."

"That's me, Mr. Latz. Not sick—just ailing. I always say that it's ridiculous that a woman in such perfect health as I am should be such a sufferer."

"Same with her and her joints."

"Why, I can outdo Alma when it comes to dancing down in the grill with the young people of an evening, or shopping."

"More like sisters than any mother and daughter I ever saw."

"Mother and daughter, but which is which from the back, some of my friends put it," said Mrs. Samstag, not without a curve to her voice, then hastily: "but the best child, Mr. Latz. The best that ever lived. A regular little mother to me in my spells."

"Nice girl, Alma."

"It snowed so the day of—my husband's funeral. Why, do you know that up to then I never had an attack of neuralgia in my life. Didn't even know what a headache was. That long drive. That windy hilltop with two men to keep me from jumping into the grave after him. Ask Alma. That's how I care when I care. But of course, as the saying is, time heals. But that's how I got my first attack. Intenseness is what the doctors called it. I'm terribly intense."

"I—guess when a woman like you—cares like—you—cared, it's not much use hoping you would ever—care again. That's about the way of it, ain't it?"

If he had known it, there was something about his own intensity of expression to inspire mirth. His eyebrows lifted to little gothic arches of anxiety, rash of tiny perspiration broke out over his blue shaved face and as he sat on the edge of his chair, it seemed that inevitably the tight sausage-like knees must push their way through mere fabric.

"That's about the way of it, ain't it?" he said again into the growing silence.

"I—when a women cares for—a man like—I did— Mr. Latz, she'll never be happy until—she cares again—like that. I always say, once an affectionate nature, always an affectionate nature."

"You mean," he said, leaning forward the imperceptible half-inch that was left of chair, "you mean—me?"

The smell of bay rum came out greenly then as the moisture sprang out on his scalp.

"I—I'm a home woman, Mr. Latz. You can put a fish in water but you cannot make him swim. That's me and hotel life."

At this somewhat cryptic apothegm Mr. Latz's knee touched Mrs. Samstag's, so that he sprang back full of nerves at what he had not intended.

"Marry me, Carrie," he said more abruptly than he might have, without the act of that knee to immediately justify.

She spread the lace out on her lap.

Ostensibly to the hotel lobby, they were casual as, "My mulligatawny soup was cold tonight" or "Have you heard the new one that Al Jolson pulls at the Winter Garden?" But actually, the roar was high in Mrs. Samstag's ears and he could feel the plethoric red rushing in flashes over his body.

"Marry me, Carrie," he said, as if to prove that his stiff lips could repeat their incredible feat.

With a woman's talent for them, her tears sprang.

"Mr. Latz——"

"Louis," he interpolated, widely eloquent of posture.

"You're proposing—Louis!" She explained rather than asked, and placed her hand to her heart so prettily that he wanted to crush it there with his kisses.

"God bless you for knowing it so easy, Carrie. A young girl would make it so hard. It's just what has kept me from asking you weeks ago, this getting it said. Carrie, will you?"

"I'm a widow, Mr. Latz—Louis——"

"Loo——"

"L—Loo. With a grown daughter. Not one of those merry widows you read about."

"That's me! A bachelor on top but a home-man underneath. Why, up to five years ago, Carrie, while the best little mother a man ever had was alive, I never had eyes for a woman or——"

"It's common talk what a grand son you were to her, Mr. La—Louis——"

"Loo!"

"Loo."

"I don't want to seem to brag, Carrie, but you saw the coat that just walked out on Mrs. Gronauer? My little mother, she was a humpback, Carrie, not a real one, but all stooped from the heavy years when she was helping my father to get his start. Well, anyway, that little stooped back was one of the reasons why I was so anxious to make it up to her. Y'understand?"

"Yes—Loo."

"But you saw that mink coat? Well, my little mother, three years before she died, was wearing one like that in sable. Real Russian. Set me back eighteen thousand. wholesale, and she never knew different than it cost eighteen hundred. Proudest moment of my life when I helped my little old mother into her own automobile in that sable coat."

"I had some friends lived in the Grenoble Apartments when you did—the Adelbergs. They used to tell me how it hung right down to her heels and she never got into the auto that she didn't pick it up so as not to sit on it."

"That there coat is packed away in cold storage, now, Carrie, waiting, without me exactly knowing why, I guess, for—the one little woman in the world besides her I would let so much as touch its hem."

Mrs. Samstag's lips parted, her teeth showing through like light.

"Oh," she said, "sable. That's my fur, Loo. I've never owned any, but ask Alma if I don't stop to look at it in every show window. Sable!"

"Carrie—would you—could you—I'm not what you would call a youngster in years, I guess, but forty-four ain't——"

"I'm—forty-one, Louis. A man like you could have younger."

"No. That's what I don't want. In my lonesomeness, after my mother's death, I thought once that maybe a young girl from the West, nice girl with her mother from Ohio—but I—funny thing, now I come to think about it—I never once mentioned my little mother's sable coat to her. I couldn't have satisfied a young girl like that or her me, Carrie any more than I could satisfy Alma. It was one of those mama-made matches that we got into because we couldn't help it and out of it before it was too late. No, no, Carrie, what I want is a woman near to my own age."

"Loo, I—I couldn't start in with you even with the

one little lie that gives every woman a right to be a liar. I'm forty-three, Louis—nearer to forty-four. You're not mad, Loo?"

"God love it! If that ain't a little woman for you! Mad? Just doing that little thing with me raises your stock fifty per cent."

"I'm—that way."

"We're a lot alike, Carrie. At heart, I'm a home man, Carrie, and unless I'm pretty much off my guess, you are, too—I mean a home woman. Right?"

"Me all over, Loo. Ask Alma if——"

"I've got the means, too, Carrie, to give a woman a home to be proud of."

"Just for fun, ask Alma, Loo, if one year since her father's death I haven't said, 'Alma, I wish I had the heart to go back housekeeping.'"

"I knew it!"

"But I ask you, Louis, what's been the incentive? Without a man in the house I wouldn't have the same interest. That first winter after my husband died I didn't even have the heart to take the summer-covers off the furniture. You can believe me or not, but half the time with just me to eat it, I wouldn't bother with more than a cold snack for supper and every one knew what a table we used to set. But with no one to come home evenings expecting a hot meal——"

"You poor little woman. I know how it is. Why, if I used to so much as telephone that I couldn't get home for supper right away I knew my little mother would turn out the gas under what was cooking and not eat enough herself to keep a bird alive."

"Housekeeping is no life for a woman alone. On the other hand, Mr. Latz—Louis—Loo, on my income, and with a daughter growing up, and naturally anxious to give her the best, it hasn't been so easy. People think I'm a rich widow and with her father's memory to consider and a young lady daughter, naturally I let them think it, but on my seventy-four hundred a year it has been hard to keep up appearances in a hotel like this. Not that I think you think I'm a rich widow, but just the same, that's me every time. Right out with the truth from the start."

"It shows you're a clever little manager to be able to do it."

"We lived big and spent big while my husband lived. He was as shrewd a jobber in knit underwear as the business ever saw, but—well, you know how it is. Pneumonia. I always say he wore himself out with conscientiousness."

"Maybe you don't believe it, Carrie, but it makes me happy what you just said about money. It means I can give you things you couldn't afford for yourself. I don't say this for publication, Carrie, but in Wall Street alone, outside of my brokerage business, I cleared eighty-six thousand last year. I can give you the best. You deserve it, Carrie. Will you say yes?"

"My daughter, Loo. She's only eighteen, but she's my shadow—I lean on her so."

"A sweet, dutiful girl like Alma would be the last to stand in her mother's light."

"She's my only. We're different natured. Alma's a Samstag through and through, quiet, reserved. But she's my all, Louis. I love my baby too much to—to marry where she wouldn't be as welcome as the day itself. She's precious to me, Louis."

"Why, of course. You wouldn't be you if she wasn't. You think I would want you to feel different?"

"I mean—Louis—no matter where I go, more than with most children, she's part of me, Loo. I—why that child won't so much as go to spend the night with a girl friend away from me. Her quiet ways don't show it, but Alma has character! You wouldn't believe it, Louis, how she takes care of me."

"Why, Carrie, the first thing we pick out in our new home will be a room for her."

"Loo!"

"Not that she will want it long the way I see that young rascal Friedlander sits up to her. A better young fellow and a better business head you couldn't pick for her. Didn't that youngster go out to Dayton the other day and land a contract for the surgical fittings for a big new hospital out there before the local firms even rubbed the sleep out of their eyes? I have it from good authority, Friedlander & Sons doubled their excess-profits tax last year."

A white flash of something that was almost fear seemed to strike Mrs. Samstag into a rigid pallor.

"No! No! I'm not like most mothers, Louis, for marrying their daughters off. I want her with me. If marrying her off is your idea, it's best you know it now in the beginning. I want my little girl with me— I have to have my little girl with me!"

He was so deeply moved that his eyes were moist.

"Why, Carrie, every time you open your mouth, you only prove to me what a grand little woman you are."

"You'll like Alma, when you get to know her, Louis."

"Why, I do now. Always have said she's a sweet little thing."

"She is quiet and hard to get acquainted with at

first, but that is reserve. She's not forward like most young girls nowadays. She's the kind of a child that would rather sit upstairs evenings with a book or her sewing than here in the lobby. She's there now."

"Give me that kind every time, in preference to all these gay young chickens that know more they oughtn't to know about life before they start than my little mother did when she finished."

"But do you think that girl will go to bed before I come up? Not a bit of it. She's been my comforter and my salvation in my troubles. More like the mother, I sometimes tell her, and me the child. If you want me, Louis, it's got to be with her too. I couldn't give up my baby—not my baby."

"Why, Carrie, have your baby to your heart's content. She's got to be a fine girl to have you for a mother and now it will be my duty to please her as a father. Carrie will you have me?"

"Oh, Louis—Loo!"

"Carrie, my dear!"

And so it was that Carrie Samstag and Louis Latz came into their betrothal.

None the less, it was with some misgivings and red lights burning high on her cheek-bones that Mrs. Samstag, at just after ten that evening, turned the knob of the door that entered into her little sitting-room, but in this case, a room redeemed by an upright piano with a green silk and gold-lace shaded floor lamp glowing by it. Two gilt-framed photographs and a cluster of ivory knickknacks on the white mantel. A heap of hand-made cushions. Art editions of the gift-poets and some circulating library novels. A fireside chair, privately owned and drawn up, ironically enough, be side the gilded radiator, its head rest worn from kindly service to Mrs. Samstag's neuralgic brow.

From the nest of cushions in the circle of lamp glow, Alma sprang up at her mother's entrance. Sure enough she had been reading and her cheek was a little flushed and crumpled from where it had been resting in the palm of her hand.

"Mama," she said, coming out of the circle of light and switching on the ceiling bulbs, "you stayed down so late."

There was a slow prettiness to Alma. It came upon you like a little dawn, palely at first and then pinkening to a pleasant consciousness that her small face was heartshaped and clear as an almond, that the pupils of her gray eyes were deep and dark like cisterns and to young Leo Friedlander, rather apt his comparison, too, her mouth was exactly the shape of a small bow that had shot its quiverful of arrows into his heart.

And instead of her eighteen she looked sixteen. There was that kind of timid adolescence about her, yet when she said, "Mama, you stayed down so late," the bang of a little pistol-shot was back somewhere in her voice.

"Why—Mr. Latz—and I—sat and talked."

An almost imperceptible nerve was dancing against Mrs. Samstag's right temple. Alma could sense, rather than see the ridge of pain.

"You're all right, mama?"

"Yes," said Mrs. Samstag, and plumped rather than sat herself down on a divan, its naked greenness relieved by a thrown scarf of black velvet, stenciled in gold.

"You shouldn't have remained down so long if your

head is hurting," said her daughter, and quite casually took up her mother's beaded hand-bag where it had fallen in her lap, but her fingers feeling lightly and furtively as if for the shape of its contents.

"Stop that," said Mrs. Samstag, jerking it back, a dull anger in her voice.

"Come to bed, mama. If you're in for neuralgia, I'll fix the electric pad."

Suddenly Mrs. Samstag shot out her arm, rather slim looking in the invariable long sleeve she affected, drawing Alma back toward her by the ribbon sash of her pretty chiffon frock.

"Alma, be good to mama tonight! Sweetheart— be good to her."

The quick suspecting fear that had motivated Miss Samstag's groping along the beaded hand-bag shot out again in her manner.

"Mama—you haven't?"

"No, no. Don't nag me. It's something else, Alma. Something mama is very happy about."

"Mama, you've broken your promise again."

"No. No. No. Alma, I've been a good mother to you, haven't I?"

"Yes, mama, yes, but what——"

"Whatever else I've been hasn't been my fault— you've always blamed Heyman."

"Mama, I don't understand."

"I've caused you worry, Alma—terrible worry. But everything is changed now. Mama's going to turn over a new leaf that everything is going to be happiness in this family."

"Dearest, if you knew how happy it makes me to hear you say that."

"Alma, look at me."

"Mama, you—you frighten me."

"You like Louis Latz, don't you, Alma?"

"Why yes, mama. Very much."

"We can't all be young and handsome like Leo, can we?"

"You mean——"

"I mean that finer and better men than Louis Latz aren't lying around loose. A man who treated his mother like a queen and who worked himself up from selling newspapers on the street to a millionaire."

"Mama?"

"Yes, baby. He asked me tonight. Come to me, Alma, stay with me close. He asked me tonight."

"What?"

"You know. Haven't you seen it coming for weeks? I have."

"Seen what?"

"Don't make mama come out and say it. For eight years I've been as grieving a widow to a man as a woman could be. But I'm human, Alma, and he—asked me tonight."

There was a curious pallor came over Miss Samstag's face, as if smeared there by a hand.

"Asked you what?"

"Alma, it don't mean I'm not true to your father as I was the day I buried him in that blizzard back there, but could you ask for a finer, steadier man than Louis Latz? It looks out of his face."

"Mama, you—what—are you saying?"

"Alma?"

There lay a silence between them that took on the roar of a simoon and Miss Samstag jumped then from her mother's embrace, her little face stiff with the clench of her mouth.

"Mama—you—no—no. Oh, mama— Oh——"

A quick spot of hysteria seemed to half strangle Mrs. Samstag, so that she slanted backward, holding her throat.

"I knew it. My own child against me. Oh, God! Why was I born? My own child against me!"

"Mama—you can't marry him. You can't marry—anybody."

"Why can't I marry anybody? Must I be afraid to tell my own child when a good man wants to marry me and give us both a good home? That's my thanks for making my child my first consideration—before I accepted him."

"Mama, you didn't accept him. Darling, you wouldn't do a—thing like that!"

Miss Samstag's voice thickened up then, quite frantically, into a little scream that knotted in her throat and she was suddenly so small and stricken, that with a gasp for fear she might crumple up where she stood, Mrs. Stamstag leaned forward, catching her again by the sash.

"Alma!"

It was only for an instant, however. Suddenly Miss Samstag was her coolly firm little self, the bang of authority back in her voice.

"You can't marry Louis Latz."

"Can't I? Watch me."

"You can't do that to a nice, deserving fellow like him!"

"Do what?"

"That!"

Then Mrs. Samstag threw up both her hands to her face, rocking in an agony of self-abandon that was rather horrid to behold.

"Oh, God, why don't you put me out of it all? My misery! I'm a leper to my own child!"

"Oh—mama——"

"Yes, a leper. Hold my misfortune against me. Let my neuralgia and Doctor Heyman's prescription to cure it ruin my life. Rob me of what happiness with a good man there is left in it for me. I don't want happiness. Don't expect it. I'm just here to suffer.

"My daughter will see to that. Oh, I know what is on your mind. You want to make me out something—terrible—because Dr. Heyman once taught me how to help myself a little when I'm nearly wild with neuralgia. Those were doctor's orders. I'll kill myself before I let you make me out something terrible. I never even knew what it was before the doctor gave his prescription. I'll kill—you hear—kill myself."

She was hoarse, she was tear splotched so that her lips were slippery with them, and while the ague of her passion shook her, Alma, her own face swept white and her voice guttered with restraint, took her mother into the cradle of her arms, and rocked and hushed her there.

"Mama, mama, what are you saying? I'm not blaming you, sweetheart. I blame him—Dr. Heyman—for prescribing it in the beginning. I know your fight. How brave it is. Even when I'm crossest with you, I realize. Alma's fighting with you, dearest, every inch of the way until—you're cured! And then——maybe—some day—anything you want! But not now. Mama, you wouldn't marry Louis Latz now!"

"I would. He's my cure. A good home with a good man and money enough to travel and forget myself. Alma, mama knows she's not an angel—sometimes when she thinks what she's put her little girl through this last year, she just wants to go out on the hill-top where she caught the neuralgia and lay down beside the grave out there and——"

"Mama, don't talk like that!"

"But now's my chance, Alma, to get well. I've too much worry in this big hotel trying to keep up big expenses on little money and——"

"I know it, mama. That's why I'm so in favor of finding ourselves a sweet, tiny little apartment with kitch——"

"No! Your father died with the world thinking him a rich man and it will never find out from me that he wasn't. I won't be the one to humiliate his memory—a man who enjoyed keeping up appearances the way he did. Oh, Alma, Alma, I'm going to get well now. I promise. So help me God, if I ever give in to—to it again."

"Mama, please. For God's sake, you've said the same thing so often only to break your promise."

"I've been weak, Alma; I don't deny it. But nobody who hasn't been tortured as I have, can realize what it means to get relief just by——"

"Mama, you're not playing fair this minute. That's the frightening part. It isn't only the neuralgia any more. It's just desire. That's what's so terrible to me, mama. The way you have been taking it these last months. Just from—desire."

Mrs. Samstag buried her face, shuddering down into her hands.

"Oh, God, my own child against me!"

"No, mama. Why, sweetheart, nobody knows better than I do how sweet and good you are when you are away—from it. We'll fight it together and win! I'm not afraid. It's been worse this last month because you've been nervous, dear. I understand now. You see, I—didn't dream of you and—Louis Latz. We'll forget—we'll take a little two room apartment of our own, darling, and get your mind on housekeeping and I'll take up stenography or social ser——"

"What good am I anyway? No good. In my own way. In my child's way. A young man like Leo Friedlander crazy to propose and my child can't let him come to the point because she is afraid to leave her mother. Oh, I know—I know more than you think I do. Ruining your life! That's what I am, and mine too!"

Tears now ran in hot cascades down Alma's cheeks.

"Why, mama, as if I cared about anything—just so you—get well."

"I know what I've done. Ruined my baby's life and now——"

"No!"

"Then help me, Alma. Louis wants me for his happiness. I want him for mine. Nothing will cure me like having a good man to live up to. The minute I find myself getting the craving for—it—don't you see, baby, fear that a good husband like Louis could find out such a thing about me would hold me back. See, Alma?"

"That's a wrong basis to start married life on——"

"I'm a woman who needs a man to baby her, Alma. That's the cure for me. Not to let me would be the same as to kill me. I've been a bad, weak woman, Alma, to be so afraid that maybe Leo Friedlander would steal you away from me. We'll make it a double wedding, baby!"

"Mama, mama, I'll never leave you."

"All right then, so you won't think your new father

and me want to get rid of you. The first thing we'll
pick out in our new home, he said it himself tonight,
is Alma's room."

"I tell you it's wrong. It's wrong!"

"The rest with Leo come later, after I've proved to
you for a little while that I'm cured. Alma, don't cry!
It's my cure. Just think, a good man. A beautiful
home to take my mind off—worry. He said tonight
he wants to spend a fortune if necessary to cure—my
neuralgia."

"Oh, mama, mama, if it were only—that!"

"Alma, if I promise on my—my life! I never felt
the craving so little as I do—now."

"You've said that before—and before."

"But never, with such a wonderful reason. It's the
beginning of a new life. I know it. I'm cured."

"Mama, if I thought you meant it."

"I do. Alma, look at me. This very minute I've a
real jumping case of neuralgia. But I wouldn't have
anything for it except the electric pad. I feel fine.
Strong! Alma, the bad times with me are over."

"Oh, mama, mama, how I pray you're right."

"You'll thank God for the day that Louis Latz proposed to me. Why, I'd rather cut off my right hand
than marry a man who could ever live to learn such
a—thing about me."

"But it's not fair. We'll have to explain to him,
dear, that we hope you're cured now, but——"

"If you do—if you do—I'll kill myself! I won't
live to bear that! You don't want me cured. You
want to get rid of me, to degrade me until I kill myself! If I was ever anything else than what I am
now—to Louis Latz—anything but his ideal—Alma,
you won't tell! Kill me, but don't tell—don't tell!"

"Why, you know I wouldn't, sweetheart, if it is so terrible to you. Never."

"Say it again."

"Never."

"As if it hasn't been terrible enough that you should have to know. But it's over, Alma. Your bad times with me are finished. I'm cured."

"But wait a little while, mama, just a year."

"No. No."

"A few months."

"Now. He wants it soon. The sooner the better at our age. Alma, mama's cured! What happiness. Kiss me, darling. So help me God, to keep my promises to you. Cured, Alma, cured."

And so in the end, with a smile on her lips that belied almost to herself the little run of fear through her heart, Alma's last kiss to her mother that night was the long one of felicitation.

And because love, even the talk of it, is so gamey on the lips of woman to woman, they lay in bed that night heart-beat to heart-beat, the electric pad under her pillow warm to the hurt of Mrs. Samstag's brow and talked, these two, deep into the stillness of the hotel night.

"My little baby, who's helped me through such bad times, it's your turn now, Alma, to be care-free, like other girls."

"I'll never leave you mama, even if—he shouldn't want me."

"He will, darling, and does! Those were his words. A room for Alma.' "

"I'll never leave you!"

"You will! Much as Louis and me want you with us every minute, we won't stand in your way! That's another reason I'm so happy, Alma. I'm not alone, any more now. Leo's so crazy over you, just waiting for the chance to—pop——"

"Shh-sh-h-h."

"Don't tremble so, darling. Mama knows. He told Mrs. Gronauer last night when she was joking him to buy a ten dollar carnation for the Convalescent Home Bazaar, that he would only take one if it was white, because little white flowers reminded him of Alma Samstag."

"Oh, mama——"

"Say, it is as plain as the nose on your face. He can't keep his eyes off you. He sells goods to Doctor Gronauer's clinic and he says the same thing about him. It makes me so happy, Alma, to think you won't have to hold him off any more."

"I'll never leave you. Never!"

None the less she was the first to drop off to sleep, pink, there in the dark, with the secret of her blushes.

Then for Mrs. Samstag the travail set in. Lying there with her raging head tossing this way and that on the heated pillow, she heard with cruel awareness, the *minutiæ*, all the faint but clarified noises that can make a night seem so long. The distant click of the elevator, depositing a night-hawk. A plong of the bed spring. Somebody's cough. A train's shriek. The jerk of plumbing. A window being raised. That creak which lies hidden in every darkness, like a mysterious knee-joint. By three o'clock she was a quivering victim to these petty concepts, and her pillow so explored that not a spot but what was rumpled to the aching lay of her cheek.

Once Alma, as a rule supersensitive to her mother's slightest unrest, floated up for the moment out of her

young sleep, but she was very drowsy and very tired
and dream-ides were almost carrying her back, as she
said.

"Mama, are you all right?"

Simulating sleep, Mrs. Samstag lay tense until her
daughter's breathing resumed its light cadence.

Then at four o'clock, the kind of nervousness that
Mrs. Samstag had learned to fear, began to roll over
her in waves, locking her throat and curling her toes
and her fingers, and her tongue up dry against the
roof of her mouth.

She must concentrate now—must steer her mind
away from the craving!

Now then: West End Avenue. Louis liked the
apartments there. Luxurious. Quiet. Residential.
Circassian walnut or mahogany dining room? Alma
should decide. A baby-grand piano. Later to be
Alma's engagement gift from, "Mama and—Papa."
No, "Mama and Louis." Better so.

How her neck and her shoulder-blade, and now her
elbow, were flaming with the pain! She cried a little, far back in her throat with the small hissing noise
of a steam-radiator, and tried a poor futile scheme for
easing her head in the crotch of her elbow.

Now then: She must knit Louis some neckties.
The silk-sweater-stitch would do. Married in a traveling suit. One of those smart dark-blue twills like
Mrs. Gronauer Junior's. Top-coat—sable. Louis'
hair thinning. Tonic. Oh God, let me sleep. Please,
God. The wheeze rising in her closed throat. That
little threatening desire that must not shape itself!
It darted with the hither and thither of a bee bumbling
against a garden wall. No. No. Ugh! The vast

chills of nervousness. The flaming, the craving chills of desire!

Just this last giving-in. This once. To be rested and fresh for him tomorrow. Then never again. The little beaded handbag. Oh God, help me. That burning ache to rest and to uncurl of nervousness. All the thousand, thousand little pores of her body, screaming each one, to be placated. They hurt the entire surface of her. That great storm at sea in her head; the crackle of lightning down that arm——

Let me see—Circassian walnut—baby-grand—the pores demanding, crying—shrieking——

It was then that Carrie Samstag, even in her lovely pink night-dress, a crone with pain, and the cables out dreadfully in her neck, began by infinitesimal processes to swing herself gently to the side of the bed, unrelaxed inch by unrelaxed inch, softly and with the cunning born of travail.

It was actually a matter of fifteen minutes, that breathless swing toward the floor, the mattress rising after her with scarcely a whisper of its stuffings and her two bare feet landing patly into the pale blue room-slippers, there beside the bed.

Then her bag, the beaded one on the end of the divan. The slow taut feeling for it and the floor that creaked twice, starting the sweat out over her.

It was finally after more tortuous saving of floor creaks and the interminable opening and closing of a door that Carrie Samstag, the beaded bag in her hand, found herself face to face with herself in the mirror of the bathroom medicine chest.

She was shuddering with one of the hot chills, the needle and little glass piston out of the hand-bag and with a dry little insuck of breath, pinching up little areas of flesh from her arm, bent on a good firm perch, as it were.

There were undeniable pock-marks on Mrs. Samstag's right forearm. Invariably it sickened her to see them. Little graves. Oh, oh, little graves. For Alma. Herself. And now Louis. Just once. Just one more little grave—

And Alma, answering her somewhere down in her heart-beats: "No, mama, no, mama. No. No. No."

But all the little pores gaping. Mouths! The pinching up of the skin. Here, this little clean and white area.

"No, mama. No, mama. No. No. No."

"Just once, darling?" Oh—oh—graves for Alma and Louis. No. No. No.

Somehow, some way, with all the little mouths still parched and gaping and the clean and white area unblemished, Mrs. Samstag found her way back to bed. She was in a drench of sweat when she got there and the conflagration of neuralgia curiously enough, was now roaring in her ears so that it seemed to her she could hear her pain.

Her daughter lay asleep, with her face to the wall, her flowing hair spread in a fan against the pillow and her body curled up cozily. The remaining hours of the night, in a kind of waking faint she could never find the words to describe, Mrs. Samstag, with that dreadful dew of her sweat constantly out over her, lay with her twisted lips to the faint perfume of that fan of Alma's flowing hair her toes curling in and out. Out and in. Toward morning she slept. Actually, sweetly and deeply as if she could never have done with deep draughts of it.

She awoke to the brief patch of sunlight that smiled

into their apartment for about eight minutes of each forenoon.

Alma was at the pretty chore of lifting the trays from a hamper of roses. She places a shower of them on her mother's coverlet with a kiss, a deeper and dearer one somehow, this morning.

There was a card and Mrs. Samstag read it and laughed:

> Good morning, Carrie.
>
> Louis

They seemed to her, poor dear, these roses, to be pink with the glory of the coming of the dawn.

On the spur of the moment and because the same precipitate decisions that determined Louis Latz's successes in Wall Street determined him here, they were married the following Thursday in Greenwich, Connecticut, without even allowing Carrie time for the blue twill traveling suit. She wore her brown velvet instead, looking quite modish, and a sable wrap, gift of the groom, lending genuine magnificence.

Alma was there, of course, in a beautiful fox scarf also gift of the groom, and locked in a white kind of tensity that made her seem more than ever like a little white flower to Leo Friendlander, the sole other attendant, and who during the ceremony yearned at her with his gaze. But her eyes were squeezed tight against his, as if to forbid herself the consciousness that life seemed suddenly so richly sweet to her—oh, so richly sweet!

There was a time during the first months of the married life of Louis and Carrie Latz, when it seemed to Alma, who in the sanctity of her lovely little ivory bedroom all appointed in rose-enamel toilet trifles, could be prayerful with the peace of it, that the old

Carrie, who could come pale and terrible out of her drugged nights, belonged to some grimacing and chimeric past. A dead past that had buried its dead and its hatchet.

There had been a month at Hot Springs in the wintergreen heart of Virginia, and whatever Louis may have felt in his heart, of his right to the privacy of these honeymoon days, was carefully belied on his lips, and at Alma's depriving him now and then of his wife's company, packing her off to rest when he wanted a climb with her up a mountain slope or a drive over piny roads, he could still smile and pinch her cheek.

"You're stingy to me with my wife, Alma," he said to her upon one of these provocations. "I don't believe she's got a daughter at all, but a little policeman instead."

And Alma smiled back, out of the agony of her constant consciousness that she was insinuating her presence upon him, and resolutely, so that her fear for him should always subordinate her fear of him, she bit down her sensitiveness in proportion to the rising tide of his growing, but still politely held in check, bewilderment.

One day, these first weeks of their marriage, because she saw the dreaded signal of the muddy pools under her mother's eyes and the little quivering nerve beneath the temple, she shut him out of her presence for a day and a night, and when he came fuming up every few minutes from the hotel veranda, miserable and fretting, met him at the closed door of her mother's darkened room and was adamant.

"It won't hurt if I tiptoe in and sit with her," he pleaded.

"No, Louis. No one knows how to get her through

these spells like I do. The least excitement will only prolong her pain."

He trotted off then down the hotel corridor with a strut to his resentment that was bantam and just a little fighty.

That night as Alma lay beside her mother, fighting sleep and watching, Carrie rolled her eyes sidewise with the plea of a stricken dog in them.

"Alma," she whispered, "for God's sake, Just this once. To tide me over. One shot—darling. Alma, if you love me?"

Later, there was a struggle between them that hardly bears relating. A lamp was overturned. But toward morning, when Carrie lay exhausted, but at rest in her daughter's arms, she kept muttering in her sleep:

"Thank you, baby. You saved me. Never leave me, Alma. Never—never—never. You saved me Alma."

And then the miracle of those next months. The return to New York. The happily busy week of furnishing and the unlimited gratifications of the well-filled purse. The selection of the limousine with the special body that was fearfully and wonderfully made in mulberry upholstery with mother-of-pearl caparisons. The fourteen-room apartment on West End Avenue. with four baths, drawing-room of pink broacaded walls and Carrie's Roman bath-room that was precisely as large as her old hotel sitting room, with two full length wall-mirrors, a dressing table canopied in white lace over white satin and the marble itself, two steps down and with the rubber curtains that swished after.

There were evenings when Carrie, who loved the tyranny of things with what must have been a survival within her of the bazaar instinct, would fall asleep almost directly after dinner her head back against her husband's shoulder, roundly tired out after a day all cluttered up with matching the blue upholstery of their bedroom with taffeta bed hangings.

Latz liked her so, with her fragrantly coiffured head, scarcely gray, back against his shoulder and with his newspapers—Wall Street journals and the comic weeklies which he liked to read—would sit an entire evening thus, moving only when his joints rebelled, and his pipe smoke carefully directed away from her face.

Weeks and weeks of this and already Louis Latz's trousers were a little out of crease and Mrs. Latz after eight o'clock and under cover of a very fluffy and very expensive négligée, would unhook her stays.

Sometimes friends came in for a game of small-stake poker, but after the second month they countermanded the standing order for Saturday night musical comedy seats. So often they discovered it was pleasanter to remain at home. Indeed, during these days of household adjustment, as many as four evenings a week Mrs. Latz dozed there against her husband's shoulder, until about ten, when he kissed her awake to forage with him in the great, white porcelain refrigerator and then to bed.

And Alma. Almost, she tiptoed through these months. Not that her scorching awareness of what must have crouched low in Louis' mind ever diminished. Sometimes, altho still never by word, she could see the displeasure mount in his face.

If she entered in on a tête-à-tête, as she did once, when by chance she had sniffed the curvative smell of spirits of camphor on the air of a room through which her mother had passed, and came to drag her off that night to share her own lace-covered and ivory bed.

Again: upon the occasion of an impulsively planned motor trip and week-end to Lakewood, her intrusion had been so obvious.

"Want to join us, Alma?"

"O—yes—thank you, Louis."

"But I thought you and Leo were——"

"No, no, I'd rather go with you and mama, Louis."

Even her mother had smiled rather strainedly. Louis' invitation, politely uttered, had said so plainly: 'Are we two never to be alone. Your mother and I?'

Oh, there was no doubt that Louis Latz was in love and with all the delayed fervor of first youth.

There was something rather throat-catching about his treatment of her mother that made Alma want to cry.

He would never tire of marveling, not alone at the wonder of her, but at the wonder that she was his.

"No man has ever been as lucky in women as I have, Carrie," he told her once in Alma's hearing. "It seemed to me that after—my little mother, there couldn't ever be another—and now you! You!"

At the business of sewing some beads on a lampshade, Carrie looked up, her eyes dewy.

"And I felt that way about one good husband," she said, "and now I see there could be two."

Alma tiptoed out.

The third month of this, she was allowing Leo Friedlander his two evenings a week. Once to the theater in a modish little sedan car which Leo drove himself. One evening at home in the rose and mauve drawing-room. It delighted Louis and Carrie slyly to have in their friends for poker over the dining-room table these evenings, leaving the young people somewhat indirectly chaperoned until as late as midnight. Louis' attitude with Leo was one of winks, quirks, slaps on the back and the curving voice of innuendo.

"Come on in, Leo, the water's fine!"

"Louis!" This from Alma stung to crimson and not arch enough to feign that she did not understand.

"Loo, don't tease," said Carrie, smiling, but then closing her eyes as if to invoke help to want this thing to come to pass.

But Leo was frankly the lover, kept not without difficulty on the edge of his ardor. A city youth with gymnasium bred shoulders, fine, pole vaulter's length of limb and a clean tan skin that bespoke cold drubbings with Turkish towels.

And despite herself, Alma, who was not without a young girl's feelings for nice detail, could thrill to this sartorial svelteness and to the patent-leather lay of his black hair which caught the light like a polished floor.

The kind of sweetness he found in Alma he could never articulate even to himself. In some ways she seemed hardly to have the pressure of vitality to match his, but on the other hand, just that slower beat to her may have heightened his sense of prowess. His greatest delight seemed to lie in her pallid loveliness. "White Honeysuckle," he called her and the names of all the beautiful white flowers he knew. And then one night, to rattle of poker chips from the remote dining-room, he jerked her to him without preamble, kissing her mouth down tightly against her teeth.

"My sweetheart. My little, white carnation sweetheart. I won't be held off any longer. I'm going to carry you away for my little moon-flower wife."

She sprang back prettier than he had ever seen her

in the dishevelment from where his embrace had
dragged at her hair.

"You musn't," she cried, but there was enough of
the conquering male in him to read easily into this a
mere plating over her desire.

"You can't hold me at arm's length any longer.
You've maddened me for months. I love you. You
love me. You do. You do," and crushed her to
him, but this time his pain and his surprize genuine
as she sprang back quivering.

"You—I—mustn't!" she said, frantic to keep her
lips from twisting, her little lacy fribble of a handkerchief a mere string from winding.

"Mustn't what?"

"Mustn't," was all she could repeat and not weep
her words.

"Won't—I—do?"

"It's—mama."

"What?"

"You see—I—she's all alone."

"You adorable, she's got a brand-new husky husband."

"No—you don't—understand."

Then, on a thunder-clap of inspiration, hitting his
knee,

"I have it. Mama-baby! That's it. My girlie is a
cry-baby, mama-baby!" And made to slide along the
divan toward her, but up flew her two small hands,
like fans.

"No," she said with the little bang back in her
voice which steadied him again. "I mustn't! You
see, we're so close. Sometimes it's more as if I were
the mother and she my little girl."

Misery made her dumb.

"Why don't you know, dear, that your mother is better able to take care of herself than you are? She's bigger and stronger. You—you're a little white flower."

"Leo—give me time. Let me think."

"A thousand thinks, Alma, but I love you. I love you and want so terribly for you to love me back."

"I—do."

"Then tell me with kisses."

Again she pressed him to arm's length.

"Please, Leo. Not yet. Let me think. Just one day. Tomorrow."

"No, no. Now."

"Tomorrow."

"When?"

"Evening."

"No, morning."

"All right Leo—tomorrow morning——"

"I'll sit up all night and count every second in every minute and every minute in every hour."

She put up her soft little fingers to his lips.

"Dear boy," she said.

And then they kissed and after a little swoon to his nearness she struggled like a caught bird and a guilty one.

"Please go, Leo," she said, "Leave me alone——"

"Little mama-baby sweetheart," he said. "I'll build you a nest right next to hers. Good night, little White Flower. I'll be waiting, and remember, counting every second of every minute and every minute of every hour."

For a long time she remained where he had left her, forward on the pink divan, her head with a listening look to it, as if waiting an answer for the prayers that she sent up.

At two o'clock that morning, by what intuition she would never know, and with such leverage that she landed out of bed plump on her two feet, Alma, with all her faculties into trace like fire-horses, sprang out of sleep.

It was a matter of twenty steps across the hall. In the white tiled Roman bathroom, the muddy circles suddenly out and angry beneath her eyes, her mother was standing before one of the full-length mirrors— snickering.

There was a fresh little grave on the inside of her right fore arm.

Sometimes in the weeks that followed, a sense of the miracle of what was happening would clutch at Alma's throat like a fear.

Louis did not know.

That the old neuralgic recurrences were more frequent again, yes. Already plans for a summer trip abroad, on a curative mission bent, were taking shape. There was a famous nerve specialist, the one who had worked such wonders on his little mother's cruelly rheumatic limbs, reassuringly foremost in his mind.

But except that there were not infrequent and sometimes twenty-four hour sieges when he was denied the sight of his wife, he had learned with a male's acquiescence to the frailties of the other sex, to submit, and with no great understanding of pain, to condone.

And as if to atone for these more or less frequent lapses there was something pathetic, even a little heart-breaking, in Carrie's zeal for his wellbeing. No duty too small. One night she wanted to unlace his shoes and even shine them, would have, in fact, except for his fierce catching of her into his arms and for some reason, his tonsils aching as he kissed her.

Once after a "spell" she took out every garment from his wardrobe and kissing them piece by piece, put them back again and he found her so, and they cried together, he of happiness.

In his utter beatitude, even his resentment of Alma continued to grow but slowly. Once, when after forty-eight hours she forbade him rather fiercely an entrance into his wife's room, he shoved her aside almost rudely, but at Carrie's little shriek of remonstrance from the darkened room, backed out shamefacedly and apologized next day in the conciliatory language of a tiny wrist-watch.

But a break came, as she knew and feared it must.

One evening during one of these attacks, when for two days Carrie had not appeared at the dinner table, Alma, entering when the meal was almost over, seated herself rather exhaustedly at her mother's place opposite her stepfather.

He had reached the stage when that little unconscious usurpation in itself could annoy him.

"How's your mother?" he asked, dourly for him.

"She's asleep."

"Funny. This is the third attack this month and each time it lasts longer. Confound that neuralgia."

"She's easier now."

He pushed back his plate.

"Then I'll go in and sit with her while she sleeps."

She who was so fastidiously dainty of manner, half rose, spilling her soup.

"No," she said, "you mustn't! Not now!" And sat down again hurriedly, wanting not to appear perturbed.

A curious thing happened then to Louis. His lower lip come pursing out like a little shelf and a hitherto unususpected look of pigginess fattened over his rather plump face.

"You quit butting into me and my wife's affairs, you, or get the hell out of here," he said, without changing his voice or his manner.

She placed her hand to the almost unbearable flutter of her heart.

"Louis! You mustn't talk like that to—me!"

"Don't make me say something I'll regret. You! Only take this tip, you! There's one of two things you better do. Quit trying to come between me and her or—get out."

"I—she's sick."

"Naw, she ain't. Not as sick as you make out. You're trying, God knows why, to keep us apart. I've watched you. I know your sneaking kind. Still water runs deep. You've never missed a chance since we're married to keep us apart. Shame!"

"I—she——"

"Now mark my word, if it wasn't to spare her, I'd have invited you out long ago. Haven't you got any pride?"

"I have. I have," she almost moaned and could have crumpled up there and swooned in her humiliation.

"You're not a regular girl. You're a she-devil. That's what you are! Trying to come between your mother and me. Ain't you ashamed? What is it you want?"

"Louis—I don't——"

"First you turn down a fine fellow like Leo Friedlander, so he don't come to the house any more and then you take out on us whatever is eating you, by trying to come between me and the finest woman that ever lived, Shame. Shame."

"Louis," she said. "Louis," wringing her hands in a dry wash of agony, "can't you understand? She'd rather have me. It makes her nervous trying to pretend to you that she's not suffering when she is. That's all, Louis. You see, she's not ashamed to suffer before me. Why, Louis—that's all. Why, should I want to come between you and her? Isn't she dearer to me than anything in the world and haven't you been the best friend to me a girl could have? That's all—Louis."

He was placated and a little sorry and did not insist further upon going into the room.

"Funny," he said. "Funny," and adjusting his spectacles, snapped open his newspaper for a lonely evening.

The one thing that perturbed Alma almost more than anything else, as the dreaded cravings grew, with each siege her mother becoming more brutish and more given to profanity, was where she obtained the drug.

The well-thumbed old doctor's prescription she had purloined even back in the hotel days, and embargo and legislation were daily making more and more furtive and prohibitive the traffic in narcotics.

Once Alma, mistakenly too, she thought later, had suspected a chauffeur of collusion with her mother and abruptly dismissed him. To Louis' rage.

"What's the idea," he said out of Carrie's hearing, of course. "Who's running this shebang anyway?"

Once after Alma had guarded her well for days, scarcely leaving her side, Carrie laughed sardonically up into her daughter's face, her eyes as glassy and without swimming fluid as a doll's.

"I get it! But wouldn't you like to know where? Yah!"

And to Alma's horror she slapped her quite roundly across the cheek.

And then one day, after a long period of quiet, when Carrie had lavished her really great wealth of contrite love upon her daughter and husband, spending on Alma and loading her with gifts of jewelry and finery to somehow express her grateful adoration of her; paying her husband the secret penance of twofold fidelity to his well-being and every whim, Alma, returning from a trip, taken reluctantly, and at her mother's bidding, down to the basement trunk room, found her gone, a modish black-lace hat and the sable coat missing from the closet.

It was early afternoon, sunlit and pleasantly cold.

The first rush of panic and the impulse to dash after, stayed, she forced herself down into a chair, striving with the utmost difficulty for coherence of procedure.

Where in the half hour of her absence had her mother gone? Matinee? Impossible! Walking. Hardly probable. Upon inquiry in the kitchen neither of the maids had seen nor heard her depart. Motoring? With hand that trembled in spite of itself, Alma telephoned the garage. Car and chauffeur were there. Incredible as it seemed, Alma, upon more than one occasion had lately been obliged to remind her mother that she was becoming careless of the old pointedly rosy hand. Manicurist? She telephoned the Bon Ton Beauty Parlor. No! Where, oh God, where? Which way to begin? That was what troubled her most. To start right, so as not to lose a precious second.

Suddenly, and for no particular reason, Alma began
a hurried search through her mother's dresser-drawers
of lovely personal appointments.

A one-inch square of newspaper clipping apparently
gouged from the sheet with a hairpin, caught her eye
from the top of one of the gold-backed hairbrushes.
Dawningly, Alma read.

It described in brief detail the innovation of a
newly equipped Narcotic Clinic on the Bowery below
Canal Street, provided to medically administer to the
pathologic cravings of addicts.

Fifteen minutes later Alma emerged from the subway at Canal Street and with three blocks toward her
destination ahead, started to run.

At the end of the first block she saw her mother,
in the sable coat and the black-lace hat, coming toward
her.

Her first impulse was to run faster and yoo-hoo,
but she thought better of it and by biting her lips and
digging her fingernails, was able to slow down to a
casual walk.

Carrie's fur coat was flaring open and because of
the quality of her attire down there where the bilge
waters of the city-tide flow and eddy, stares followed
her.

Once, to the stoppage of Alma's heart, she halted
and said a brief word to a truckman as he crossed
the sidewalk with a bill of lading. He hesitated,
laughed and went on.

Then she quickened her pace and went on, but as if
with a sense of being followed, because constantly
as she walked, she jerked a step, to look back, and then
again, over her shoulder.

A second time she stopped, this time to address a

little nub of a woman without a hat and lugging one-sidedly a stack of men's basted waistcoats, evidently for home-work in some tenement. She looked and muttered her un-understanding of whatever Carrie had to say and shambled on.

Then Mrs. Latz spied her daughter, greeting her without surprize or any particular recognition.

"Thought you could fool me! Heh, Louis! Alma."

"Mama, it's Alma. It's all right. Don't you remember, we had this appointment? Come dear."

"No, you don't! That's a man following. Shh-h-h, Louis. I was fooling. I went up to him (snicker) and I said to him, 'Give you five dollars for a doctor's certificate.' That's all I said to him, or any of them. He's in a white carnation, Louis. You can find him by the — it's on his coat lapel. He's coming! Quick——"

"Mama, there's no one following. Wait, I'll call a taxi!"

"No, you don't! He tried to put me in a taxi, too. No, you don't!"

"Then the subway, dearest. You'll sit quietly beside Alma in the subway, won't you, Carrie. Alma's so tired."

Suddenly Carrie began to whimper.

"My baby! Don't let her see me. My baby. What am I good for? I've ruined her life. My precious sweetheart's life. I hit her once—Louis—in the mouth. God won't forgive me for that."

"Yes, He will, dear, if you come."

"It bled. Alma, tell him mama lost her doctor's certificate. That's all I said to him—give you five dollars for a doctor's certificate—he had a white carnation—right lapel—stingy! Quick! He's following!"

"Sweetheart, please, there's no one coming."

"Don't tell! Oh, Alma darling—mama's ruined your life. Her sweetheart baby's life."

"No, darling, you haven't. She loves you if you'll come home with her, dear, to bed, before Louis gets home and——"

"No. No. He mustn't see. Never this bad—was I, darling—oh—oh——"

"No, mama—never—this bad. That's why we must hurry."

"Best man that ever lived. Best baby. Ruin. Ruin."

"Mama, you—you're making Alma tremble so that she can scarcely walk if you drag her back so. There's no one following, dear. I won't let any one harm you. Please, sweetheart—a taxicab."

"No. I tell you he's following. He tried to put me into a taxicab."

"Then mama, listen. Do you hear! Alma wants you to listen. If you don't—she'll faint. People are looking. Now I want you to turn square around and look. No, look again. You see now, there's no one following. Now, I want you to cross the street over there to the subway. Just with Alma, who loves you. There's nobody following. Just with Alma who loves you."

And then Carrie, whose lace hat was crazily on the back of her head, relaxed enough so that through the enormous maze of the traffic of trucks and the heavier drags of the lower city, she and her daughter could wind their way.

"My baby. My poor Louis," she kept saying. "The worst I've ever been. Oh—Alma—Louis—waiting—before we get there—Louis."

It was in the tightest tangle of the crossing and apparently on this conjuring of her husband, that Carrie jerked suddenly free of Alma's frailer hold.

"No—no—not home—now. Him. Alma!" And darted back against the breast of the down side of the traffic.

There was scarcely more than the quick rotation of her arm around with the spoke of a truck wheel, so quickly she went down.

It was almost a miracle, her kind of death, because out of all that jam of tonnage, she carried only one bruise, a faint one, near the brow.

And the wonder was that Louis Latz in his grief was so proud.

"To think," he kept saying over and over again and unabashed at the way his face twisted, "to think they should have happened to me. Two such women in one lifetime, as my little mother—and her. Fat little old Louis to have had those two. Why just the memory of my Carrie—is almost enough—to think old me should have a memory like that—it is almost enough—isn't it, Alma?"

She kissed his hand.

That very same, that dreadful night, almost without her knowing it, her throat-tearing sobs broke loose, her face to the waistcoat of Leo Friedlander.

He held her close. Very, very close.

"Why sweetheart," he said, "I could cut out my heart to help you. Why, sweetheart. Shh-h-h, remember what Louis says. Just the beautiful memory—of —her—is—wonderful——"

"Just—the b-beautiful—memory—you'll always have it too—of her—my mama—won't you, Leo? Won't you?"

"Always," he said, when the tight grip in his throat had eased enough.

"Say—it again—Leo."

"Always."

She could not know how dear she became to him then, because not ten minutes before, from the very lapel against which her cheek lay pressed, he had unpinned a white carnation.

SOLITUDE

By BEN AMES WILLIAMS

The lonely reaches of the wilderness, motionless in
the bonds of winter, extended to the utmost horizon
The black blur of the forests were mottled by snow
which clung to the great trees, and the even blackness
of their masses was somewhat palliated by the fact that
a blanket of snow lay on the ground beneath them
faintly modifying their hue with glimpses of white here
and there. In the great cup formed by the surrounding mountains there were miles by the score and the
hundred where spruce and pine stood in solid ranks;
there were other reaches of barren land white with the
snow except where a bush or a patch of scrub growth
broke the glaring surfaces with a speck of black.

Above the sun blazed cold as ice from a sky pellucid
blue at the zenith, shading imperceptibly into a cold
white mist that blurred a little the horizon—a mist that
suggested sparkling crystals of frost suspended in the
air above the winter-prisoned world. The sunlight rebounded from the earth, reflected from billions and
billions of snow particles in a blinding torrent of radiance, no more to be endured by human eye than a
glance from the sun itself. Against the mountain flanks
there were scars, bare slopes of rock swept clean by
wind or slide, and these scars assumed fantastic and
unbelievable colors in the interplay of light, sometimes

black, sometimes gray, sometimes crimson, sometimes purple, sometimes as white as the snow itself.

Here and there the forest gave way to an expanse of swamp where the pointed plumes of the tamaracks rose above the level of the surrounding cedars, and here and there stood the stark trunk of a tree long since dead, waiting the completion of those processes of decay which, eating at its roots, would level it to earth again. A tree three hundred years in the growing, condemned to stand like a skeleton at the feast among its still living fellows, fated to sweep down at last in a single splitting, crashing second, ruining so swiftly the structure centuries had built!

A thread of more even white, now visible, now broken by intervening forest growths, marked where the river ran.

Irregularly it widened; lakes lay with breathless bosoms bound in a scarf of snow. And between the eye and all these things hung the air; a definite thing, a thing to be taken into account; not the forgotten and disregarded air of more kindly scenes, but a biting, needlelike, razor-edged substance fit to wound and maim. This still and cold air was like a faint blue curtain drawn across a gigantic canvas; a canvas which bore a scene that might fitly have been called "Solitude."

There was, near the southern end of one of the more extensive tracts of white which might be recognized as the snow-covered surface of a lake, a small spot; a dark spot, appearing black against the snow. This spot was infinitely small.

The lake itself was not large—it may have been as large as your hand—and diverging coves at the northern end suggested this simile. The thumb was not apparent, but at least three fingers of the hand could be seen. This small dark spot, appearing black against the snow, was at a point corresponding to the ball of the thumb. It was very small, no more than a pin prick— so small that the eye swept over it without stopping, had to return and search to discover it again; as hard to see as a flock of geese disappearing in the mist miles away along the shore; as hard to keep within the focus of one's vision as an airplane going straight away from the beholder, a mile in every thirty seconds' time. Even more difficult, perhaps, to see this spot and keep it in view, for the geese move and the airplane moves, tho it be so slightly, but this spot did not move at all! Visible now at a certain point upon the frozen surface of the lake, its position an hour later had not perceptibly changed. It was, to all intents and purposes, motionless.

Yet that it was not altogether motionless time at length revealed. Toward midday it seemed to have descended from the ball of the thumb into the palm of the hand which the lake represented; by dusk it had approached the base of the index finger. A little after daybreak the next morning it was apparent that the spot was certainly moving, following the index finger toward its end. Toward mid-afternoon it disappeared, merging in the shadows of the forest which cloaked the lake's end and lay like a slipping mantle up the steep slopes of a ridge of higher ground, perceptible from a distance only as a hair line of snow between the forest in the one valley and in the next. On the third day the spot was for a time visible upon this ridge; then it disappeared once more. But the day subsequent, upon a wide expanse of barren land beyond the ridge, the

painfully advancing speck of black again came into
view.

There was a suggestion of persistence about this spot.
It did not wander to and fro, as an animal might be
expected to wander; instead it moved steadfastly and
in a line more or less direct, suggesting that it was
guided by intelligence. It became necessary to suspect
that this moving spot was a man. The spectacle of a
single man set alone in the immensity of this solitude
inevitably excited a certain ironic mirth; it was so
ridiculous that it was somehow sublime.

The spot was, in fact, a man—a man alone. His
progress across the face of this enormous wilderness
was, on any comparative basis, superlatively slow, but
as a matter of fact the man seemed to be making what
haste he could. A somewhat closer view revealed the
fact that he was evidently accustomed to such journeys
as this one was. His heavy garments, increasing his
apparent breadth, made him seem almost squat; the
snowshoes on his feet were like heavy clogs, stumbling
through the loose snow; his hood muffled his face, and
from its opening there appeared only a red glint of a
nose burned by the snowlight. Across his eyes a black
band was drawn to protect them from the blinding
radiance of the snow. In his hand he carried a rifle
in a skin case, shifting the weapon from this side to
that, occasionally resting it upon his shoulder. There
was a small pack upon his back, but he seemed unconscious of its presence there. A cooking pot and a fry
pan hung against this pack. The man himself, concealed within such a mass of accouterments, kept a
steady, shuffling pace, threading his way among the
inequalities of the ground, moving at times circuitously,

yet nevertheless advancing day by day. If you had marked his progress by pin pricks on the map, the tiny holes would have been so near together as almost to overlap; yet a week would have shown a perceptible gain.

The colossal forces, at times inert, at times overpowering, with which he was surrounded, seemed unconscious of this man's existence. He was like a Lilliputian among Brobdingnags, a pygmy among giants; and it was forever necessary that he go cautiously lest ever their casual and unstudied movements overwhelm him. Where the giant that was the wind had breathed a gentle sigh, a swath of down timber barred his passage and forced him to a wide detour. Where the giant that was the snow had played at sliding downhill, it was necessary that he pick a cautious way lest he be precipitated into a gulf full of destruction.

He crawled across the sleeping bosom of the giantess who was the earth; he became entangled in the thickets of her hair; he had to go a day's walk out of his way to avoid the precipice that was her chin, and it required another day for him to descend into the ravine formed by her lips and climb out to level ground once more. The fact that the universe seemed to slumber made his task no easier, for one of the colossal forces asleep about him might so easily turn in its sleep. The twitch of one of their fingers was, for the man, calamity; and even in sleep they presented almost insurmountable difficulties to his passage.

The snow itself had fallen in a mood of riot, playing with the wind a game which left them both exhausted, so that the snow lay in the tumbled abandon of a sleeping child, and the wind too was still. But passively sleeping tho it might be, the snow dragged at his feet, reared lofty drifts like ridges which he could not pass, concealed pits into which he might by a careless movement be precipitated, slid down from either side in a swift stroke as a sleeping child brushes at a troublesome fly. His way was beset by these perils, by the peril of a tree falling in the still forest, by the peril of a mishap to his own tiny but effective mechanism. A twisted ankle would destroy him.

The man within his wrappings, inching his way across the face of the universe, felt himself completely at the mercy of these colossal forces among which he picked his way. It was not that they were malicious; it was simply that they disregarded him. He was in their eyes of no account at all; the snow slide that buried him would lie as serenely waiting for the suns of spring as that which he escaped by the most desperate and scrambling haste. The trees, whispering above his head, did not observe his passage past their feet; the mountains never knew he crawled across their flanks; the winds blew over him without feeling that his head tickled their bellies as they passed, and he thought they were huge and reptilian monsters scurrying to and fro above him, whose feet might descend upon him crushingly and lift again without knowing what they had done.

During the day his consciousness of the world about him was not so overwhelming; it was at night, when he made his camp in the forest, that he was most utterly alone. He was lonely because he was so naked and so helpless and so completely disregarded. There is no loneliness like that of one caught up in a throng of persons engaged upon their own affairs; and this was his portion.

When he made his little fire and huddled over it, he could hear the wind rushing toward him from a thousand miles away; he could look up through the interlocked branches of the trees and discover the stars, so like eyes. But the wind rushed past him, and these stars seemed to the man to be looking not at him but just beyond his brow, as tho he did not exist, as tho his existence were merely a delusion under which he suffered. The great trees over his head brushed together, whispered together; they were full of little murmurous voices, calmly discussing matters beyond his knowledge or understanding.

If he had had a tent he might have shut out the universe, for this is the function of a habitation. Not to shut ourselves in, but to shut the world outside the door. But he had no tent. He was traveling light. He had a little food, and he was able to shoot some game as he advanced; he had matches and an ax and cooking gear, and he had a single blanket. At night he scooped away snow to make walls around his little fire, and he bedded himself, half recumbent, on boughs laid upon this heaped snow; and he woke every few minutes to replenish his fire. But the walls of snow did not shut out the forest. The trees over his head could look down upon him if they chose to do so; it was the more maddening because they did not choose. The stars could see him, but their attention seemed to be fixed on a point just past his brow.

He could not even banish the cold with his little fire; the air, full of icy particles, wreathed itself around him; crystals of ice formed and grew upon his beard and the collar of his hood; cold stole up into his body from the snow; cold stabbed him from above; he had not sufficient food, and he ate sparingly, so that not even when he was moving did warmth fill his veins. He was always in this embrace of the cold, and tho he fought against her like a sluggish lover, she still twined her arms about him and he felt her cold breast forever against his own, beseeching him to yield himself to her.

He began at last to permit himself to look forward to the end of his journey. Four days would do it; then three; then two; and finally, huddling shiveringly beside his fire, he saw the dawn of the day that, barring mischance, should bring him to haven.

Impatience began to stir in his blood; he was in such haste to be forward that at noon he did not even stop to boil the kettle, but pressed on. A little after noon he came down into the ravine of a brook where once he had set his traps, and as he moved steadily forward he saw now and then a leaning tree, an old windfall, or a great bowlder which marked the location where one of these sets had been. The very familiarity of these scenes comforted him like a home-coming. There was, he knew, no one trapping here now; the man with whom for two winters he had shared the cabin ahead had gone to other fields. But he and his partner had left provender in the hidden cabin; he counted on being able to sustain himself there, to live through the winter. The stout walls would shut out the vastness of the wilderness, and within the cabin he would have memories for companions—would not be so lonely there.

He debouched from the ravine into a wider, where the small stream joined a greater, and so pursued his way, and he came to the dead water above the beaver dam where he and his partner had once taken many

beaver. His glance turned that way as he passed, and
then abruptly the man stopped and tried to focus his
weary eyes. For better vision he removed from his
face the dark handkerchief which he had worn like a
veil, as a protection against the glare from the snow.
Out in the pond a stake protruded through the ice; a
stake to which he had secured traps. The thing which
had caught his eye was the fact that about this stake
there were low mounds of snow. A moment's scrutiny
satisfied him that his first glance had told the truth.
Someone had been trapping here this winter; had been
here, no doubt, before the last fall of snow; must be
in the cabin now.

The discovery awoke in the desperate and lonely
man a tumult of conjecture. His need was great and
instant; he must find shelter and warmth and food.
Yet he was under the necessity of avoiding his fellow
men, avoiding their accusing eyes, avoiding their rumor
and report. The alternatives confronting him were
critical and he tried to weigh them in cool blood, but
his weariness was too great. His attempts to think
clearly, to judge accurately, resulted merely in a more
complete fuddling of his mental processes. He was
not even conscious that he had moved forward until he
discovered that his feet were following an old trail
beneath the later fallen snow.

The fact that this trail must lead to the cabin he
sought came home to him with maddening force, de-
stroying all his caution, nullifying his inhibitions, as
the first sip of water wakes a devil of desire in one
dying of thirst. Even tho destruction lay just
ahead, this man had no strength left to avoid it; he
plunged onward more swiftly along the trodden trail.

By the cabin door he kicked off his rackets, threw

ımself down the tunnellike slope of snow and grasped the latch. Even then, before opening, he hesitated once more, despairingly certain that his own destruction lay within.

But when he opened the door and the man in the cabin turned to look at him, the fugitive suffered such a flood of relief that it was almost more than he could bear. He had been so unutterably lonely; he had striven so desperately to reach the poor comfort of familiar scenes, of a once-known shelter, of a solitude a little less alien than the vast solitude through which ne journeyed; he had known despair in the discovery that this goal of his had already been seized upon by another, presumably a stranger; had taken counsel of desperation and chosen to risk destruction for the small portion of comfort he might find within these walls; and then, when all his hopes were at an ebb, fortune had granted him an inexpressible reassurance and relief.

For the man in the cabin, who looked up at his entrance, was his partner, a friend he counted stanch and true.

His name was Mat Rullen, this patient and indomitable traveler through the wilderness. A rude, strong man, who had known the rough spots of the North. He had washed gold and he had mined gold; he had worked for hire and he had slaved like a serf for his own ends he had fought and won; he had fought and been vanquished. He had striven through a long winter to earn the price of a week's debauch; he had won and lost a fortune in a dozen hours across a split-slab table littered with greasy cards. He had loved a woman, his mother, and she died; he had loved another, his wife, and she died. He had loved men and they died or went away from the place in which he dwelt. He had moved restlessly from one camp to another, one post to another.

There was in him a curiously sensitive imaginative streak; it made him the prey of hours of bitter depression, when he was but poor company. It made him draw back when those among whom his days were cast would have gone forward; it made him go forward when they drew back. In the casual encounters of life it had lost him many friends; but one man had understood and borne with him; one man he had served well and loved as we love those whom we serve.

This man was Charlie Day; and Charlie Day it was whose countenance he saw when his dazed eyes learned to see through the gloom within the cabin.

They had met in a barroom brawl; had found themselves by chance back to back while a whirling group of men fought all about them; they had buffeted their way into the clear and struck hands and bunked that night together in Mat Rullen's tent. They worked a placer one long summer; they thawed and dug and washed a winter through; they abandoned that enterprize for this trapping territory and wintered together without a bitter hour; they parted at last when one of his moods of black regret drove Mat to harsh and ugly words—parted in a surface hatred. But that hatred on Mat's part was forgotten now; he only remembered the Charlie Day whom he had loved; and he saw Charlie's face with a great lump of happiness choking in his throat, with eyes so moisted that he could not see the lack of response in Charlie's steady glance returning his.

He said through cracked and swollen lips, "Charlie, old man!" and sat down limply upon the floor, half crawling toward the beautiful warmth of the stove. And Charlie stood by, neither assisting nor opposing him, while he warmed himself back to life again and while he eased off the pack and tugged the heavy parka over his head. And Mat talked to his old partner garrulously, senselessly, rejoicing in the sound of his own voice and in the certainty that there was someone to hear what he said; some human ear at hand attending to his words. He was at first conscious of no lack, no failure on the other's part; he desired merely to talk and to be heard.

"I heard you'd gone outside," he said over and over. "I never looked to find you here. I heard you'd gone outside, Charlie, old man. They said so. They said you'd took the last boat out." He looked at the other more attentively. "Somebody said you'd broke a leg; said you went out on crutches, Charlie; said you went home with a crutch under your arm."

Charlie asked at last, in a stony voice, "How come you here?"

And Mat told him, rambling and incoherently. 'Overland," he said. "Overland. From the gulch. I had a placer there, working it alone. I come from there. Two weeks on the way. I pulled out of there and headed for the cabin here. I never looked to find you here, Charlie."

"What made you pull out of there?" Charlie insisted.

Mat made a gesture of despair. "One of those things," he explained. "It was old Willie Beam. Old Willie. He always was an old fool, and too much of a fool this time. He kep' pestering at me, in Nick's place, one night. There was a crowd there, but I didn't want to do with any of them. They bothered me; all I wanted was to be left alone. And Old Willie was drunk. Yes, he was drunk—and making big talk to me and the others; and they laughed at him. But he made me sick, Charlie. He made me sick. I didn't want him bothering. I tried to tell him so, Charlie." His tone was a plea. "I told him to leave me alone. I tried to get away from him, and I started to go out and go down to Dave's. But they laughed at that, and they said Old Willie was running me. So I stayed and he crowed over it. Yes, sir, Old Willie was right tickled because he bothered me."

He wiped a hand slowly across his forehead. "I got mad at him—and madder," he said laboriously. "And I talked to him. Yes, sir; I laid him out, talking to him. And Old Willie began to hop. He got mad, his own self. He hopped like a crow. And I was sick of him. And I told him so; and then he dragged that gun of his. Tried to stick it on me. I was too mad to fool with him. And then he was down, and the smoke in my nostrils, and my gun in my hand. And Old Willie down and gasping and dying on the floor—and hard looks for me."

He seemed to shudder. "He had his gun out," he repeated. "Had his gun on me. It was up to him. But they said Old Willie wouldn't harm anybody; said I knew it; said I ought to have took his gun and slapped his face and left him be. I dared them all to take it up, but none of them did. They wouldn't go after their guns, Charlie. They just pulled back from me and lugged Old Willie home and buried him. Folks liked him, Charlie; and they never liked me."

"You hadn't any need of killing him," said Charlie.

Mat looked up at his old partner curiously. "He had <u>his</u> gun on me," he protested. "That's what they

said too, but he had his gun on me. There wasn't
anybody would take it up with me, Charlie. They just
let me alone. Never come near me. Pulled back when
I come around. I tried to laugh at it, and then I begun
to get lonesome, and nobody can stand that, Charlie.
I couldn't talk to them. They'd say, 'Sure, you had a
right to. If you wanted to,' they'd say. 'If you wanted
to,' they'd say. But he had his gun on me, Charlie."

He sat a moment silent, squatting on his hunkers,
warming his hands about the stove, embracing it with
his whole body, bathing in its heat. "They wouldn't
talk to me, Charlie," he repeated. "They wouldn't
even listen to me. The story went down-river. It
went around. Nick told me it would go all over.
'They'll know about you anywhere you go,' he told me.
'You better go outside,' he said. 'There won't anybody
hook up with you here.' And I said to him, 'He had
his gun out,' I said. 'I had a right to drop him.' And
Nick just spit and says, 'Sure, if you wanted to,' he
says. So I couldn't stick it there, Charlie. And I hit
out for the cabin here. Figured to stay here the winter
and make a stake of fur maybe and go outside in the
spring."

He suddenly beamed with recollection. "But I never
looked to find you here, Charlie. It's great, finding
you. We can work together this winter now."

His wits were returning; he had the wit to expect an
answer from Charlie, agreeing to this plan. But no
answer came, so that he looked up at his old partner
querulously; and Charlie met his eyes and said at last,
steadily enough, shaking his head:

"No, Mat; you can't stay here."

Mat Rullen seemed not to hear this; he muttered,
"Like old times, together here, Charlie."

And Charlie said again, more steadily, "You can't stay here."

There was silence then for a time while Mat chewed this and savored its bitter flavor. "Can't stay here, Charlie?" he repeated at last.

Charlie Day shook his head. "Why not, pardner?" Mat asked gently.

"Moll's here with me," said Charlie.

"Moll?"

"She's here with me," the other repeated; and Mat fell silent again, to chew upon this for a while.

She had no other name, this Moll. But Mat knew her. A woman. A woman impossible in any other surroundings save those which for years had been the background of his life—a woman large, ample, mild and beneficent: stalwart as a man, strong as a man, and as tender as a woman too. Not a promiscuous woman, but an itinerant.

She had come north with a man by the name of Sladen, a small man, a weakling, ill, who nagged at her unceasingly, fretted at her in an ill-tempered and irascible way. In spite of which she lived with him and took care of him, cooked for him and tended him till his cough disappeared and his flabby muscles hardened and he became able to hold his own with men. And one day he told her he was sick to death of her, and Moll left him. She ran for a season a rude boarding house, till one Wally Hurd drank himself into dementia and became her charge; for him she gave herself fully, sleeping neither night nor day so long as he needed her solicitude.

There must have been much of the mother in this woman, this Moll. To her, it was evident enough, men were children still; she cared for them, humored them, disciplined them in mild ways, gave them what they desired, all with the same large, impersonal and benign generosity, always forgetful of herself, seeking only the need that she might fill. Men spoke of her with scorn —until they fell ill and needed her. She was unlovely —had too much the appearance of a man for beauty's sake—but there was in her broad countenance something eternal and calm and full of peace. Yes, Mat remembered Moll.

His eyes searched the cabin. "Where's she at?" he asked.

And Charlie Day explained. "She went out yesterday morning on the south loop of traps," he said. "My leg's bad still; I can't cover much ground. She does the heft of it."

"Here with you?" Mat asked uncertainly.

"She took care of my leg," Charlie replied, as tho this would explain all to the other. "Staked me then and fetched me in here. Freighted our grub and all up the river before the freeze. I could get around now if I had to, but she's willing. Works more'n a man would. I let her." His eyes shone with a curiously petty light. "Might as well, long as she wants it so," he explained.

"The south loop?" Mat repeated. "She's due back here any time."

Charlie nodded. "So you got to move along," he repeated.

"I figured on staying here," Mat urged helplessly. "When I see you, I figured you'd want me. I can get along with Moll."

"We got only just enough to carry us," Charlie insisted. "Need what we've got."

"I can take some grub we left here," Mat insisted, clinging to straws.

"We allowed for that when we outfitted," Charlie told him. "Figure on using all there is. There ain't room for you here, Mat. You better hit for outside."

Mat sat for a moment very still; then a long shudder ran through his body and he huddled to the stove. "It's damned lonesome traveling," he pleaded.

"I never asked you to come here. I never asked you to kill Old Willie."

"I had a right to," Mat insisted plaintively.

"If you wanted to," Charlie agreed, unmoved.

And there was again silence then, and at its end Mat got slowly to his feet and began to beat the snow off his garments and off his pack traps. He said thoughtfully, "I was glad, finding you here, Charlie."

"You can see yourself you can't stay," Charlie implacably replied.

So Mat got into his gear, with slow and labored movements. "I might rest up a night," he suggested.

"She'll be back any time."

Mat glanced at the two bunks. "I can roll up on the floor."

"You'd do a lot of talking," Charlie told him.

Mat nodded. "I get a comfort out of talking," he agreed. "Ain't had anybody to listen for a long time now."

But Charlie showed no yielding, and Mat saw he would not yield. So a little later he went out through the cabin door and found a little wind was blowing, a little whispering, jeering wind which struck at his warmed cheeks with stabbing fingers and slashed at them with knives of driven snow. He stuck his feet into the loops of his snowshoes and looked down at the cabin door for a last glimpse of Charlie.

But Charlie Day had shut the door; so Mat turned patiently away.

It was late afternoon when he left the cabin; dusk was already fallen, but the snowlight guided his footsteps. And at first he went uncertainly with no definite goal in mind. This cabin had been his goal; in his thoughts for a fortnight past the world had ended here; there was nothing beyond.

But here he could not stay; instead must venture into that world beyond, that world which was nothing. And till now he had been sustained by the knowledge that his infinitely laborious progress was directed to a certain end, but now there was no such knowledge to support him. He was going nowhere; was simply going away from the cabin. There had been no time for a new plan to form in his thoughts. He was purposeless —and alone—and his estate was forlorn as Adam's, fleeing from the flaming sword.

His thoughts kept turning backward to the cabin and to Charlie; to the warm cabin, with its stores of food and its soft bunks and Charlie comfortable there. Another man might have felt anger, but Mat Rullen was broken past resentment. He was in the full grip of overpowering loneliness and melancholy sorrow; his faltering footsteps lagged; it was only the habit of progress which kept him from halting, slumping down in the snow, submitting himself to be trodden by the galloping hoofs of the wind-driven snow. So he moved on, a derelict, adrift, lacking either home port or destination; and about him lay the great wilderness, calm in its own concerns, and the wind that blew disregarded him, brushed him carelessly; and the hurrying

snow drifting on the wind stumbled and jostled past
him, scurrying on. The trees over his head whispered
pleasantly together like old women gossiping.

He came to a little corner under a bank where there
was some shelter from the wind; and he made camp
there, moving automatically. Kicked aside the snow
with his rackets till he could tread down a more solid
area; then removed the snowshoes and completed his
excavation. Almost within reach of his hand two or
three young pines, dead from overcrowding, stood
ready for his fire. He broke a handful of twigs and
started the little blaze and huddled over it, melting
snow to boil his tea. The provisions in his pack were
low. He thought he should have begged matches and
salt and tea; these at least Charlie might have spared.
For more substantial food he would have to trust his
rifle, watch a chance on the morrow.

He ate a little, and broke some green boughs from a
low-growing spruce and bedded them against the snow
blanket about his fire and so lay down, seeking what
measure of warmth he could find. Overhead the inter-
lacing branches whispered; between them he could see
the far, impersonal glances of the stars; past him
flowed the wind. The pale light of his fire seemed to
escape him, to radiate far through the night, through
the branches into the bitter current of the outer airs,
over the banked snow into the forest. There was
nothing to keep it here where it would comfort him;
the room in which he slept was the universe; his bed-
fellows were the trees in their ranks for miles, the
mountains on the horizon's rim, the infinitely distant
stars. He was no more than a mote fallen from a
sunbeam, a speck of dust waiting to be obliterated or
swept away.

He drew his head within his blankets and tried thus to secure a counterfeit of privacy; to build for himself a small world in which tho he might be alone he would still be of some consequence. But snow dusted against his cheek and the cold night wind burned him bitterly and the trees still whispered above his bed and the far stars pierced him with their gaze. He huddled closer, pressing the blanket against his eyes, and a stupor crept over him, a stupor that was no more than the noisome counterpart of sleep.

This man, this Mat Rullen, woke from his miserable slumber and dragged the blanket off his face and opened his eyes to see a figure revealed in the light of the fire — the figure of a woman, of the woman called Moll.

He rubbed at his face with his hands, and he watched while the woman busied herself. She put fresh boughs upon the fire till it crackled warmly. He saw beyond her a light hand sledge, upon which there was a load. Food, perhaps; blankets; the necessities of existence.

She did not speak, but he at last found words. "That you, Moll?" he asked.

She nodded. "Charlie told me," she explained briefly. "Don't you bother now."

"Where's Charlie?" he asked.

"He can get along," she replied.

She had, he saw, a kettle boiling; presently held toward him the scalding tea and bade him drink. "You'll sleep better," she said.

"What did you come for?" he asked.

"I'm coming to take care of you," she replied.

The tea ran through him like revivifying fire. It raced through his veins in a scorching flood; he welcomed the agonizing pain. Peace stole through him.

He was surprised to discover a curious phenomenon. The radiance and the heat of the fire no longer escaped into the illimitable universe. It was reflected from the lowest branches of the trees over his head; it rebounded from the banked snow; it clotted about the little fire itself. He could bathe his hands in it. The stirring wind went past them overhead, but it did not dip into the hollow where they were. He found that he could not even see the stars.

Moll took a fur robe from the sledge. She spread it over him and beside him, and she lay down and took him in her arms. He nestled against her warm body. Her coming had driven out the world; it was as tho she brought with her a habitation, a haven, a home. And in this home the man was no longer lonely.

He slept in her arms, safely and secure.

P. & O.

By W. Somerset Maugham

Mrs. Hamlyn lay on her long chair and lazily watched the passengers come along the gangway. The ship had reached Singapore in the night and since dawn had been taking on cargo; the winches had been grinding away all day, but by now her ears were accustomed to their insistent clamor. She had lunched at the Europe and for lack of anything better to do had driven in a rickshaw through the gay, multitudinous streets of the city. Singapore is the meeting-place of many races. The Malays, tho natives of the soil, dwell uneasily in towns, and are few; and it is the Chinese, supple, alert and industrious, who throng the streets, the dark-skinned Tamils walk on their silent, naked feet as tho they were but brief sojourners in a strange land, but the Bengalis, sleek and prosperous, are easy in their surroundings and self-assured; the sly and obsequious Japanese seem busy with pressing and secret affairs; and the English in their topees and white ducks, speeding past in motor-cars or at leisure in their rickshaws, wear a nonchalant and careless air. The rulers of these teeming peoples take their authority with a smiling unconcern. And now, tired and hot, Mrs. Hamlyn waited for the ship to set out again on her long journey across the Indian Ocean.

She waved a rather large hand, for she was a big

woman, to the doctor and Mrs. Linsell as they came on board. She had been on the ship since she left Yokohama, and had watched with acid amusement the intimacy which had sprung up between the two. Linsell was a naval officer who had been attached to the British Embassy at Tokio, and she had wondered at the indifference with which he took the attentions that the doctor paid his wife. Two men came along the gangway, new passengers, and she amused herself by trying to discover from their demeanor whether they were married or single. Close by, a group of men were sitting together on rattan chairs, planters she judged by their khaki suits and wide-brimmed double felt hats, and they kept the deck-steward busy with their orders. They were talking loudly and laughing, for they had all drunk enough to make them somewhat foolishly hilarious, and they were evidently giving one of their number a send-off; but Mrs. Hamlyn could not tell which it was that was to be a fellow-passenger. The time was growing short. More passengers arrived, and then Mr. Jephson with dignity strolled up the gangway. He was a consul and was going home on leave. He had joined the ship at Shanghai and had immediately set about making himself agreeable to Mrs. Hamlyn. But just then she was disinclined for anything in the nature of a flirtation. She frowned as she thought of the reason which was taking her back to England. She would be spending Christmas at sea, far from any one who cared two straws for her, and for a moment she felt a little twist at her heartstrings; it vexed her that a subject which she was so resolute to put away from her should so constantly intrude on her unwilling mind.

But a warning bell clanged loudly and there was a general movement among the men who sat beside her.

"Well, if we don't want to be taken on we'd better be toddling," said one of them.

They rose and walked towards the gangway. Now that they were all shaking hands she saw who it was that they had come to see the last of. There was nothing very interesting about the man on whom Mrs. Hamlyn's eyes rested, but because she had nothing better to do she gave him more than a casual glance. He was a big fellow, well over six feet high, broad and stout; he was dressed in a bedraggled suit of khaki drill and his hat was battered and shabby. His friends left him, but they bandied chaff from the quay, and Mrs. Hamlyn noticed that he had a strong Irish brogue; his voice was full, loud and hearty.

Mrs. Linsell had gone below and the doctor came and sat down beside Mrs. Hamlyn. They told one another their small adventures of the day. The bell sounded again and presently the ship slid away from the wharf. The Irishman waved a last farewell to his friends and then sauntered towards the chair on which he had left papers and magazines. He nodded to the doctor.

"Is that some one you know?" asked Mrs. Hamlyn.

"I was introduced to him at the club before tiffin. His name is Gallagher. He's a planter."

After the hubbub of the port and the noisy bustle of departure, the silence of the ship was marked and grateful. They steamed slowly past green-clad, rocky cliffs (the P. & O. anchorage was in a charming and secluded cove), and came out into the main harbor. Ships of all nations lay at anchor, a great multitude, passenger boats, tugs, lighters, tramps; and beyond, behind the breakwater, you saw the crowded masts, a bare straight forest, of the native junks. In the soft light of the evening the busy scene was strangely touched with mystery, and you felt that all those vessels, their activity for the moment suspended, waited for some event of a peculiar significance.

Mrs. Hamlyn was a bad sleeper and when the dawn broke she was in the habit of going on deck. It rested her troubled heart to watch the last faint stars fade before the encroaching day and at that early hour the glassy sea had often an immobility which seemed to make all earthly sorrows of little consequence. The light was wan, and there was a pleasant shiver in the air. But next morning when she went to the end of the promenade deck, she found that some one was up before her. It was Gallagher. He was watching the low coast of Sumatra which the sunrise like a magician seemed to call forth from the dark sea. She was startled and a little vexed, but before she could turn away he had seen her and nodded.

"Up early," he said. "Have a cigaret?"

He was in pyjamas and slippers. He took his case from his coat pocket and handed it to her. She hesitated. She had on nothing but a dressing-gown and a little lace cap which she had put over her tousled hair, and she knew that she must look a sight; but she had her reasons for scourging her soul.

"I suppose a woman of forty has no right to mind how she looks," she smiled, as tho he must know what vain thoughts occupied her. She took the cigaret. "But you're up early too."

"I'm a planter. I've had to get up at five in the morning for so many years that I don't know how I'm going to get out of the habit."

"You'll not find it will make you very popular at home."

She saw his face better now that it was not shadowed by a hat. It was agreeable without being handsome. He was of course much too fat, and his features which must have been good enough when he was a young man were thickened. His skin was red and bloated. But his dark eyes were merry; and tho he could not have been less than five and forty his hair was black and thick. He gave you an impression of great strength. He was a heavy, ungraceful, commonplace man, and Mrs. Hamlyn, except for the promiscuity of shipboard, would never have thought it worth while to talk to him.

"Are you going home on leave?" she hazarded.

"No, I'm going home for good."

His black eyes twinkled. He was of a communicative turn, and before it was time for Mrs. Hamlyn to go below in order to have her bath he had told her a good deal about himself. He had been in the Federated Malay States for twenty-five years, and for the last ten had managed an estate in Selantan. It was a hundred miles from anything that could be described as civilization and the life had been lonely; but he had made money; during the rubber boom he had done very well and with an astuteness which was unexpected in a man who looked so happy-go-lucky he had invested his savings in Government stock. Now that the slump had come he was prepared to retire.

"What part of Ireland do you come from?" asked Mrs. Hamlyn.

"Galway."

Mrs. Hamlyn had once motored through Ireland and she had a vague recollection of a sad and moody town with great stone warehouses, deserted and crumbling, which faced the melancholy sea. She had a sen-

sation of greenness and of soft rain, of silence and of
resignation. Was it here that Mr. Gallagher meant to
spend the rest of his life? He spoke of it with boyish
eagerness. The thought of his vitality in that gray
world of shadows was so incongruous that Mrs. Hamlyn
was intrigued.

"Does your family live there?" she asked.

"I've got no family. My mother and father are dead.
So far as I know I haven't a relation in the world."

He had made all his plans, he had been making them
for twenty-five years, and he was pleased to have some
one to talk to of all these things that he had been
obliged for so long only to talk to himself about. He
meant to buy a house and he would keep a motor-car.
He was going to breed horses. He didn't much care
about shooting; he had shot a lot of big game during
his first years in the F. M. S.; but now he had ? t his
zest. He didn't see why the beasts of the jungle shoul ?
be killed; he had lived in the jungle so long. But he
could hunt.

"Do you think I'm too heavy?" he asked.

Mrs. Hamlyn, smiling, looked him up and down with
appraising eyes.

"You must weigh a ton," she said.

He laughed. The Irish horses were the best in the
world, and he'd always kept pretty fit. You had a
devil of a lot of walking exercise on a rubber estate
and he'd played a good deal of tennis. He'd soon
get thin in Ireland. Then he'd marry. Mrs. Hamlyn
looked silently at the sea, colored now with the tender-
ness of the sunrise. She sighed.

"Was it easy to drag up all your roots? Is there
no one you regret leaving behind? I should have
thought after so many years, however much you'd

looked forward to going home, when the time came at last to go it must have given you a pang."

"I was glad to get out. I was fed up. I never want to see the country again or any one in it."

One or two early passengers now began to walk round the deck and Mrs. Hamlyn, remembering that she was scantily clad, went below.

During the next day or two she saw little of Mr. Gallagher, who passed his time in the smoking-room. Owing to a strike the ship was not touching at Colombo and the passengers settled down to a pleasant voyage across the Indian Ocean. They played deck games, they gossiped about one another, they flirted. The approach of Christmas gave them an occupation, for some one had suggested that there should be a fancy-dress dance on Christmas day, and the ladies set about making their dresses. A meeting was held of the first-class passengers to decide whether the second-class passengers should be invited, and notwithstanding the heat the discussion was animated. The ladies said that the second-class passengers would only feel ill-at-ease. On Christmas day it was to be expected that they would drink more than was good for them and unpleasantness might ensue. Every one who spoke insisted that there was in his (or her) mind no idea of class distinction, no one would be so snobbish as to think there was any difference between first and second-class passengers as far as that went, but it would really be kinder to the second-class passengers not to put them in a false position. They would enjoy themselves much more if they had a party of their own in the second-class cabin. On the other hand, no one wanted to hurt their feelings, and of course one had to be more democratic nowadays (this was in reply to the wife of a missionary in China

who said she had travelled on the P. & O. for thirty-
five years and she had never heard of the second-class
passengers being invited to a dance in the first-class
saloon) and even tho they wouldn't enjoy it, they
might like to come. Mr. Gallagher, dragged unwill-
ingly from the card-table, because it had been foreseen
that the voting would be close, was asked his opinion
by the consul. He was taking home in the second-class
a man who had been employed on his estate. He raised
his massive bulk from the couch on which he sat.

"As far as I'm concerned I've only got this to say:
I've got the man who was looking after our engines
with me. He's a rattling good fellow and he's just
as fit to come to your party as I am. But he won't
come because I'm going to make him so drunk on
Christmas day that by six o'clock he'll be fit for nothing
but to be put to bed."

Mr. Jephson, the consul, gave a distorted smile. On
account of his official position he had been chosen
to preside at the meeting and he wished the matter
to be taken seriously. He was a man who often said
that if a thing was worth doing it was worth doing
well.

"I gather from your observations," he said, not without acidity, "that the question before the meeting does
not seem to you of great importance."

"I don't think it matters a tinker's curse," said
Gallagher, with twinkling eyes.

Mrs. Hamlyn laughed. The scheme was at last
devised to invite the second-class passengers, but to
go to the captain privily and point out to him the
advisability of withholding his consent to their coming into the first-class saloon. It was on the evening
of the day on which this happened that Mrs. Ham-

lyn, having dressed for dinner, came on deck at the same time as Mr. Gallagher.

"Just in time for a cocktail, Mrs. Hamlyn," he said jovially.

"I'd like one. To tell you the truth I need cheering up."

"Why?" he smiled.

Mrs. Hamlyn thought his smile attractive, but she did not want to answer his question.

"I told you the other morning," she answered cheerfully. "I'm forty."

"I never met a woman who insisted on the fact so much."

They went into the lounge and the Irishman ordered a dry Martini for her and a gin pahit for himself. He had lived too long in the East to drink anything else.

"You've got hiccups," said Mrs. Hamlyn.

"Yes, I've had them all the afternoon," he answered carelessly. "It's rather funny, they came on just as we got out of sight of land."

"I daresay they'll pass off after dinner."

They drank, the second bell rang, and they went into the dining-saloon.

"You don't play bridge?" he said, as they parted.

"No."

Mrs. Hamlyn did not notice that she saw nothing of Gallagher for two or three days. She was occupied with her own thoughts. They crowded upon her when she was sewing; they came between her and the novel with which she sought to cheat their insistence. She had hoped that as the ship took her further away from the scene of her unhappiness the torment of her mind would be eased; but contrariwise, each day that brought her nearer England increased her distress. She looked forward with dismay to the bleak emptiness of the life that awaited her; and then, turning her exhausted wits from a prospect that made her flinch she considered, as she had done she knew not how many times before, the situation from which she had fled.

She had been married for twenty years. It was a long time and of course she could not expect her husband to be still madly in love with her; she was not madly in love with him; but they were good friends and they understood one another. Their marriage, as marriages go, might very well have been looked upon as a success. Suddenly she discovered that he had fallen in love. She would not have objected to a flirtation, he had had those before, and she had chaffed him about them; he had not minded that, it somewhat flattered him, and they had laughed together at an inclination which was neither deep nor serious. But this was different. He was in love as passionately as a boy of eighteen. He was fifty-two. It was ridiculous. It was indecent. And he loved without sense or prudence: by the time the hideous fact was forced upon her all the foreigners in Yokohama knew it. After the first shock of astonished anger, for he was the last man from whom such a folly might have been expected, she tried to persuade herself that she could have understood, and so have forgiven, if he had fallen in love with a girl. Middle-aged men often make fools of themselves with flappers, and after twenty years in the Far East she knew that the fifties were the dangerous age for men. But he had no excuse. He was in love with a woman eight years older than herself. It was grotesque, and it made her, his wife, perfectly absurd. Dorothy

Lacom was hard on fifty. He had known her for eighteen years, for Lacom, like her own husband, was a silk merchant in Yokohama. Year in, year out, they had seen one another three or four times a week, and once, when they happened to be in England together, had shared a house at the seaside. But nothing! Not till a year ago had there been anything between them but a chaffing friendship. It was incredible. Of course Dorothy was a handsome woman; she had a good figure, overdeveloped, perhaps, but still comely; with bold black eyes and a red mouth and lovely hair; but all that she had had years before. She was forty-eight. Forty-eight!

Mrs. Hamlyn tackled her husband at once. At first he swore that there was not a word of truth in what she accused him of, but she had her proofs; he grew sulky; and at last he admitted what he could no longer deny. Then he said an astonishing thing.

"Why should you care?" he asked.

It maddened her. She answered him with angry scorn. She was voluble, finding in the bitterness of her heart wounding things to say. He listened to her quietly.

"I've not been such a bad husband to you for the twenty years we've been married. For a long time now we've only been friends. I have a great affection for you and this hasn't altered it in the very smallest degree. I'm giving Dorothy nothing that I take away from you."

"But what have you to complain of in me?"

"Nothing. No man could want a better wife."

"How can you say that when you have the heart to treat me so cruelly?"

"I don't want to be cruel to you. I can't help myself."

"But what on earth made you fall in love with her?"

"How can I tell? You don't think I wanted to, do you?"

"Couldn't you have resisted?"

"I tried. I think we both tried."

"You talk as tho you were twenty. Why, you're both middle-aged people. She's eight years older than I am. It makes me look such a perfect fool."

He did not answer. She did not know what emotions seethed in her heart. Was it jealousy that seemed to clutch at her throat, anger, or was it merely wounded pride?

"I'm not going to let it go on. If only you and she were concerned I would divorce you, but there's her husband and then there are the children. Good heavens, does it occur to you that if they were girls instead of boys she might be a grandmother by now?"

"Easily."

"What a mercy that we have no children!"

He put out an affectionate hand as tho to caress her, but she drew back with horror.

"You've made me the laughing-stock of all my friends. For all our sakes I'm willing to hold my tongue, but only on the condition that everything stops now, at once, and forever."

He looked down and played reflectively with a Japanese knick-knack that was on the table.

"I'll tell Dorothy what you say," he replied at last.

She gave him a little bow, silently, and walked past him out of the room. She was too angry to observe that she was somewhat melodramatic.

She waited for him to tell her the result of his interview with Dorothy Lacom, but he made no further reference to the scene. He was quiet, polite, and silent; and at last she was obliged to ask him.

"Have you forgotten what I said to you the other day?" she enquired frigidly.

"No. I talked to Dorothy. She wishes me to tell you that she is desperately sorry that she has caused you so much pain. She would like to come and see you, but she is afraid you wouldn't like it."

"What decision have you come to?"

He hesitated. He was very grave, but his voice trembled a little.

"I'm afraid there's no use in our making a promise we shouldn't be able to keep."

"That settles it then," she answered.

"I think I should tell you that if you brought an action for divorce we should have to contest it. You would find it impossible to get the necessary evidence and you would lose your case."

"I wasn't thinking of doing that. I shall go back to England and consult a lawyer. Nowadays these things can be managed fairly easily and I shall throw myself on your generosity. I daresay you will enable me to get my freedom without bringing Dorothy Lacom into the matter."

He sighed.

"It's an awful muddle, isn't it? I don't want you to divorce me, but of course I'll do anything I can to meet your wishes."

"What on earth do you expect me to do?" she cried, her anger rising again. "Do you expect me to sit still and be made a damned fool of?"

"I'm awfully sorry to put you in a humiliating

position." He looked at her with harassed eyes. "I'm quite sure we didn't want to fall in love with one another. We're both of us very conscious of our age. Dorothy, as you say, is old enough to be a grandmother and I'm a baldish, stoutish gentleman of fifty-two. When you fall in love at twenty you think your love will last for ever, but at fifty you know so much about life and about love, and you know that it will last so short a time." His voice was low and rueful. It was as tho before his mind's eye he saw the sadness of autumn and the leaves falling from the trees. He looked at her gravely. "And at that age you feel that you can't afford to throw away the chance of happiness which a freakish destiny has given you. In five years it will certainly be over, and perhaps in six months. Life is rather drab and gray, and happiness is so rare. We shall be dead so long."

It gave Mrs. Hamlyn a bitter sensation of pain to hear her husband, a matter-of-fact and practical man, speak in a strain which was quite new to her. He had gained on a sudden a wistful and tragic personality of which she knew nothing. The twenty years during which they had lived together had no power over him and she was helpless in face of his determination. She could do nothing but go, and now, resentfully determined to get the divorce with which she had threatened him, she was on her way to England.

The smooth sea, upon which the sun beat down so that it shone like a sheet of glass, was as empty and hostile as life in which there was no place for her. For three days no other craft had broken in upon the solitariness of that expanse. Now and again its even surface was scattered for the twinkling of an eye by the scurry of flying fish. The heat was so great that even the most energetic of passengers had given up deck games and now (it was after luncheon) such as were not resting in their cabins lay about on chairs. Linsell strolled towards her and sat down.

"Where's Mrs. Linsell?" asked Mrs. Hamlyn.

"Oh, I don't know. She's about somewhere."

His indifference exasperated her. Was it possible that he did not see that his wife and the surgeon were falling in love with one another? Yet, not so very long ago, he must have cared. Their marriage had been romantic. They had become engaged when Mrs. Linsell was still at school and he little more than a boy. They must have been a charming, handsome pair, and their youth and their mutual love must have been touching. And now, after so short a time, they were tired of one another. It was heartbreaking. What had her husband said?

"I suppose you're going to live in London when you get home?" asked Linsell lazily, for something to say.

"I suppose so," said Mrs. Hamlyn.

It was hard to reconcile herself to the fact that she had nowhere to go and where she lived mattered not in the least to any one alive. Some association of ideas made her think of Gallagher. She envied the eagerness with which he was returning to his native land, and she was touched, and at the same time amused, when she remembered the exuberant imagination he showed in describing the house he meant to live in and the wife he meant to marry. Her friends in Yokohama, apprised in confidence of her determination to divorce her husband, had assured her that she would marry again. She did not much want to enter a second time upon a state which had once

so disappointed her, and besides, most men would
think twice before they suggested marriage to a woman
of forty. Mr. Gallagher wanted a buxom young person.

"Where is Mr. Gallagher?" she asked the submis-
sive Linsell. "I haven't seen him for the last day
or two."

"Didn't you know? He's ill."

"Poor thing. What's the matter with him?"

"He's got hiccups."

Mrs. Hamlyn laughed.

"Hiccups don't make one ill, do they?"

"The surgeon is rather worried. He's tried all sorts
of things, but he can't stop them."

"How very odd."

She thought no more about it, but next morning,
chancing upon the surgeon, she asked him how Mr.
Gallagher was. She was surprised to see his boyish,
cheerful face darken and grow perplexed.

"I'm afraid he's very bad, poor chap."

"With hiccups?" she cried in amazement.

It was a disorder that really it was impossible to
take seriously.

"You see, he can't keep any food down. He can't
sleep. He's fearfully exhausted. I've tried everything I can think of." He hesitated. "Unless I can
stop them soon—I don't quite know what'll happen."

Mrs. Hamlyn was startled.

"But he's so strong. He seemed so full of vitality."

"I wish you could see him now."

"Would he like me to go and see him?"

"Come along."

Gallagher had been moved from his cabin into the
ship's hospital, and as they approached it they heard

a loud hiccup. The sound, perhaps owing to its connection with insobriety, had in it something ludicrous. But Gallagher's appearance gave Mrs. Hamlyn a shock. He had lost flesh and the skin hung about his neck in loose folds; under the sunburn his face was pale. His eyes, before, full of fun and laughter, were haggard and tormented. His great body was shaken incessantly by the hiccups, and now there was nothing ludicrous in the sound; to Mrs. Hamlyn, for no reason that she knew, it seemed strangely terrifying. He smiled when she came in.

"I'm sorry to see you like this," she said.

"I shan't die of it, you know," he gasped. "I shall reach the green shores of Erin all right."

There was a man sitting beside him and he rose as they entered.

"This is Mr. Pryce," said the surgeon. "He was in charge of the machinery on Mr. Gallagher's estate."

Mrs. Hamlyn nodded. This was the second-class passenger to whom Gallagher had referred when they had discussed the party which was to be given on Christmas day. He was a very small man, but sturdy, with a pleasantly impudent countenance and an air of self-assurance.

"Are you glad to be going home?" asked Mrs. Hamlyn.

"You bet I am, lady," he answered.

The intonation of the few words told Mrs. Hamlyn that he was a cockney and, recognizing the cheerful, sensible, good-humored and careless type, her heart warmed to him.

"You're not Irish?" she smiled.

"Not me, miss. London's my 'ome and I shan't be sorry to see it again, I can tell you."

Mrs. Hamlyn never thought it offensive to be called miss.

"Well, sir, I'll be getting along," he said to Gallagher, with the beginning of a gesture as tho he were going to touch a cap which he hadn't got on.

Mrs. Hamlyn asked the sick man whether she could do anything for him and in a minute or two left him with the doctor. The little cockney was waiting outside the door.

"Can I speak to you a minute or two, miss?" he asked.

"Of course."

The hospital cabin was aft and they stood, leaning against the rail, and looked down on the well-deck where lascars and stewards off duty were lounging about on the covered hatches.

"I don't know exactly 'ow to begin," said Pryce, uncertainly, a serious look strangely changing his lively, puckered face. "I've been with Mr. Gallagher for four years now and a better gentleman you wouldn't find in a week of Sundays."

He hesitated again.

"I don't like it and that's the truth."

"What don't you like?"

"Well, if you ask me 'e's for it, and the doctor don't know it. I told 'im, but 'e won't listen to a word I say."

"You musn't be too depressed, Mr. Pryce. Of course the doctor's young, but I think he's quite clever, and people don't die of hiccups, you know. I'm sure Mr. Gallagher will be all right in a day or two."

"You know when it come on? Just as we was out of sight of land. She said 'e'd never see 'is 'ome."

Mrs. Hamlyn turned and faced him. She stood a good three inches taller than he.

"What do you mean?"

"My belief is, it's a spell been put on 'im, if you understand what I mean. Medicine's going to do 'im no good. You don't know them Malay women like what I do."

For a moment Mrs. Hamlyn was startled, and because she was startled she shrugged her shoulders and laughed.

"Oh, Mr. Pryce, that's nonsense."

"That's what the doctor said when I told 'im. But you mark my words, 'e'll die before we see land again."

The man was so serious that Mrs. Hamlyn, vaguely uneasy, was against her will impressed.

"Why should any one cast a spell on Mr. Gallagher?" she asked.

"Well, it's a bit awkward speakin' of it to a lady."

"Please tell me."

Pryce was so embarrassed that at another time Mrs. Hamlyn would have had difficulty in concealing her amusement.

"Mr. Gallagher's lived a long time up-country, if you understand what I mean, and of course it's lonely, and you know what men are, miss."

"I've been married for twenty years," she replied, smiling.

"I beg your pardon, ma'am. The fact is he had a Malay girl living with him. I don't know 'ow long, ten or twelve years, I think. Well, when he made up 'is mind to come 'ome for good she didn't say nothing. She just sat there. He thought she'd carry on no end, but she didn't. Of course 'e provided for 'er all right, 'e gave 'er a little 'ouse for herself, an' 'e fixed it up so as so much should be paid 'er every month; 'e wasn't mean, I will say that for 'im, an' she knew all along, as 'e'd be going some time. She didn't cry or anything. When 'e packed up all 'is things and sent them off he just sat there an' watched 'em go. And when 'e sold 'is furniture to the Chinks she never said a word. He'd give 'er all she wanted. And when it was time for 'im to go so as to catch the boat she just kep' on sitting, on the steps of the bungalow, you know, and she just looked an' said nothing. He wanted to say good-by to 'er, same as any one would, an', would you believe it? she never even moved. 'Aren't you going to say good-by to me?' he says. A rare funny look came over 'er face. And do you know what she says? 'You go,' she says; they 'ave a funny way of talking, them natives, not like we 'ave; 'you go,' she says, 'but I tell you that you will never come to your own country. When the land sinks into the sea death will come upon you, an' before them as goes with you sees the land again, death will have took you.' It gave me quite a turn."

"What did Mr. Gallagher say?" asked Mrs. Hamlyn.

"Oh, well, you know what 'e is. He just laughed. 'Always merry an' bright,' he says and he jumps into the motor, an' off we go."

Mrs. Hamlyn saw the bright and sunny road that ran through the rubber estates, with their trim green trees, carefully spaced, and their silence, and then wound its way up hill and down through the tangled jungle. The car raced on, driven by a reckless Malay, with its white passengers, past Malay houses that stood away from the road among the coconut trees, sequestered and taciturn, and through busy villages where the market-place was crowded with dark-skinned little people in gay sarongs. Then towards evening it reached the trim, modern town, with its clubs and its golf links, its well-ordered rest-house, its white people, and its railway station, from which the two men could take the train to Singapore. And the woman sat on the steps of the bungalow, empty till the new manager moved in, and watched the road down which the car had panted, watched the car as it sped on, and watched till at last it was lost in the shadow of the night.

"What was she like?" Mrs. Hamlyn asked.

"Oh, well, to my way of thinking them Malay women are all very much alike, you know," Pryce answered. "Of course she wasn't so young any more and you know what they are, them natives, they run to fat something terrible."

"Fat?"

The thought, absurdly enough, filled Mrs. Hamlyn with dismay.

"Mr. Gallagher was always one to do himself well, if you understand what I mean."

The idea of corpulence at once brought Mrs. Hamlyn back to common sense. She was impatient with herself because for an instant she had seemed to accept the little cockney's suggestion.

"It's perfectly absurd, Mr. Pryce. Fat women can't throw spells on people at a distance of a thousand miles. In fact life is very difficult for a fat woman any way."

"You can laugh, miss, but unless something's done, you mark my words, the governor's for it. And medicine ain't goin' to save him, not white man's medicine."

"Pull yourself together, Mr. Pryce. This fat lady had no particular grievance against Mr. Gallagher. As

these things are done in the East he seems to have
treated her very well. Why should she wish him any
harm?"

"We don't know 'ow they look at things. Why, a
man can live there for twenty years with one of them
natives, and d'you think 'e knows what's goin' on in
that black heart of hers? Not 'im!"

She could not smile at his melodramatic language,
for his intensity was impressive. And she knew, if
any one did, that the hearts of men, whether their
skins are yellow or white or brown, are incalculable.

"But even if she felt angry with him, even if she
hated him and wanted to kill him, what could she
do?" It was strange that Mrs. Hamlyn with her
questions was trying now, unconsciously, to reassure
herself. "There's no poison that could start working after six or seven days."

"I never said it was poison."

"I'm sorry, Mr. Pryce," she smiled, "but I'm not
going to believe in a magic spell, you know."

"You've lived in the East."

"Off and on for twenty years."

"Well, if you can say what they can do and what
they can't, it's more than I can." He clenched his
fist and beat it on the rail with sudden, angry violence. "I'm fed up with the bloody country. It's
got on my nerves, that what it is. We're no match
for them, us white men, and that's a fact. If you'll
excuse me I think I'll go an' 'ave a tiddley. I've got
the jumps."

He nodded abruptly and left her. Mrs. Hamlyn
watched him, a sturdy, shuffling little man in shabby
khaki slither down the companion into the waist of
the ship, walk across it with bent head, and disap-

pear into the second-class saloon. She did not know why he left with her a vague uneasiness. She could not get out of her mind that picture of a stout woman, no longer young, in a sarong, a colored jacket and gold ornaments, who sat on the steps of a bungalow looking at an empty road. Her heavy face was painted, but in her large, tearless eyes there was no expression. The men who drove in the car were like schoolboys going home for the holidays. Gallagher gave a sigh of relief. In the early morning, under the bright sky, his spirits bubbled. The future was like a sunny road that wandered through a wide-flung, wooded plain.

Later in the day Mrs. Hamlyn asked the doctor how his patient did. The doctor shook his head.

"I'm done. I'm at the end of my tether." He frowned unhappily. "It's rotten luck, striking a case like this. It would be bad enough at home, but on board ship . . ."

He was an Edinburgh man, but recently qualified, and he was taking this voyage as a holiday before settling down to practise. He felt himself aggrieved. He wanted to have a good time and, faced with this mysterious illness, he was worried to death. Of course he was inexperienced, but he was doing everything that could be done and it exasperated him to suspect that the passengers thought him an ignorant fool.

"Have you heard what Mr. Pryce thinks?" asked Mrs. Hamlyn.

"I never heard such rot. I told the captain and he's right up in the air. He doesn't want it talked about. He thinks it'll upset the passengers."

"I'll be as silent as the grave."

The surgeon looked at her sharply.

"Of course you don't believe that there can be any truth in nonsense of that sort?" he asked.

"Of course not." She looked out at the sea which shone, blue and oily and still, all round them. "I've lived in the East a long time," she added. "Strange things happen there."

"This is getting on my nerves," said the doctor.

Near them two little Japanese gentlemen were playing deck quoits. They were trim and neat in their tennis shirts, white trousers and buckram shoes. They looked very European, they even called the score to one another in English, and yet somehow to look at them filled Mrs. Hamlyn at that moment with a vague disquiet. Because they seemed to wear so easily a disguise there was about them something sinister. Her nerves too were on edge.

And presently, no one quite knew how, the notion spread through the ship that Gallagher was bewitched. While the ladies sat about on their deck-chairs, stitching away at the costumes they were making for the fancy-dress party on Christmas day, they gossiped about it in undertones, and the men in the smoking-room talked of it over their cocktails. A good many of the passengers had lived long in the East and from the recesses of their memory they produced strange and inexplicable stories. Of course it was absurd to think seriously that Gallagher was suffering from a malignant spell, such things were impossible, and yet this and that was a fact and no one had been able to explain it. The doctor had to confess that he could suggest no cause for Gallagher's condition, he was able to give a physiological explanation, but why these terrible spasms should have suddenly assailed him he did not say. Feeling vaguely to blame, he tried to defend himself.

"Why, it's the sort of a case you might never come across in the whole of your practice," he said. "It's rotten luck."

He was in wireless communication with passing ships and suggestions for treatment came from here and there.

"I've tried everything they tell me," he said irritably. "The doctor of the Japanese boat advised adrenalin. How the devil does he expect me to have adrenalin in the middle of the Indian Ocean?"

There was something impressive in the thought of this ship speeding through a deserted sea while to her from all parts came unseen messages. She seemed at that moment strangely alone and yet the center of the world. In the lazaret the sick man, shaken by the cruel spasms, gasped for life. Then the passengers became conscious that the ship's course was altered and they heard that the captain had made up his mind to put in at Aden. Gallagher was to be landed there and taken to the hospital where he could have attention which on board was impossible. The chief engineer received orders to force his engines. The ship was an old one and she throbbed with the greater effort. The passengers had grown used to the sound and feel of her engines and now the greater vibration shook their nerves with a new sensation. It would not pass into each one's unconsciousness, but beat on their sensibilities so that each felt a personal concern. And still the wide sea was empty of traffic so that they seemed to traverse an empty world. And now the uneasiness which had descended upon the ship, but which no one had been willing to acknowledge, became

a definite malaise. The passengers grew irritable, and
people quarrelled over trifles which at another time
would have seemed insignificant. Mr. Jephson made
his hackneyed jokes, but no one any longer repaid him
with a smile. The Linsells had an altercation and
Mrs. Linsell was heard late at night walking around the
deck with her husband, and uttering in a low, tense
voice a stream of vehement reproaches. There was a
violent scene in the smoking-room one night over a
game of bridge, and the reconciliation which followed it
was attended with general intoxication. People talked
little of Gallagher, but he was seldom absent from
their thoughts. They examined the route map. The
doctor said now that Gallagher could not live more than
three or four days and they discussed acrimoniously
what was the shortest time in which Aden could be
reached. What happened to him after he was landed
was no affair of theirs; they did not want him to
die on board.

Mrs. Hamlyn saw Gallagher every day. With the
suddenness with which after tropical rain in the spring
you seem to see the herbage grow before your very
eyes, she saw him go to pieces. Already his skin
hung loosely on his bones and his double chin was
like the wrinkled wattle of a turkey-cock. His cheeks
were sunken. You saw now how large his frame was
and through the sheet under which he lay his bony
structure was like the skeleton of a prehistoric giant.
For the most part he lay with his eyes closed, torpid
with morphia, but shaken still with terrible spasms, and
when now and again he opened his eyes they were
preternaturally large; they looked at you vaguely, perplexed and troubled, from the depths of their bony
sockets. But when, emerging from his stupor, he

recognized Mrs. Hamlyn he forced a gallant smile to his lips.

"How are you, Mr. Gallagher?" she said.

"Getting along, getting along. I shall be all right when we get out of this confounded heat. Lord, how I look forward to a dip in the Atlantic. I'd give anything for a good long swim. I want to feel the cold gray sea of Galway beating against my chest."

Then the hiccup shook him from the crown of his head to the sole of his foot. Mr. Pryce and the stewardess shared the care of him. The little cockney's face wore no longer its look of impudent gaiety, but instead was sullen.

"The captain sent for me yesterday," he told Mrs. Hamlyn when they were alone. "He gave me a rare talking to."

"What about?"

"He said 'e wouldn't 'ave all this hoodoo stuff. He said it was frightening the passengers and I'd better keep a watch on me tongue or I'd 'ave 'im to reckon with. It's not my doing. I never said a word except to you and the doctor."

"It's all over the ship."

"I know it is. D'you think it's only me that's saying it? All them lascars and the Chinese, they all know what's the matter with him. You don't think you can teach them much, do you? They know it ain't a natural illness."

Mrs. Hamlyn was silent. She knew through the amahs of some of the passengers that there was no one on the ship, except the whites, who doubted that the woman whom Gallagher had left in distant Selantan was killing him with her magic. All were convinced that as they sighted the barren rocks of Arabia his soul would be parted from his body.

"The captain says if he hears of me trying any hanky-panky he'll confine me to my cabin for the rest of the voyage," said Pryce suddenly, a surly frown on his puckered face.

"What do you mean by hanky-panky?"

He looked at her for a moment fiercely as tho she too were an object of the anger he felt against the captain.

"The doctor's tried every damned thing he knows, and he's wirelessed all over the place, and what good 'as 'e done? Tell me that. Can't 'e see the man's dying? There's only one way to save him now."

"What do you mean?"

"It's magic what's killing 'im, and it's only magic what'll save him. Oh, don't you say it can't be done. I've seen it with me own eyes." His voice rose, irritable and shrill. "I've seen a man dragged from the jaws of death, as you might say, when they got in a *pawang*, what we call a witch-doctor, an' 'e did 'is little tricks. I seen it with me own eyes, I tell you."

Mrs. Hamlyn did not speak. Pryce gave her a searching look.

"One of them lascars on board, he's a witch-doctor, same as the *pawang* thet we 'ave in the F. M. S. An' 'e says he'll do it. Only he must 'ave a live animal. A cock will do."

"What do you want a live animal for?" Mrs. Hamlyn asked, frowning a little.

The cockney looked at her with quick suspicion.

"If you take my advice you won't know anything about it. But I tell you what, I'm going to leave no stone unturned to save my governor. An' if the captain 'ears of it and shuts me up in me cabin, well, let 'im."

At that moment Mrs. Linsell came up and Pryce with his quaint gesture of salute left them. Mrs. Linsell wanted Mrs. Hamlyn to fit the dress she had been making herself for the fancy-dress ball, and on the way down to the cabin she spoke to her anxiously about the possibility that Mr. Gallagher might die on Christmas day. They could not possibly have the dance if he did. She had told the doctor that she would never speak to him again if this happened, and the doctor had promised her faithfully that he would keep the man alive over Christmas day somehow.

"It would be nice for him, too," said Mrs. Linsell.

"For whom?" asked Mrs. Hamlyn.

"For poor Mr. Gallagher. Naturally no one likes to die on Christmas day. Do they?"

"I don't really know," said Mrs. Hamlyn.

That night, after she had been asleep a little while, she awoke weeping. It dismayed her that she should cry in her sleep. It was as tho when the weakness of the flesh mastered her, and, her will broken, she was defenseless against a natural sorrow. She turned over in her mind, as so often before, the details of the disaster which had so profoundly affected her; she repeated the conversations with her husband, wishing she had said this and blaming herself because she had said the other. She wished with all her heart that she had remained in comfortable ignorance of her husband's infatuation, and asked herself whether she would not have been wiser to pocket her pride and shut her eyes to the unwelcome truth. She was a woman of the world and she knew too

well how much more she lost in separating herself
from her husband than his love; she lost the settled establishment and the assured position, the ample
means and the support of a recognized background.
She had known of many separated wives, living
equivocally on smallish incomes, and knew how quickly
their friends found them tiresome. And she was
lonely. She was as lonely as the ship that throbbed her
hasting way through an unpeopled sea, and lonely as
the friendless man who lay dying in the ship's lazaret.
Mrs. Hamlyn knew that her thoughts had got the
better of her now and that she would not easily sleep
again. It was very hot in her cabin. She looked at
the time; it was between four and half-past; she must
pass two mortal hours before broke the reassuring
day.

She slipped into a kimono and went on deck. The
night was somber and altho the sky was unclouded
no stars were visible. Panting and shaking, the old
ship under full steam lumbered through the darkness.
The silence was uncanny. Mrs. Hamlyn with bare feet
groped her way slowly along the deserted deck. It was
so black that she could see nothing. She came to the
end of the promenade deck and leaned against the
rail. Suddenly she started and her attention was fixed,
for on the lower deck she caught a fitful glow. She
leaned forward cautiously. It was a little fire, and she
saw only the glow because the naked backs of men,
crouched round, hid the flame. At the edge of the
circle she divined, rather than saw, a stocky figure in
pyjamas. The rest were natives, but this was a European. It must be Pryce and she guessed immediately
that some dark ceremony of exorcizm was in progress.
Straining her ears she heard a voice muttering a

string of secret words. She began to tremble. She was aware that they were too intent upon their business to think that any one was watching them, but she dared not move. Suddenly, rending the sultry silence of the night like a piece of silk violently torn in two, came the crowing of a cock. Mrs. Hamlyn almost shrieked. Mr. Pryce was trying to save the life of his friend and master by a sacrifice to the strange gods of the East. The voice went on, low and insistent. Then in the dark circle there was a movement, something was happening, she knew not what; there was a cluck-cluck from the cock, angry and frightened, and then a strange, indescribable sound; the magician was cutting the cock's throat; then silence; there were vague doings that she could not follow, and in a little while it looked as tho some one was stamping out the fire. The figures she had dimly seen were dissolved in the night and all once more was still. She heard again the regular throbbing of the engines.

Mrs. Hamlyn stood still for a little while, strangely shaken, and then walked slowly along the deck. She found a chair and lay down on it. She was trembling still. She could only guess what had happened. She did not know how long she lay there, but at last she felt that the dawn was approaching. It was not yet day, but it was no longer night. Against the darkness of the sky she could now see the ship's rail. Then she saw a figure come towards her. It was a man in pyjamas.

"Who's that?" she cried nervously.

"Only the doctor," came a friendly voice.

"Oh! What are you doing here at this time of night?"

"I've been with Gallagher." He sat down beside
her and lit a cigaret. "I've given him a good strong
hypodermic and he's quiet now."

"Has he been very ill?"

"I thought he was going to pass out. I was watching him, and suddenly he started up on his bed and
began to talk Malay. Of course I couldn't understand a thing. He kept on saying one word over and
over again."

"Perhaps it was a name, a woman's name."

"He wanted to get out of bed. He's a damned
powerful man even now. By George, I had a struggle with him. I was afraid he'd throw himself overboard. He seemed to think some one was calling
him."

"When was that?" asked Mrs. Hamlyn slowly.

"Between four and half-past. Why?"

"Nothing."

She shuddered.

Later in the morning when the ship's life was set
upon its daily round, Mrs. Hamlyn passed Pryce on
the deck, but he gave her a brief greeting and walked
on with quickly averted gaze. He looked tired and
overwrought. Mrs. Hamlyn thought again of that
fat woman, with golden ornaments in her thick, black
hair, who sat on the steps of the deserted bungalow
and looked at the road which ran through the trim
lines of the rubber trees.

It was fearfully hot. She knew now why the night
had been so dark. The sky was no longer blue, but
a dead, level white; its surface was too even to give
the effect of cloud; it was as tho in the upper air
the heat hung like a pall. There was no breeze and
the sea, as colorless as the sky, was smooth and

shining like the dye in a dyer's vat. The passengers were listless; when they walked round the deck they panted and beads of sweat broke out on their foreheads. They spoke in undertones. Something uncanny and disquieting brooded over the ship, and they could not bring themselves to laugh. A feeling of resentment arose in their hearts; they were alive and well, and it exasperated them that, so near, a man should be dying and by the fact (which was after all no concern of theirs) so mysteriously affect them. A planter in the smoking-room over a gin sling said brutally what most of them felt, tho none had confessed.

"Well, if he's going to peg out," he said, "I wish he'd hurry up and get it over. It gives me the creeps."

The day was interminable. Mrs. Hamlyn was thankful when the dinner hour arrived. So much time, at all events, was passed. She sat at the doctor's table.

"When do we reach Aden?" she asked.

"Some time to-morrow. The captain says we shall sight land between five and six in the morning."

She gave him a sharp look. He stared at her for a moment, then dropped his eyes and reddened. He remembered that the woman, the fat woman sitting on the bungalow steps, had said that Gallagher would never see the land. Mrs. Hamlyn wondered whether he, the skeptical, matter-of-fact young doctor, was wavering at last. He frowned a little, and then, as tho he sought to pull himself together, looked at her once more.

"I shan't be sorry to hand over my patient to the hospital people at Aden, I can tell you," he said.

Next day was Christmas eve. When Mrs. Hamlyn awoke from a troubled sleep the dawn was break-

ing. She looked out of her porthole and saw that
the sky was clear and silvery; during the night the
haze had melted, and the morning was brilliant. With
a lighter heart she went on deck. She walked as far
forward as she could go. A late star twinkled palely
close to the horizon. There was a shimmer on the
sea as tho a loitering breeze passed playful fingers
over its surface. The light was exquisitely soft, ten-
uous like a budding wood in spring, and crystalline
so that it reminded you of the bubbling of water in a
mountain brook. She turned to look at the sun rising
rosy in the east, and saw coming towards her the
doctor. He wore his uniform; he had not been to
bed all night; he was dishevelled and he walked, with
bowed shoulders, as tho he were dog-tired. She knew
at once that Gallagher was dead. When he came up
to her she saw that he was crying. He looked so young
then that her heart went out to him. She shook his
hand.

"You poor dear," she said. "You're tired out."

"I did all I could," he said. "I wanted so awfully
to save him."

His voice shook and she saw that he was almost
hysterical.

"When did he die?" she asked.

He closed his eyes, trying to control himself, and
his lips trembled.

"A few minutes ago."

Mrs. Hamlyn sighed. She found nothing to say.
Her gaze wandered across the calm, dispassionate and
ageless sea. It stretched on all sides of them as infinite
as human sorrow. But on a sudden her eyes were held,
for there, ahead of them, on the horizon, was something which looked like a precipitous and massy cloud.

But its outline was too sharp to be a cloud's. She touched the doctor on the arm.

"What's that?"

He looked at it for a moment and under his sunburn she saw him grow white.

"Land."

Once more Mrs. Hamlyn thought of the fat Malay woman who sat silent on the steps of Gallagher's bungalow. Did she know?

They buried him when the sun was high in the heavens. They stood on the lower deck and on the hatches, the first- and second-class passengers, the white stewards and the European officers. The missionary read the burial service.

"Man that is born of woman hath but a short time to live, and is full of misery. He cometh up, and is cut down, like a flower; he fleeth as it were a shadow, and never continueth in one stay."

Pryce looked down at the deck with knit brows. His teeth were tightly clenched. He did not grieve, for his heart was hot with anger. The doctor and the consul stood side by side. The consul bore to a nicety the expression of an official regret, but the doctor, clean-shaven now, in his neat fresh uniform and his gold braid, was pale and harassed. From him Mrs. Hamlyn's eyes wandered to Mrs. Linsell. She was pressed against her husband, weeping, and he was holding her hand tenderly. Mrs. Hamlyn did not know why this sight singularly affected her. At that moment of grief, her nerves distraught, the little woman went by instinct to the protection and support of her husband. But then Mrs. Hamlyn felt a little shudder pass through her and she fixed her eyes on the seams in the deck, for she did not want to see what was

toward. There was a pause in the reading. There
were various movements. One of the officers gave an
order. The missionary's voice continued.

*"Forasmuch as it has pleased Almighty God of
His great mercy to take unto himself the soul of our
dear brother here departed; we therefore commend his
body to the deep, to be turned into corruption, looking
for the resurrection of the body when the sea shall
give up its dead."*

Mrs. Hamlyn felt the hot tears flow down her cheeks.
There was a dull splash. The missionary's voice went
on.

When the service was finished the passengers scattered; the second-class passengers returned to their
quarters and a bell rang to summon them to luncheon.
But the first-class passengers sauntered aimlessly about
the promenade deck. Most of the men made for the
smoking-room and sought to cheer themselves with
whiskies and sodas and with gin slings. But the consul
put up a notice on the board outside the dining-saloon
summoning the passengers to a meeting. Most of
them had an idea for what purpose it was called and
at the appointed hour they assembled. They were
more cheerful than they had been for a week and
they chattered with a gaiety which was only subdued
by a mannerly reserve. The consul, an eye-glass in his
eye, said that he had gathered them together to dis-
cuss the question of the fancy-dress ball on the following day. He knew they all had the deepest sympathy for Mr. Gallagher and he would have proposed
that they should combine to send an appropriate mes-
sage to the deceased's relatives; but his papers had been
examined by the purser and no trace could be found of
any relative or friend with whom it was possible to

communicate. The late Mr. Gallagher appeared to be quite alone in the world. Meanwhile he (the consul) ventured to offer his sincere sympathy to the doctor who, he was quite sure, had done everything that was possible in the circumstances.

"Hear, hear," said the passengers.

They had all passed through a very trying time, proceeded the consul, and to some it might seem that it would be more respectful to the deceased's memory if the fancy-dress ball were postponed till New Year's eve. This, however, he told them frankly was not his view, and he was convinced that Mr. Gallagher himself would not have wished it. Of course it was a question for the majority to decide. The doctor got up and thanked the consul and the passengers for the kind things that had been said of him, it had of course been a very trying time, but he was authorized by the captain to say that the captain expressly wished all the festivities to be carried out on Christmas day as tho nothing had happened. He (the doctor) tolu them in confidence that the captain felt the passengers had got into a rather morbid state and thought it would do them all good if they had a jolly good time on Christmas day. Then the missionary's wife rose and said they mustn't think only of themselves; it had been arranged by the Entertainment Committee that there should be a Christmas tree for the children immediately after the first-class passengers' dinner, and the children had been looking forward to seeing every one in fancy dress; it would be too bad to disappoint them; she yielded to no one in her respect for the dead and she sympathized with any one who felt too sad to think of dancing just then. Her own heart was very heavy, but she did feel it would be merely selfish to give way to a feeling

which could do no good to any one. Let them think
of the little ones. This very much impressed the passengers. They wanted to forget the brooding terror
which had hung over the boat for so many days, they
were alive and they wanted to enjoy themselves; but
they had an uneasy notion that it would be decent to
exhibit a certain grief. It was quite another matter if
they could do as they wished from altruistic motives.
When the consul called for a show of hands every one,
but Mrs. Hamlyn and one old lady who was rheumatic,
held up an eager arm.

"The ayes have it," said the consul. "And I venture
to congratulate the meeting on a very sensible decision."

It was just going to break up when one of the planters
got on his feet and said he wished to offer a suggestion.
In the circumstances didn't they all think it would be
as well to invite the second-class passengers? They
had all come to the funeral that morning. The missionary jumped up and seconded the motion. The
events of the last few days had drawn them all together,
he said, and in the presence of death all men were
equal. The consul again addressed them. This matter
had been discussed at a previous meeting and the con-
clusion had been reached that it would be pleasanter
for the second-class passengers to have their own party,
but circumstances alter cases, and he was distinctly of
opinion that their previous decision should be reversed.

"Hear, hear," said the passengers.

A wave of democratic feeling swept over them and
the motion was carried by acclamation. They separated
light-heartedly, they felt charitable and kindly. Every
one stood every one else drinks in the smoking-room.

And so, on the following evening, Mrs. Hamlyn put
on her fancy-dress. She had no heart for the gaiety

before her, and for a moment had thought of feigning illness, but she knew no one would believe her, and was afraid to be thought affected. She was dressed as Carmen and she could not resist the vanity of making herself as attractive as possible. She darkened her eyelashes and rouged her cheeks. The costume suited her. When the bugle sounded and she went into the saloon she was received with flattering surprize. The consul (always a humorist) was dressed as a ballet-girl and was greeted with shouts of delighted laughter. The missionary and his wife, self-conscious but pleased with themselves, were very grand as Manchus. Mrs. Linsell, as Columbine, showed all that was possible of her very pretty legs. Her husband was an Arab sheik and the doctor was a Malay sultan.

A subscription had been collected to provide champagne at dinner and the meal was hilarious. The company had provided crackers in which were paper hats of various shapes and these the passengers put on. There were paper streamers too which they threw at one another and little balloons which they beat from one to the other across the room. They laughed and shouted. They were very gay. No one could say that they were not having a good time. As soon as dinner was finished they went into the saloon where the Christmas tree, with candles lit, was ready, and the children were brought in, shrieking with delight, and given presents. Then the dance began. The second-class passengers stood about shyly round the part of the deck reserved for dancing and occasionally danced with one another.

"I'm glad we had them," said the consul, dancing with Mrs. Hamlyn. "I'm all for democracy, and I think they're very sensible to keep themselves to themselves."

But she noticed that Pryce was not to be seen, and when an opportunity presented asked one of the second-class passengers where he was.

"Blind to the world," was the answer. "We put him to bed in the afternoon and locked him up in his cabin."

The consul claimed her for another dance. He was very facetious. Suddenly Mrs. Hamlyn felt that she could not bear it any more, the noise of the amateur band, the consul's jokes, the gaiety of the dancers. She knew not why, but the merriment of those people passing on their ship through the night and the solitary sea affected her on a sudden with horror. When the consul released her she slipped away and, with a look to see that no one had noticed her, ascended the companion to the boat-deck. Here everything was in darkness. She walked softly to a spot where she knew she would be safe from all intrusion. But she heard a faint laugh and she caught sight in a hidden corner of a Columbine and a Malay sultan. Mrs. Linsell and the doctor had resumed already the flirtation which the death of Gallagher had interrupted.

Already all those people had put out of their minds with a kind of ferocity the thought of that poor lonely man who had so strangely died in their midst. They felt no compassion for him, but resentment rather, because on his account they had been ill-at-ease. They seized upon life avidly. They made their jokes, they flirted, they gossiped. Mrs. Hamlyn remembered what the consul had said, that among Mr. Gallagher's papers no letter could be found, not the name of a single friend to whom the news of his death might be sent, and she knew not why this seemed to her unbearably tragic. There was something mysterious in a man who could pass through the world in such solitariness. When she remembered how he had come on deck in Singapore, so short a while since, in such rude health, full of vitality, and his arrogant plans for the future, she was seized with dismay. Those words of the burial service filled her with a solemn awe: *Man that is born of woman hath but a short time to live, and is full of misery. He cometh up, and is cut down, like a flower.* . . . Year in, year out, he had made his plans for the future, he wanted to live so much and he had so much to live for, and then just when he stretched out his hand—oh, it was pitiful; it made all the other distresses of the world of small account. Death with its mystery was the only thing that really mattered. Mrs. Hamlyn leaned over the rail and looked at the starry sky. Why did people make themselves unhappy? Let them weep for the death of those they loved, death was terrible always, but for the rest, was it worth while to be wretched, to harbor malice, to be vain and uncharitable? She thought again of herself and her husband and the woman he so strangely loved. He too had said that we live to be happy so short a time and we are so long dead. She pondered long and intently, and suddenly, as summer lightning flashes across the darkness of the night, she made a discovery which filled her with tremulous surprise; for she found that in her heart was no longer anger with her husband nor jealousy of her rival. A notion dawned on some remote horizon of her consciousness and like the morning sun suffused her soul with a tender, blissful glow. Out of the tragedy of that unknown Irishman's death she gathered elatedly the courage for a desperate resolution. Her heart beat quickly, she was impatient to carry it into effect. A passion for self-sacrifice seized her.

The music had stopped, the ball was over; most of

the passengers would have gone to bed and the rest would be in the smoking-room. She went down to her cabin and met no one on the way. She took her writing-pad and wrote a letter to her husband.

> *My dear. It is Christmas day and I want to tell you that my heart is filled with kindly thoughts towards both of you. I have been foolish and unreasonable. I think we should allow those we care for to be happy in their own way, and we should care for them enough not to let it make us unhappy. I want you to know that I grudge you none of the joy that has so strangely come into your life. I am no longer jealous, nor hurt, nor vindictive. Do not think I shall be unhappy or lonely. If ever you feel that you need me, come to me, and I will welcome you with a cheerful spirit and without reproach or ill-will. I am most grateful for all the years of happiness and of tenderness that you gave me, and in return I wish to offer you an affection which makes no claim on you and is, I hope, utterly disinterested. Think kindly of me and be happy, happy, happy.*

She signed her name and put the letter into an envelop. Tho it would not go till they reached Port Said she wanted to place it at once in the letter-box. When she had done this, beginning to undress, she looked at herself in the glass. Her eyes were shining and under her rouge her color was bright. The future was no longer desolate, but bright with a fair hope. She slipped into bed and fell at once into a sound and dreamless sleep.

THE WOMAN AND HER BONDS

By Edwin Lefevre

It seemed to Fullerton F. Colwell, of the famous
Stock-Exchange house of Wilson & Graves, that he
had done his full duty by his friend Harry Hunt.
He was a director in a half-score of companies—
financial *débutants*—which his firm had "brought out"
and over whose stock-market destinies he presided.
His partners left a great deal to him, and even the
clerks in the office ungrudgingly acknowledged that Mr.
Colwell was "the hardest working man in the place,
barring none"—an admission that means much to those
who know it is always the downtrodden clerks who do
all the work and their employers who take all the profit
and credit. Possibly the important young men who
did all the work in Wilson & Graves' office bore wit-
ness to Mr. Colwell's industry so cheerfully, because
Mr. Colwell was ever inquiring, very courteously, and,
above all, sympathetically, into the amount of work
each man had to perform, and suggesting, the next
moment, that the laborious amount in question was
indisputably excessive. Also, it was he who raised sal-
aries; wherefore he was the most charming as well as
the busiest man there. Of his partners, John G. Wilson
was a consumptive, forever going from one health-
resort to another, devoting his millions to the purchase
of railroad tickets in the hope of out-racing Death.

(From "Wall Street Stories," by Edwin Lefevre; copyright, 1916,
by Harper & Bros.)

George B. Graves was a dyspeptic, nervous, irritable, and, to boot, penurious; a man whose chief recommendation at the time Wilson formed the firm had been his cheerful willingness to do all the dirty work—not an inconsiderable portion of the every-day business of a big Wall Street house. Frederick R. Denton was busy in the "Board Room"—the Stock-Exchange—all day, executing orders, keeping watch over the market behavior of the stocks with which the firm was identified, and from time to time hearing things not meant for his ears, being the truth regarding Wilson & Graves. But Fullerton F. Colwell had to do everything—in the stock-market and in the office. He conducted the manipulation of the Wilson & Graves stocks, took charge of the un-nefarious part of the numerous pools formed by the firm's customers—Mr. Graves attending to the other details—and had a hand in the actual management of various corporations. Also, he conferred with a dozen people daily—chiefly "big people," in Wall Street parlance—who were about to "put through" stock-market "deals." He had devoted his time, which was worth thousands, and his brain, which was worth millions, to disentangling his careless friend's affairs, and when it was all over and every claim adjusted, and he had refused the executor's fees to which he was entitled, it was found that poor Harry Hunt's estate not only was free from debt, but consisted of $38,000 in cash, deposited in the Trolleyman's Trust Company, subject to Mrs. Hunt's order, and drawing interest at the rate of 2½ per cent. per annum. He had done his work wonderfully well, in addition to the cash, the widow owned an unencumbered house Harry had given her during his lifetime.

Not long after the settlement of the estate Mrs.

Hunt called at his office. It was a very busy day. The bears were misbehaving—and misbehaving mighty successfully. Alabama Coal & Iron—the firm's great specialty—was under heavy fire from "Sam" Sharpe's Long Tom as well as from the room-traders' Maxims. All that Colwell could do was to instruct Denton, who was on the ground to "support" *Ala. C. & I* sufficiently to discourage the enemy, and not enough to acquire the company's entire capital stock. He was himself at that moment practising that peculiar form of financial dissimulation which amounts to singing blithely at the top of your voice when your beloved sackful of gold has been ripped by bear-paws and the coins are pouring out through the rent. Every quotation was of importance; a half-inch of tape might contain an epic of disaster. It was not wise to fail to read every printed character.

"Good morning, Mr. Fullerton."

He ceased to pass the tape through his fingers, and turned quickly, almost apprehensively, for a woman's voice was not heard with pleasure at an hour of the day when distractions were undesirable.

"Ah, good morning, Mrs. Hunt," he said, very politely. "I am very glad indeed to see you. And how do you do?" He shook hands, and led her, a bit ceremoniously, to a huge arm-chair. His manners endeared him even to the big Wall Street operators, who were chiefly interested in the terse speech of the ticker.

"Of course, you are very well, Mrs. Hunt. Don't tell me you are not."

"Ye-es," hesitatingly. "As well as I can hope to be since—since Harry left me."

"Time alone, dear Mrs. Hunt, can help us. You

must be very brave. It is what he would have liked."

"Yes, I know," she sighed. "I suppose I must."

There was a silence. He stood by, deferentially, sympathetic.

"Ticky-ticky-ticky-tick," said the ticker.

What did it mean, in figures? Reduced to dollars and cents, what did the last three brassy taps say? Perhaps the bears were storming the Alabama Coal & Iron intrenchments of "scaled buying orders"; perhaps Colwell's trusted lieutenant, Fred Denton, had repulsed the enemy. Who was winning? A spasm, as of pain, passed over Mr. Fullerton F. Colwell's grave face. But the next moment he said to her, slightly conscience-strickenly, as if he reproached himself for thinking of the stock-market in her presence: "You must not permit yourself to brood, Mrs. Hunt. You know what I thought of Harry, and I need not tell you how glad I shall be to do what I may, for his sake, Mrs. Hunt, and for your own."

"Ticky-ticky-ticky-tick!" repeated the ticker.

To avoid listening to the voluble little machine, he went on. "Believe me, Mrs. Hunt, I shall be only too glad to serve you."

"You are so kind, Mr. Colwell," murmured the widow; and after a pause: "I came to see you about that money."

"Yes?"

"They tell me in the trust company that if I leave the money there without touching it I'll make $79 a month."

"Let me see; yes; that is about what you may expect."

"Well, Mr. Colwell, I can't live on that. Willie's school costs me $50, and then there's Edith's clothes."

she went on, with the air of a martyr, which implies
that as for herself she wouldn't care at all. "You see,
he was so indulgent, and they are used to so much.
Of course, it's a blessing we have the house; but taxes
take up so much; and—isn't there some way of invest-
ing the money so it could bring more?"

"I might buy some bonds for you. But for your
principal to be absolutely safe at all times, you will
have to invest in very high-grade securities, which will
return to you about 3½ per cent. That would mean,
let's see, $110 a month."

"And Harry spent $10,000 a year," she murmured,
complainingly.

"Harry was always—er—rather extravagant."

"Well, I'm glad he enjoyed himself while he lived,"
she said, quickly. Then, after a pause: "And, Mr.
Colwell, if I should get tired of the bonds, could I always get my money back?"

"You could always find a ready market for them.
You might sell them for a little more or for a little
less than you paid."

"I shouldn't like to sell them," she said, with a
business air, "for less than I paid. What would be
the sense?"

"You are right, Mrs. Hunt," he said encouragingly.
"It wouldn't be very profitable, would it?"

"*Ticky-ticky-ticky-ticky-ticky-ticky-tick!*" said the
ticker. It was whirring away at a furious rate. Its
story is always interesting when it is busy. And Colwell had not looked at the tape in fully five minutes!

"Couldn't you buy something for me, Mr. Colwell,
that when I came to sell it I could get more than it
cost me?"

"No man can guarantee that, Mrs. Hunt."

"I shouldn't like to lose the little I have," she said, hastily.

"Oh, there is no danger of that. If you will give me a check for $35,000, leaving $3,000 with the trust company for emergencies, I shall buy some bonds which I feel reasonably certain will advance in price within a few months."

"Ticky-ticky-ticky-tick," interrupted the ticker. In some inexplicable way it seemed to him that the brassy sound had an ominous ring, so he added: "But you will have to let me know promptly, Mrs. Hunt. The stock-market, you see, is not a polite institution. It waits for none, not even for your sex."

"Gracious me, must I take the money out of the bank to-day and bring it to you?"

"A check will do." He began to drum on the desk nervously with his fingers, but ceased abruptly as he became aware of it.

"Very well. I'll send it to you to-day. I know you're very busy, so I won't keep you any longer. And you'll buy good, cheap bonds for me?"

"Yes, Mrs. Hunt."

"There's no danger in losing, is there, Mr. Colwell?"

"None whatever. I have bought some for Mrs. Colwell, and I would not run the slightest risk. You need have no fear about them."

"It's exceedingly kind of you. Mr. Colwell, I am more grateful than I can say. I—I——"

"The way to please me is not to mention it, Mrs. Hunt. I am going to try to make some money for you, so that you can at least double the income from the trust company."

"Thanks, ever so much. Of course, I know you are thoroughly familiar with such things. But I've heard so much about the money everybody loses in Wall Street that I was half afraid."

"Not when you buy good bonds, Mrs. Hunt."

"Good morning, Mr. Colwell."

"Good morning, Mrs. Hunt. Remember, whenever I may be of service you are to let me know immediately."

"Oh, thank you so much, Mr. Colwell. Good morning."

"Good morning, Mrs. Hunt."

Mrs. Hunt sent him a check for $35,000, and Colwell bought 100 five-per cent. gold bonds of the Manhattan Electric Light, Heat & Power Company, paying 96 for them.

"These bonds," he wrote to her, "will surely advance in price, and when they touch a good figure I shall sell a part, and keep the balance for you as an investment. The operation is partly speculative, but I assure you the money is safe. You will have an opportunity to increase your original capital and your entire funds will then be invested in these same bonds— Manhattan Electric 5s—as many as the money will buy. I hope within six months to secure for you an income of twice as much as you have been receiving from the trust company."

The next morning she called at his office.

"Good morning, Mrs. Hunt, I trust you are well."

"Good morning, Mr. Colwell. I know I am an awful bother to you, but——"

"You are greatly mistaken, Mrs. Hunt."

"You are very kind. You see, I don't exactly understand about these bonds. I thought you could tell me. I'm so stupid," archly.

"I won't have you prevaricate about yourself, Mrs. Hunt. Now, you gave me $35,000, didn't you?"

"Yes." Her tone indicated that she granted that much and nothing more.

"Well, I opened an account for you with our firm. You were credited with the amount. I then gave an order to buy one hundred bonds of $1,000 each. We paid 96 for them."

"I don't follow you quite, Mr. Colwell. I told you"—another arch smile—"I was so stupid!"

"It means that for each $1,000-bond $960 was paid. It brought the total up to $96,000."

"But I only had $35,000 to begin with. You don't mean I've made that much, do you?"

"Not yet, Mrs. Hunt. You put in $35,000; that was your margin, you know; and we put in the other $61,-000 and kept the bonds as security. We owe you $35,-000, and you owe us $61,000, and——"

"But—I know you'll laugh at me, Mr. Colwell—but I really can't help thinking it's something like the poor people you read about, who mortgage their houses, and they go on, and the first thing you know some real-estate agent owns the house and you have nothing. I have a friend, Mrs. Stilwell, who lost hers that way," she finished, corroboratively.

"This is not a similar case, exactly. The reason why you use a margin is that you can do much more with the money that way than if you bought outright. It protects your broker against a depreciation in the security purchased, which is all he wants. In this case you owe us $61,000, but the bonds are in your name, and they are worth $96,000, so that if you want to pay us back, all you have to do is to order us to sell the bonds, return the money we have advanced, and keep

the balance of your margin; that is, of your original
sum."

"I don't understand why I should owe the firm. I
shouldn't mind so much owing you, because I know
you'd never take advantage of my ignorance of business matters. But I've never met Mr. Wilson nor
Mr. Graves. I don't even know how they look."

"But you know me," said Mr. Colwell, with patient
courtesy.

"Oh, it isn't that I'm afraid of being cheated, Mr.
Colwell," she said, hastily and reassuringly; "but I
don't wish to be under obligations to any one, particularly utter strangers; tho of course, if you say
it is all right, I am satisfied."

"My dear Mrs. Hunt, don't worry about this matter.
We bought these bonds at 96. If the price should
advance to 110, as I think it will, then you can sell
three-fifths for $66,000 pay us back $61,000, and
keep $5,000 for emergencies in savings-banks drawing
4 per cent. interest, and have in addition 40 bonds
which will pay you $2,000 a year."

"That would be lovely. And the bonds are now 96?"

"Yes; you will always find the price in the financial
page of the newspapers, where it says BONDS. Look
for *Man. Elec. 5s*," and he showed her.

"Oh, thanks, ever so much. Of course, I am a
great bother, I know——"

"You are nothing of the kind, Mrs. Hunt. I'm only
too glad to be of the slightest use to you."

"Good morning, Mr. Colwell."

"Good morning, Mrs. Hunt."

Mr. Colwell, busy with several important "deals,"
did not follow closely the fluctuations in the price of
Manhattan Electric Light, Heat & Power Company 5s.

The fact that there had been any change at all was made clear to him by Mrs. Hunt. She called a few days after her first visit, with peturbation written large on her face. Also, she wore the semi-resolute look of a person who expects to hear unacceptable excuses.

"Good morning, Mr. Colwell."

"How do you do, Mrs. Hunt? Well, I hope."

"Oh, I am well enough. I wish I could say as much for my financial matters." She had acquired the phrase from the financial reports which she had taken to reading religiously every day.

"Why, how is that?"

"They are 95 now," she said, a trifle accusingly.

"Who are *they*, pray, Mrs. Hunt?" in surprise.

"The bonds. I saw it in last night's paper."

Mr. Colwell smiled. Mrs. Hunt almost became indignant at his levity.

"Don't let that worry you, Mrs. Hunt. The bonds are all right. The market is a trifle dull; that's all."

"A friend," she said, very slowly, who knows all about Wall Street, told me last night that it made a difference of $1,000 to me."

"So it does, in a way; that is, if you tried to sell your bonds. But as you are not going to do so until they show you a handsome profit, you need not worry. Don't be concerned about the matter, I beg of you. When the time comes for you to sell the bonds I'll let you know. Never mind if the price goes off a point or two. You are amply protected. Even if there should be a panic I'll see that you are not sold out, no matter how low the price goes. You are not to worry about it; in fact, you are not to think about it at all."

"Oh, thanks, ever so much, Mr. Colwell. I didn't sleep a wink last night. But I knew——"

A clerk came in with some stock-certificates and stopped short. He wanted Mr. Colwell's signature in a hurry, and at the same time dared not interrupt. Mrs. Hunt thereupon rose and said: "Well, I won't take up any more of your time. Good morning, Mr. Colwell. Thanks ever so much."

"Don't mention it, Mrs. Hunt. Good morning. You are going to do very well with those bonds if you only have patience."

"Oh, I'll be patient now that I know all about it; yes, indeed. And I hope your prophecy will be fulfilled. Good morning, Mr. Colwell."

"Good morning."

Little by little the bonds continued to decline. The syndicate in charge was not ready to move them. But Mrs. Hunt's unnamed friend—her Cousin Emily's husband—who was employed in an up-town bank, did not know all the particulars of that "deal." He knew the Street in the abstract, and had accordingly implanted the seed of insomnia in her quaking soul. Then, as he saw values decline, he did his best to make the seed grow, fertilizing a naturally rich soil with ominous hints and head-shakings and with phrases that made her firmly believe he was gradually and considerately preparing her for the worst. On the third day of her agony Mrs. Hunt walked into Colwell's office. Her face was pale and she looked distressed. Mr. Colwell sighed involuntarily—a scarcely perceptible and not very impolite sigh—and said: "Good morning, Mrs. Hunt."

She nodded gravely and silently, gasped twice, and said, tremulously: "The bonds!"

"Yes? What about them?"

She gasped again, and said: "The p-p-papers!"

"What do you mean, Mrs. Hunt?"

She dropped into a chair nervelessly, as if exhausted. After a pause she said: "It's in all the papers. I thought the *Herald* might be mistaken, so I bought the *Tribune* and the *Times* and the *Sun*. But no. It was the same in all. It was," she added, tragically, "93!"

"Yes?" he said, smilingly.

The smile did not reassure her; it irritated her and aroused her suspicions. By him, of all men, should her insomnia be deemed no laughing matter.

"Doesn't that mean a loss of $3,000?" she asked. There was a deny-it-if-you-dare inflection in her voice of which she was not conscious. Her cousin's husband had been a careful gardener.

"No, because you are not going to sell your bonds at 93, but at 110, or thereabouts."

"But if I did want to sell the bonds now, wouldn't I lose $3,000?" she queried, challengingly. Then she hastened to answer herself: "Of course I would, Mr. Colwell. Even I can tell that."

"You certainly would, Mrs. Hunt; but—"

"I knew I was right," with irrepressible triumph.

"But you are not going to sell the bonds."

"Of course, I don't want to, because I can't afford to lose any money, much less $3,000. But I don't see how I can help losing it. I was warned from the first," she said, as if that made it worse. "I certainly had no business to risk my all." She had waived the right to blame some one else, and there was something consciously just and judicial about her attitude that was eloquent. Mr. Colwell was moved by it.

"You can have your money back, Mrs. Hunt, if you

wish it," he told her, quite unprofessionally. "You seem to worry about it so much."

"Oh, I am not worrying, exactly; only, I do wish I hadn't bought them—I mean, the money was so safe in the Trolleyman's Trust Company, that I can't help thinking I might just as well have let it stay where it was, even if it didn't bring me in so much. But, of course, if you want me to leave it here," she said, very slowly to give him every opportunity to contradict her, "of course, I'll do just as you say."

"My dear Mrs. Hunt," Colwell said very politely, "my only desire is to please you and to help you. When you buy bonds you must be prepared to be patient. It may take months before you will be able to sell yours at a profit, and I don't know how low the price will go in the meantime. Nobody can tell you that, because nobody knows. But it need make no difference to you whether the bonds go to 90, or even to 85, which is unlikely."

"Why, how can you say so, Mr. Colwell? If the bonds go to 90, I'll lose $6,000—my friend said it was one thousand for every number down. And at 85 that would be"—counting on her fingers—"eleven numbers, that is, *eleven—thousand—dollars!*" And she gazed at him, awe-strickenly, reproachfully. "How *can* you say it would make no difference, Mr. Colwell?"

Mr. Colwell fiercely hated the unnamed "friend," who had told her so little and yet so much. But he said to her, mildly: "I thought that I had explained all that to you. It might hurt a weak speculator if the bonds declined ten points, tho such a decline is utterly improbable. But it won't affect you in the slightest, since, having an ample margin, you would not be forced to sell. You would simply hold on until the price rose again. Let me illustrate. Supposing your house cost $10,000 and—"

"Harry paid $32,000," she said, correctly. On second thought she smiled, in order to let him see that she knew her interpolation was irrelevant. But he might as well know the actual cost.

"Very well," he said, good-humoredly, "we'll say $32,000, which was also the price of every other house in that block. And suppose that, owing to some accident, or for any reason whatever, nobody could be found to pay more than $25,000 for one of the houses and three or four of your neighbors sold theirs at that price. But you wouldn't, because you knew that in the fall, when everybody came back to town, you would find plenty of people who'd give you $50,000 for your house; you wouldn't sell it for $25,000, and you wouldn't worry. Would you, now?" he finished cheerfully.

"No," she said slowly, "I wouldn't worry. But," hesitatingly, for, after all, she felt the awkwardness of her position, "I wish I had the money instead of the bonds." And she added, self-defensively: "I haven't slept a wink for three nights thinking about this."

The thought of his coming emancipation cheered Mr. Colwell immensely. "Your wish shall be gratified, Mrs. Hunt. Why didn't you ask me before, if you felt that way?" he said, in mild reproach. And he summoned a clerk.

"Make out a check for $35,000 payable to Mrs. Rose Hunt, and transfer the 100 Manhattan Electric Light 5s to my personal account."

He gave her the check and told her: "Here is the money. I am very sorry that I unwittingly caused you some anxiety. But all's well that ends well. Any time that I can be of service to you—Not at all. Don't thank me, please; no. Good morning."

But he did not tell her that by taking over her account he paid $96,000 for bonds he could have bought in the open market for $93,000. He was the politest man in Wall Street; and, after all, he had known Hunt many years.

A week later Manhattan Electric 5-per cent. bonds sold at 96 again. Mrs. Hunt called on him. It was noon, and she evidently had spent the morning mustering up courage for the visit. They greeted one another, she embarrassed and he courteous and kindly as usual.

"Mr. Colwell, you still have those bonds, haven't you?"

"Why, yes."

"I—I think I'd like to take them back."

"Certainly, Mrs. Hunt. I'll find out how much they are selling for." He summoned a clerk to get a quotation on Manhattan Electric 5s. The clerk telephoned to one of their bond-specialists, and learned that the bonds could be bought at 96½. He reported to Mr. Colwell, and Mr. Colwell told Mrs. Hunt, adding: "So you see they are practically where they were when you bought them before."

She hesitated. "I—I—didn't you buy them from me at 93? I'd like to buy them back at the same price I sold them to you."

"No, Mrs. Hunt," he said; "I bought them from you at 96."

"But the price was 93." And she added, corroboratively: "Don't you remember it was in all the papers?"

"Yes, but I gave you back exactly the same amount that I received from you, and I had the bonds transferred to my account. They stand on our books as having cost me 96."

"But couldn't you let me have them at 93?" she persisted.

"I'm very sorry, Mrs. Hunt, but I don't see how I could. If you buy them in the open market now, you will be in exactly the same position as before you sold them, and you will make a great deal of money, because they are going up now. Let me buy them for you at 96½."

"At 93, you mean," with a tentative smile.

"At whatever price they may be selling for," he corrected, patiently.

"Why did you let me sell them, Mr. Colwell?" she asked, plaintively.

"But, my dear madam, if you buy them now, you will be no worse off than if you had kept the original lot."

"Well, I don't see why it is that I have to pay 96½ now for the very same bonds I sold last Tuesday at 93. If it was some other bonds," she added, "I wouldn't mind so much."

"My dear Mrs. Hunt, it makes no difference which bonds you hold. They have all risen in price, yours and mine and everybody's; your lot was the same as any other lot. You see that, don't you?"

"Ye-es; but——"

"Well, then, you are exactly where you were before you bought any. You've lost nothing, because you received your money back intact."

"I'm willing to buy them," she said resolutely, "at 93."

"Mrs. Hunt, I wish I could buy them for you at

that price. But there are none for sale cheaper than 96½."

"Oh, why did I let you sell my bonds!" she said, disconsolately.

"Well, you worried so much because they had declined that——"

"Yes, but I didn't know anything about business matters. You know I didn't, Mr. Colwell," she finished, accusingly.

He smiled in his good-natured way. "Shall I buy the bonds for you?" he asked. He knew the plans of the syndicate in charge, and being sure the bonds would advance, he thought she might as well share in the profits. At heart he felt sorry for her.

She smiled back. "Yes," she told him, "at 93." It did not seem right to her, notwithstanding his explanations, that she should pay 96½ for them, when the price a few days ago was 93.

"But how can I, if they are 96½?"

"Mr. Colwell, it is 93 or nothing." She was almost pale at her own boldness. It really seemed to her as if the price had only been waiting for her to sell out in order to advance. And tho she wanted the bonds she did not feel like yielding.

"Then I very much fear it will have to be nothing."

"Er—good morning, Mr. Colwell," on the verge of tears.

"Good morning, Mrs. Hunt." And before he knew it, forgetting all that had gone before, he added: "Should you change you mind, I should be glad to—"

"I know I wouldn't pay more than 93 if I lived to be a thousand years." She looked expectantly at him, to see if he had repented, and she smiled—the smile that is a woman's last resort, that says, almost articu lately: "I know you will, of course, do as I ask. My question is only a formality. I know your nobility, and I fear not." But he only bowed her out, very politely.

On the Stock-Exchange the price of *Man. Elec. L. H. & P. Co. 5s* rose steadily. Mrs. Hunt, too indignant to feel lachrymose, discussed the subject with her Cousin Emily and her husband. Emily was very much interested. Between her and Mrs. Hunt they forced the poor man to make strange admissions, and, deliberately ignoring his feeble protests, they worked themselves up to the point of believing that, while it would be merely generous of Mr. Colwell to let his friend's widow have the bonds at 93, it would be only his obvious duty to let her have them at 96½. The moment they reached this decision Mrs. Hunt knew how to act. And the more she thought the more indignant she became. The next morning she called on her late husband's executor and friend.

Her face wore the look often seen on those ardent souls who think their sacred and inalienable rights have been trampled upon by the tyrant Man, but who at the same time feel certain the hour of retribution is near.

"Good morning, Mr. Colwell. I came to find out exactly what you propose to do about my bonds." Her voice conveyed the impression that she expected violent opposition, perhaps even bad language, from him.

"Good morning, Mrs. Hunt. Why, what do you mean?"

His affected ignorance deepened the lines on her face. Instead of bluster he was using *finesse!*

"I think *you* ought to know, Mr. Colwell," she said, meaningly.

"Well, I really don't. I remember you wouldn't heed my advice when I told you not to sell out, and again when I advised you to buy them back."

"Yes, at 96½," she burst out, indignantly.

"Well, if you had, you would to-day have a profit of over $7,000."

"And whose fault is it that I haven't?" She paused for a reply. Receiving none, she went on: "But never mind; I have decided to accept your offer," very bitterly, as if a poor widow could not afford to be a chooser; "I'll take those bonds at 96½." And she added, under her breath: "Altho it really ought to be 93."

"But, Mrs. Hunt," said Colwell, in measureless astonishment, "you can't do that, you know. You wouldn't buy them when I wanted you to, and I can't buy them for you now at 96½. Really, you ought to see that."

Cousin Emily and she had gone over a dozen imaginary interviews with Mr. Colwell—of varying degrees of storminess—the night before, and they had, in an idle moment, and not because they really expected it, represented Mr. Colwell as taking that identical stand. Mrs. Hunt was, accordingly, prepared to show both that she knew her moral and technical rights, and that she was ready to resist any attempt to ignore them. So she said, in a voice so ferociously calm that it should have warned any guilty man: "Mr. Colwell, will you answer me one question?"

"A thousand, Mrs. Hunt, with pleasure."

"No; only one. Have you kept the bonds that I bought, or have you not?"

"What difference does that make, Mrs. Hunt?"

He evaded the answer!

"Yes or no, please. Have you, or have you not those same identical bonds?"

"Yes; I have. But——"

"And to whom do those bonds belong, by rights?" She was still pale, but resolute.

"To me, certainly."

"To *you*, Mr. Colwell?" She smiled. And in her smile were a thousand feelings; but not mirth.

"Yes, Mrs. Hunt, to me."

"And do you propose to keep them?"

"I certainly do."

"Not even if I pay 96½ will you give them to me?"

"Mrs. Hunt," Colwell said with warmth, "when I took those bonds off your hands at 93 I took an actual loss of $3,000——"

She smiled in pity—pity for his judgment in thinking her so hopelessly stupid.

"And when you wanted me to sell them back to you at 93 after they had risen to 96½, if I had done as you wished, it would have meant an additional loss of $3,500 to me."

Again she smiled—the same smile, only the pity was now mingled with rising indignation.

"For Harry's sake I was willing to pocket the first loss, in order that you might not worry. But I didn't see why I should make you a present of $3,500," he said, very quietly.

"I never asked you to do it," she retorted, hotly.

"If you had lost any money through my fault, it would have been different. But you had your original capital unimpaired. You had nothing to lose, if you bought back the same bonds at practically the same price. Now you come and ask me to sell you the bonds at 96½ that are selling in the market for 104 which means that I should make you another present of $7,000 or $8,000—as a reward, I suppose, for your refusal to take my advice."

"Mr. Colwell, you take advantage of my position to insult me. And Harry trusted you so much! But let me tell you that I am not going to let you do just as you please. No doubt you would like to have me go home and forget how you've acted toward me. But I am going to consult a lawyer, and see if I am to be treated this way by a *friend* of my husband's. You've made a mistake, Mr. Colwell."

"Yes, madam, I certainly have. And, in order to avoid making any more, you will oblige me greatly by never again calling at this office. By all means consult a lawyer. Good morning, madam," said the politest man in Wall Street.

"We'll see," was all she said; and she left the room.

Colwell paced up and down his office nervously. It was seldom that he allowed himself to lose his temper, and he did not like it. The ticker whirred away excitedly, and in an absent-minded, half-disgusted way he glanced sideways at it.

"*Man. Elec. 5s, 106⅛*," he read on the tape.

THE END OF CANDIA

By GABRIELE D'ANNUNZIO

Chapter I

Three days after the Easter banquet, which was
traditionally a great occasion in the Lamonica household, both in its lavishness and in the number of its
guests, Donna Cristina Lamonica was counting the
table linen and silver service, and replacing them one
by one, methodically, in drawer and cupboard, in readi-
ness for future banquets.

As usual, she had with her, to help in the task, the
chambermaid, Maria Bisaccia, and the laundress, Can-
dida Marcanda, familiarly known as Candia. The huge
hampers, filled with fine linen, stood in a row upon the
floor. The silver platters and other table service gleamed
brightly from the sideboard—massive vessels, somewhat
crudely wrought by rustic silversmiths, and of more or
less liturgical design, like all the plate which rich pro-
vincial families hand down from generation to generation.
A fresh fragrance of soapy water pervaded the room.

From the hampers Candia took tablecloths, napkins,
and towels; she made the mistress take note that each
piece was intact, and then passed them over to Maria,
who laid them away in the drawers, while the mistress
sprinkled lavender between them and entered the numbers in a book. Candia was a tall, lean, angular woman

of fifty, with back somewhat bent from the habitual attitude of her calling, with arms of unusual length, and the head of a bird of prey mounted on a turtle's neck. Maria Bisaccia was a native of Ortona, a trifle stout, with a fresh complexion and the clearest of eyes; she had a soft fashion of speech, and the light, leisurely touch of one whose hands were almost always busy over cakes and sirups, pastry and preserves. Donna Cristina, also an Ortonese, and educated in a Benedictine convent, was of small stature, with a somewhat too generous expanse of bosom, a face overstrewn with freckles, a large, long nose, poor teeth, and handsome eyes cast downward in a way that made one think of a priest in woman's clothing.

The three women were performing their task with the utmost care, giving up to it the greater part of the afternoon. All at once, just as Candia was leaving with the empty baskets, Donna Cristina, in the course of counting the small silver, found that a spoon was missing.

"Maria! Maria!" she cried, in utter dismay, "count these! There's a spoon missing! Count them yourself!"

"But how could it? That's impossible, Signora!" replied Maria, "let me have a look." And she in turn began to count the small pieces, telling off the numbers aloud, while Donna Cristina looked on, shaking her head. The silver gave forth a clear, ringing sound.

"Well, it's a fact!" Maria exclaimed at last, with a gesture of despair; "what's to be done about it!"

She herself was safe from all suspicion. For fifteen years she had given proofs of her fidelity and honesty in this very household. She had come from Ortona together with Donna Cristina at the time of the wedding, almost as tho she were a part of the marriage settlement; and from the first she had acquired a certain authority in the house, through the indulgence of her mistress. She was full of religious superstitions, devoted to the saint and the belfry of her birthplace, and possessed of great shrewdness. She and her mistress had formed a sort of offensive alliance against Pescara and all pertaining to it, and more particularly against the saint of the Pescarese. She never missed a chance to talk of her native town, to vaunt its beauty and its riches, the splendor of its basilica, the treasures of San Tommaso, the magnificence of its religious ceremonies, as compared with the poverty of San Cetteo, that possessed only one single little silver cross

Donna Cristina said:

"Take a good look in there."

Maria left the room to extend the search. She explored every nook and corner of the kitchen and the balcony, but in vain. She came back empty-handed.

"It isn't there! It isn't there!"

Then the two together tried to think, to make conjectures, to ransack their memories. They went out upon the balcony that communicated with the court, the balcony back of the laundry, to make one last research. As they talked together in loud tones, women's heads began to appear at the windows of the surrounding houses.

"What has happened, Donna Cristina? Tell us about it."

Donna Cristina and Maria related the occurrence with many words and many gestures.

"Lord, Lord! Then there have been thieves here?"

In a moment the report of the theft had spread through the neighborhood, through all Pescara. Men and women fell to discussing, to imagining who could have been the thief. By the time the news had reached the most distant houses of Sant' Agostino, it had gathered volume; it was no longer a question of a mere spoon, but of all the silver plate in the house of Lamonica.

Now, since the weather was fine and roses were beginning to bloom upon the balcony, and a pair of linnets were singing in their cage, the women lingered at their windows, for the pleasure of gossiping across the grateful warmth of the outdoor air. Female heads continued to appear from behind the pots of sweet basil, and a chatter arose that must have rejoiced the cats upon the housetops.

Clasping her hands, Donna Cristina asked: "Who could it have been?"

Donna Isabella Sertale, nicknamed the Polecat, who had the lithe and stealthy movements of a breast of prey, asked in a strident voice: "Who did you have with you, Donna Cristina? It seems to me that I saw Candia on her way——"

"Ahah!" exclaimed Donna Felicetta Margasanta, nicknamed the Magpie because of her continuous garrulity. "Ahah!" repeated the other gossips.—"And you hadn't thought of it?"—"And you never noticed?" —"And you don't know about Candia?"—"We can tell you about Candia!"—"Indeed we can!"—"Oh, yes, we can tell you about her!"

"She washes clothes well, there is no denying it. She is the best laundress in Pescara, there's no question about it. But the trouble with her is that she is too light-fingered—didn't you know that, my dear?"

"She got a couple of towels from me once."—"And a napkin from me."—"And a night-gown from me."— "And three pairs of stockings from me."—"And a new

petticoat from me."—"And I never got them back
again."—"Nor I."—"Nor I."

"But I didn't discharge her. Whom could I get?
Silvestra?"

"Oh! oh!"

"Angelantonia? The African?"

"Each one worse than the other!"

"We must put up with it."

"But it's a spoon this time!"

"That's a little too much!"

"Don't you let it pass, Donna Cristina, don't you let
it pass!"

"Let it pass, or not let it pass!" burst forth Maria
Bisaccia, who, in spite of her placid and benign appearance, never let an opportunity pass for displaying
her superiority over her fellow servants. "That is for
us to decide, Donna Isabella, that is for us to decide!"

And the chatter continued to flow back and forth
from windows to balcony. And the accusation spread
from lip to lip throughout the whole countryside.

Chapter II

The following morning, Candia Marcanda already
had her arms in a tubful of clothes, when the village
constable, Biagio Pesce, nicknamed the Little Corporal,
appeared at her door.

"His Honor, the mayor, wants you up at his office
right away," he told the laundress.

"What's that?" demanded Candia, wrinkling her brows
into a frown, yet without interrupting the task before her.

"His Honor, the mayor, wants you up at his office,
right away."

"Wants me? What does he want me for?" Candia

demanded rather sharply, for she was at a loss to understand this unexpected summons, and it turned her as stubborn as a horse balking at a shadow.

"I can't tell you what for," replied the Little Corporal, "those were my orders."

"What were your orders?" From an obstinacy that was natural to her, she would not cease from asking questions. She could not convince herself that it was a reality. "The mayor wants me? What for? What have I done, I should like to know? I'm not going? I haven't done anything."

The Little Corporal, losing his temper, answered: "Oh, you won't go, won't you? We'll see about that!" and he went off, muttering, with his hand upon the hilt of the ancient sword he wore.

Meanwhile there were others along the narrow street who had overheard the conversation and came out upon their doorsteps, where they could watch Candia vigorously working her arms up and down in the tubful of clothes. And since they knew about the silver spoon, they laughed meaningly and interchanged ambiguous phrases, which Candia could not understand. But this laughter and these phrases awoke a vague forboding in the woman's mind. And this forboding gathered strength when the Little Corporal reappeared, accompanied by another officer.

"Step lively," said the Little Corporal peremptorily.

Candia wiped her arms, without replying, and went with them. In the public square, people stopped to look. One of her enemies, Rosa Panura, called out from the door of her shop, with a hateful laugh: "Drop your stolen bone!"

The laundress, dazed by this persecution for which she could find no reason, was at a loss for a reply.

Before the mayor's office a group of curious idlers had gathered to watch her as she went in. Candia, in an access of anger, mounted the steps in a rush and burst into the mayor's presence, breathlessly demanding: "Well, what is it you want of me?"

Don Silla, a man of peaceful proclivities, was for the moment perturbed by the laundress's strident tones, and cast a glance at the two faithful custodians of his official dignity. Then, taking a pinch of tobacco from his horn snuff-box, he said to her: "My daughter, be seated."

But Candia remained standing. Her beak-like nose was inflated with anger, and her wrinkled cheeks quivered curiously. "Tell me, Don Silla."

"You went yesterday to take back the wash to Donna Cristina Lamonica?"

"Well, and what of it? What of it? Was there anything missing? All of it counted, piece by piece—and not a thing missing. What's the matter with it now?"

"Wait a moment, my daughter! In the same room there was the table silver—"

Candia, comprehending, turned like an angry hawk, about to swoop upon its prey. Her thin lips twitched convulsively.

"The silver was in the room, and Donna Cristina found that a spoon was missing. Do you understand, my daughter? Could you have taken it—by mistake?"

Candia jumped like a grasshopper before the injustice of this accusation. As a matter of fact she had stolen nothing.

"Oh, it was I, was it? I? Who says so? Who saw me? I am astonished at you, Don Silla! I am astonished at you! I, a thief? I? I?"

And there was no end to her indignation. She was all the more keenly stung by the unjust charge, because she knew herself to be capable of the action they attributed to her.

"Then it was you who took it?" interrupted Don Silla, prudently sinking back into the depths of his spacious judicial chair.

"I am astonished at you!" snarled the woman once more, waving her long arms around as tho they had been two sticks.

"Very well, you may go. We will see about it."

Candia went out without a salutation, blindly bumping into the doorpost. She had turned fairly green; she was beside herself. As she set foot in the street and saw the crowd which had gathered, she realized that already public opinion was against her; that no one was going to believe in her innocence. Nevertheless, she began to utter a vociferous denial. The crowd continued to laugh as it dispersed. Full of fury, she returned home, and hopelessly began to weep upon her doorstep.

Don Donato Brandimarte, who lived next door, said mockingly: "Cry louder, cry louder! There are people passing by!"

Since there were heaps of clothing still waiting for the suds, she finally calmed herself, bared her arms, and resumed her task. As she worked, she thought out her denials, elaborated a whole system of defense, sought out in her shrewd woman's brain an ingenious method of establishing her innocence; racking her brain for specious subtleties, she had recourse to every trick of rustic dialectic to construct a line of reasoning that would convince the most incredulous.

Then, when her day's work was ended, she went out, deciding to go first to see Donna Cristina.

Donna Cristina was not to be seen. It was Maria Bisaccia who listened to Candia's flood of words, shaking her head but answering nothing, and withdrawing in dignified silence.

Next, Candia made the circuit of all her clients. To each in turn she related the occurrence, to each she unfolded her defense, continually adding some new argument, amplifying her words, growing constantly more excited, more desperate, in the face of incredulity and distrust. And all in vain; she felt that from now on there was no further defense possible. A sort of blind hopelessness took possession of her—what more was there to do? What more was there to say?

Chapter III

Meanwhile Donna Cristina Lamonica gave orders to send for Cinigia, a woman of the people, who practised magic and empirical medicine with considerable success. Cinigia had several times before discovered stolen goods; and it was said that she was secretly in league with the thieves.

"Find that spoon for me," Donna Cristina told her, "and you shall have a big reward."

"Very well," Cinigia replied; "twenty-four hours are all I need."

And twenty-four hours later she brought back her answer; the spoon was to be found in a hole in the courtyard, near the well.

Donna Cristina and Maria descended to the courtyard, made search, and, to their great amazement, found the spoon.

Swiftly the news spread throughout Pescara.

Then triumphantly Candia Marcanda went the rounds of all the streets. She seemed to have grown taller; she held her head erect; she smiled, looking every one straight in the eye, as if to say, "I told you so! I told you so!"

The people in the shops, seeing her pass by, would murmur something and then break forth into a significantly sneering laugh. Filippo La Selvi, who sat drinking a glass of liqueur brandy in the Café d'Ange, called Candia in.

"Another glass for Candia, the same as mine!"

The woman, who was fond of strong spirits, pursed up her lips covetously.

"You certainly deserve it, there's no denying that!" added Filippo La Selvi.

An idle crowd had gathered in front of the café. They all had the spirit of mischief in their faces. While the woman drank, Filippo La Selvi turned and addressed his audience:

"Say, she knew how to work it, didn't she? Isn't she the foxy one?" and he slapped the laundress familiarly upon her bony shoulder.

The crowd laughed. A little dwarf, called Magnafave, or "Big Beans," weak-minded and stuttering, joined the forefinger of his right hand to that of his left, and striking a grotesque attitude and dwelling upon each syllable, said:

"Ca—ca—ca—Candia—Ci—ci—Cinigia!" and he continued to make gestures and to stammer forth vulgar witticisms, all implying that Candia and Cinigia were in league together. His spectators indulged in contortions of merriment.

For a moment Candia sat there bewildered, with the

glass still in her hand. Then in a flash she understood —they did not believe in her innocence. They accused her of having brought back the silver spoon secretly, by agreement with the sorceress, to save herself further trouble.

An access of blind anger came upon her. Speechless with passion, she flung herself upon the weakest of them, upon the little hunchback, in a hurricane of blows and scratches. And the crowd, at the sight of this struggle, formed a circle and jeered at them in cruel glee, as at a fight between two animals, and egged on the two combatants with voice and gesture.

Big Beans, badly scared by her unexpected violence, tried to escape, hopping about like a little ape; and held fast by the laundress's terrible arms, whirled round and round with increasing velocity, like a stone in a sling, until at last he fell violently upon his face.

Some of the men hastened to pick him up. Candia withdrew in the midst of hisses, shut herself within her house, and flung herself across her bed, sobbing and gnawing her fingers, in the keenness of her suffering. The new accusation cut her deeper than the first, and all the more that she knew herself capable of such a subterfuge. How was she to clear herself now? How was she to establish the truth? She grew hopeless as she realized that she could not allege in defense any material difficulties that might have interfered with carrying out the deception. Access to the courtyard was perfectly simple; a door, that was never fastened, opened from the ground floor of the main stairway; people came and went freely through that door, to remove the garbage, or for other causes. So it was impossible for her to close the lips of her accusers by saying, "How could I have got in?" The means of successfully carrying out such a plan were many and easy.

Candia proceeded to conjure up new arguments to convince them; she sharpened up her wits; she invented three, four, five different cases to prove that the spoon never could have been found in that hole in the courtyard; she split hairs with marvelous ingenuity. Next she took to making the rounds of the shops and the houses, seeking in every possible way to overcome the people's incredulity. They listened to her, greatly entertained by her captious reasoning; and they would end by saying, "Oh, it's all right!"

But there was a certain tone in their voice that left Candia annihilated. So, then, all her trouble was for nothing! No one would believe her! Yet with marvelous persistence she would return to the attack, spending whole nights in thinking out new arguments. And little by little, under this continued strain, her mind gave way; she could no longer follow any sustained thought but that of the silver spoon.

Neglecting her work, she had sunk to a state of actual want. When she went down to the river bank, under the iron bridge, where the other wash-women congregated, she would sometimes let slip from between her fingers the garments that the current swept away forever. And she would talk continually, unweariedly, of the one single subject. In order not to hear her, the young laundresses would begin to sing, and would mock her with the improvised rimes of their songs. And she meanwhile would shout and gesticulate like a crazy woman.

No one could give her work any longer. Out of pity, some of her former employers would send her food. Little by little she fell into the habit of begging, and wandered through the streets, bowed over, unkempt,

and all in rags. The street urchins would tag behind
her, shouting: "Tell us the story of the spoon, 'cause
we never heard it, Auntie Candia!"

She would stop strangers sometimes as they passed
by, to tell them the story and to argue out her defense.
Young fellows would sometimes send for her, and
pay her a copper to tell it all over, two, three, or
four times; they would raise up difficulties against
her argument; they would hear her all the way
through, and then at last stab her with a final word.
She would shake her head, and go on her way; she
found companionship among other beggars and would
reason with them endlessly, indefatigably, invincibly.
Her chosen friend was a deaf woman, whose skin was
a mass of angry blotches, and who limped on one leg.

In the winter of 1874 she was at last stricken with
serious illness. The woman with the blotches cared for
her. Donna Cristina Lamonica sent her a cordial and
a scuttle of coals.

The sick woman, lying on her pallet, still raved of
the silver spoon. She would raise herself on her elbow
and struggle to wave her arm, to give emphasis to her
fevered arguments.

And at the last, when her staring eyes already seemed
overspread with a veil of troubled waters that rose
from within, Candia gasped forth:

"It wasn't I, madam—because you see—the spoon—"

THAT FAMOUS LOVE AFFAIR

By STEPHEN FRENCH WHITMAN

Toward sunset on an afternoon in August, Cleopatra, the seventh and last of that name, sat in a marble portico of her palace on the Lochias peninsula, looking out at the Great Harbor. Twenty war galleys were moored to the naval quays below the terraces blossoming with oleanders; there were more behind the Island of Antirrhodus, and a hum of life arose from all those tall vessels with their many banks of oars, their prows studded with spikes and their decks encumbered with towers and catapults.

A saline freshness began to pervade these still, transparent waters that had shimmered all day in the heat.

Across the haven, on Pharos Island, the Temple of Isis gleamed amid its groves. To the right, at the harbor entrance, the marble lighthouse, the seventh wonder of the world rose high in the sunshine, its lower story square, its next octagonal, its third cylindrical, its last composed of columns. Beyond, the Mediterranean Sea spread out as if illimitably its deep blue flood covered with sparkling points. But that illimi-

For the historical data which formed the basis for this new treatment of the two principal characters, the author is indebted to "The Life and Times of Cleopatra, Queen of Egypt," by A. E. P. B. Weigall (Putnam).

tableness was a deception. There, to the north, lay the constant enemy, Rome.

The Queens' gaze returned to her ships.

Motionless in the portico, she had watched the First Royal Squadron come back from its maneuvers. Her blue, far-seeing eyes had noted even the knotting of the hawsers. Everything had been smartly done, and now the swarms of galley slaves were streaming away along the water front, under the escort of troops, toward their barracks by the Harbor of Happy Return. The dark masses of figures, surrounded by twinkling helmets, undulated like serpents at the base of the sumptuous buildings that fronted the Great Harbor. One heard a faint roaring of voices raised in a route song.

Those servile hordes, however, propelled only a portion of the Egyptian fleet. The Second Squadron was cruising off Pelusium; the Third was being re-equipped at the Cibctos docks. One hundred and eighty men-of-war were preparing for combat. The Queen pondered on the day when all those sea fortresses must fight at her order for the empire of the earth.

Would her Egyptians stand fast against the stubborn Romans?

"But I," she reflected, "shall have Romans, too."

Nevertheless, that thought did not brighten her eyes today.

The sea breeze caressed her face, as if tempting her to smile. The odors of the flowering terraces mingled with the perfumes dispelled by her Greek garments. In her ebony chair inlaid with mother-of-pearl, alone in the portico of green and pinkish marble, Cleopatra looked a fragile little figure, gentle and harmless, a prey to nothing more than some passing feminine sadness.

Had she, as men said, been beautiful in her youth; or had her enchantment even then consisted in exquisiteness of manner, a temperament that seemed at one moment subtle and the next capricious, a pride that made her cold immediately following her jolly laughter? She was still dainty, elegant, flawless from constant care of her appearance—she still appeared nearly girlish because of two great treasures that she had not lost, her sense of humor and her audacity. And perhaps no queen had ever shown herself to be a women in so many charming ways.

Silence fell on the ships and the harbor. From the mainland, behind the great palace, rose the noises of Alexandria, that frivolous and fickle city packed with all races and religions, all splendors and vices, more regal and more corrupt than Rome itself.

A dark-eyed woman in amethyst-colored Greek robes appeared in the portico.

"Cæsarion and Antyllus haven't come home," she remarked. "I hear that they've sneaked off again to the fairground at Eleusis."

The Queen, her slender lips tightening, replied: "Send both of those boys to me as soon as they return. My little Iras, do you know where my husband may be?"

"Throwing dice with his Romans in the old blue peristyle. He has complained of a headache."

"Why should he complain? He was drinking till daylight, wasn't he? I heard them singing atrociously on the terraces after the first hour this morning. I want to see him, too. He may find me presently in the children's apartment."

"Is there anything else?" the lady-in-waiting asked.

"Yes, my dear, the kitchens. They have been using Carian honey in the cooking. Have the bees of Hybla stopped working? No; but somebody is turning a dishonest penny in this house. And what's the matter with the pastry lately? And yesterday Antony got a half-spoiled oyster! I am not in the field with my army; I am at home. If these things continue, I'll see the cooks themselves, and they will not enjoy the conversation. Warn them."

"The chief cook is ill," Iras ventured.

"He has evidently been sampling the food intended for me."

Iras, quizzically smiling, departed on her sandaled feet without a sound.

The Queen continued to gaze out to sea. A pearly light, faintly tinctured with pink and green filled the shaded portico, softening the hue of Cleopatra's auburn hair, which was arranged on her little head, according to the current Greek fashion, in nine parts running back to the disklike knot at the rear. Her delicate and aquiline features remained serene, as she thought:

"Dice at the present moment. Tonight more heavy drinking. Tomorrow another headache. Tell me Marcus Antonius, are you still enough of a man to lead the host that I am conjuring up?"

The lighthouse across the Great Harbor was flushing in the first rays of the sunset when Cleopatra rose and went into the palace.

The immense house of the Ptolemies had been much embellished since the Egyptian marriage of Cleopatra and Marc Antony. Everywhere one saw walls covered with the rarest marbles, fretted ceilings encrusted with gold, doors lined with tortoise-shell and studded with emeralds, pavements of onyx and alabaster. On tables of chiseled ivory stood priceless bric-à-brac from the remotest lands, the invaluable black-and-red vases of an earlier Greece and those unheard-of curiosities in art which pleased the Queen so much. But the beautiful slaves, of all colors and accomplishments, who moved through the rooms over the shining floors, were as costly as the porphyry pillars inlaid with garlands of rubies, or the old statues from Athens and Olympia.

Compared with this house of hers, the best of the dwellings that Cleopatra had seen in Rome were fit only for emancipated slaves.

As she passed through each suite—the portals guarded by mercenaries of the Macedonian Household Troops, the anterooms full of gossiping pages and women—her clear eyes missed nothing. Here she noted the upholsterers from Sidon, hanging fresh curtains of Tyrian dye stitched with vivid flowers and birds. There she saw, in gardens, the Sicilians, clipping the bushes. In a pillared court, dark-browed Sporadean girls, in the transparent, sea-green robes of Cos, were feeding peacocks at the appointed hour.

She was pleased to see everything running like clockwork, as things always ran in her house.

Here was the endless repetition of splendid vistas, the alternating odors of perfumes, incense, and blooms transplanted from exotic lands. But what she noticed especially was that the soot of last night's lamps had been washed away, that the pavements showed no foot tracks and that the pedestals of the statues were free from dust.

Cleopatra turned in at a door tended by two negroes with effeminate faces. She heard, rising above a clamor of remonstrances, the bawling of a child: "Aie! Aie! Aie!"

She halted on the threshold of the nursery.

"I want to go home!" wailed a big-eyed, puny girl of six, running to Cleopatra in an agony of resentment. Her black braids, interwoven with tiny silver images, were all disordered; her narrow chest was heaving under the pleated black robe. She was Iotapa, the daughter of the King of Media. It was she who, for reasons of state, had been married a year ago to Cleopatra's seven-year-old son, Alexander Helios.

The curly-headed Alexander was there, planted defiantly on his small bare feet, scowling, with his tunic torn at the neck. His twin sister, Cleopatra Selene, immaculate in a lemon-colored chiton, sat on a stool regarding the fracas with intense excitement. The three-year-old Ptolemy was howling in sympathy with the little Median princess.

Without effort the Queen lifted Iotapa into her arms.

"There, there; it's all right now. If Alexander has been wicked, he shall be punished."

The two Macedonian nurses, robust in the costume of their native mountains, the Median nurse with her headdress and many bangles, the Athenian tutors and the Chamberlain of the Royal Children subsided with smiles of relief. The walls of the room were painted with animals. The rug-strewn floor was littered with dolls, hobby-horses and miniature armor.

"He ate my piece of candy!" wailed Iotapa, her face pressed against the Queen's bosom.

'She is my wife," Alexander Helios retorted, with a dramatic gesture, "and what is hers is mine."

"Being your wife, in Egypt," said Cleopatra calmly, "she is also your equal. Besides, one piece of candy is your full allowance. You have not only affronted the daughter of a king; you have also disobeyed the orders of a queen. Tomorrow you shall have no candy at all; but today—and tomorrow too—Iotapa shall eat her share before your eyes."

"I will not watch her!" declared Alexander, after a moment of stupefaction and horror. He turned on them his little back that imitated so well, in diminished form, his father's burly back.

"You shall watch her, my son, or I'll know the reason why. About face. How will you ever be a soldier, if you do it so slovenly?"

Cleopatra sat down sidewise on a hobby-horse with the foreign child in her arms. There was an awful silence as the Median nurse, her dark visage alight with triumph, brought to Iotapa on a platter the piece of rose-colored candy. Gulping down her tears, the wife of Alexander Helios tried a nibble, then crowed in exultation:

"I am eating it, Alexander. Look and see me eating it!"

The other, without flinching under the torture, answered contemptuously: "Bah! I have had two pieces, which nobody can take away from me."

Lowering her head, the Queen kissed Iotapa's cheek to hide her smile.

"Henceforth," she said, when the candy had disappeared, "remember that hospitality is a holy virtue, failure in which is an offense to the gods. Years ago the great Pompey came as a stranger asking hospi-

tality of certain men, who used him most unkindly.
The gods were incensed at such rudeness. Where are
those men now? All, all have met a bad end. Take
warning, especially as the Princess Iotapa has gods
of her own nation to care for her and avenge her
even here in Egypt. Lick your fingers, child, before
you smear my dress! Now then, let me hear from
you three, each in turn, about the fine things that
you've done and learned today. You first, Alexander. No sulking, my boy! You're not yet too
old to be spanked."

While she was still engaged in her catechism, Marc
Antony entered.

"Good evening, my treasure."
"Good evening, Bacchus," she answered.

That was the name which had been given him without irony by the ironical Alexandrians, who seemed
to perceive in this Roman lord of theirs an incarna-
tion of the gay Dionysus. Yet nowadays Antony
flushed when Cleopatra addressed him so, feeling that
from her lips a sting issued with the word.

He kissed the children, who all adored him, then
looked round the nursery for the chair that would
bear his weight.

"You were not in very good voice at daybreak
this morning," the Queen remarked.

"Did we wake you up? Forgive me. It was a
folly, that business."

"Never mind: I was awake already, and busy at
our plans."

This added reproach made him hang his handsome
head, covered thickly with dark curls, amid which
some gray hairs were appearing.

Having now for the most part abandoned Roman dress, he had on a purple tunic of Chinese silk adorned with golden moons. His large forearms, from which the hair had been removed by a depilatory, emerged from short sleeves hemmed with fringes of gold. On his left wrist he wore a gold-and-sapphire bracelet; on his feet were boots of purple kid ornamented with gold tags.

In the last five years his appearance had changed greatly for the worse.

This big body of an athlete was becoming flabby. The heavy neck and jaws—once ridiculed by Cicero, perhaps from jealousy—were covered over with fat. But it was Antony's face that showed the accelerated progress of his faults. The hard countenance of the victorious general had grown indulgent. The eyes that had flashed so dangerously, on battlefield and rostrum, were haunted by the memory of certain defeats. The mouth, especially, had come to reveal the corrosion of his manhood—his unconquerable love of indolence and wine, his pride reduced to bombast, his force of will crumbled into self-distrust. But he was, at least, still fearless of personal danger, still chivalrous and easily touched in the heart, still the idol of his army, even that of the disastrous Parthian campaign.

He was jiggling the baby Ptolemy up and down on his knee.

"How is your headache?" Cleopatra asked him, with a twinge of pity.

"Wretched! I've been in torture ever since I woke up. Imagine: we began with light Egyptian, then switched to Greek, and by midnight we were drinking it unmixed. As if that wasn't enough, some fool called for this year's Vesuvium! I understand that later on the dancers from Gades came in—a show for the dead; they had to applaud themselves. By the way, somebody knocked over the Vase of Pericles and smashed it to smithereens."

Cleopatra was silent from indignation.

"There also occurred a brawl," he continued, languidly massaging his scalp with his fingers, while little Ptolemy pulled at his golden fringes. "We made Plancus to represent the sea god: he painted his body blue and danced on the tables naked. That is to say, he had on a wreath of seaweed and a fish tail. Marcus Silanus, declaring that such conduct was outrageous in a Roman, threw a glass dish at him and cut him rather badly. The next minute both of them were yelling for their swords. But in the midst of it Plancus went to sleep. Taking a table for a funeral bed, we marched him all over the northern wing, with the proper lamentations. Really, Cleo, that part of it would have tickled you. We gave him a funeral wreath of garlic and radishes, and, instead of the penny for Charon—"

"Be still!" Cleopatra commanded under her breath. "What sots do you want your children to think their father's friends are?"

Antony sighed and wagged his head.

"Whatever my children may think of them, they are a very sick man's friends, a very foolish man's friends, but a penitent man's. This time I am through with the cups. No, never again!"

He turned to his son Alexander Helios, who was pinching his arm. "What do you want, O King of Media?"

"I want to be Hannibal on his elephant," said Alexander.

"This evening? Ye gods! Well, then, come on, and be sharp about it, because it's nearly bedtime. Are the others in it too?"

"Yes! yes! yes!" screamed Cleopatra Selene, Iotapa and the baby Ptolemy. All came crowding around Antony, who, on his hands and knees, let them climb upon his back, Alexander in front, his sister behind him, Iotapa next, and Ptolemy half sliding off at the rear. It was growing dusky. The smiling nurses began to light the tapers in the stands.

"All right?" asked Antony. And in a hollow voice, "This is the elephant of Hannibal the Carthaginian and on the elephant is Hannibal, riding Hannibal's Carthaginian elephant. Is that clear? Then off we go."

He began to crawl forward, swaying from side to side and trumpeting as much like an elephant as possible.

Squeals resounded as one child or another, on the point of slipping off, hugged the child in front more tightly. Their small flushed faces in a line, their shining eyes and open mouths, kept turning toward the Queen for approbation. She clapped them, seated on the rump of the hobby-horse, like a spectator at the games.

"He climbs the lofty and most perilous mountains!" Antony bellowed, as he heaved himself up on a cedar-wood couch full of cushions. "And descends into the dreadful depths of the sea!" he moaned, regaining the rugs. "Whew!" he gasped under his breath, "my brain is bursting."

"That's enough for tonight, children," the Queen quickly interposed.

But Antony was going to end the game properly.

"How graceful is his Carthaginian waddle!" he cried. All the children immediately tried to waggle themselves on his back in imitation of him. "How beautiful the flapping of his Carthaginian ears!" Alexander reached forward to make his father's ears flap. "But alas!" Antony roared, "he has caught sight of a Roman. Alas! he is running away." At this point Ptolemy fell off behind. "Woe to Hannibal! Woe to all the little Hannibals and Hannibalesses! The Carthaginian elephant is carthaginiously turning his tail to the terrible Roman from Rome!"

Uttering screams of alarm and ecstasy the children tumbled off to right and left as the elephant galloped into the vestibule.

There, with a groan, he bumped his head into the knees of Iras, the lady-in-waiting.

"Cæsarion and Antyllus have returned," that injured woman announced to Cleopatra, when Antony had helped her to her feet.

"I will see them at once. Let the children be put to bed. Did he hurt you, Iras?"

"Aside from my kneecaps, which I think he knocked off, I am as well as ever."

"Tomorrow," Alexander Helios remarked, before retiring with his grinning retinue, "I want to be the terrible Roman from Rome, and kill the elephant."

"You needn't bother—you have all but killed him today," Antony muttered weakly, holding his head in his hands.

The two boys were awaiting the Queen in the Egyptian hall—the only apartment of its kind in all the great Greek palace. They came forward reluctantly as Cleopatra and Antony entered, to divulge, in the light of the bronze candelabra set between the pillars, their tired faces, sunburnt foreheads and guilty smiles.

The Queen impassively compared them with each other.

The fourteen-year-old Cæsarion already resembled his father, Julius Cæsar.

The son of Antony by Fulvia had a bolder air, was even more handsome, perhaps, and, tho a year the other's junior, already looked stronger.

But Cleopatra, seeing in each boy the shadow of his father, knew that her Cæsarion could hope, as his companion never could, for a truly glorious future.

Antyllus and Cæsarion each held a big bunch of ranunculi and asphodels, which they had gathered on their homeward way—no doubt stealing them from the villas of Nicopolis. Now they offered the flowers as a peace gift to the Queen, who had in her gardens the blossoms of a world.

She was touched by this naïveté, tho her face remained severe.

When she had accepted the two bouquets, in the hall insufficiently lighted by clusters of candles, with the painted human gods and beast gods of Egypt everywhere looming forth from the obscurity, she spoke in low accents, so that her words might not reach the slaves who prowled behind the pillars:

"You ran away from your lesson in oratory and fencing. You did no Homer, and learned not even one maxim. Instead, you went to Eleusis. Am I right?"

"Yes, Mother," Cæsarion confessed. "We were so weary of lessons!"

"But you did it by stealth, which shows that you

knew it was wrong. Now tell me why I've asked you not to go there."

The boys stole an imploring look at Antony. From behind Cleopatra's back he gave them a solemn wink.

After waiting in vain, she continued:

"I have reminded you that the booths and inns of Eleusis attract nothing but the scum of Alexandria. Is there any private gentleman in the city who would not be ashamed to go there? You have perhaps been sitting with the vilest acrobats, flute players and tavern waitresses—you, Antyllus, the son of the most powerful man alive—you, Cæsarion, you are to be crowned on the Capitol at Rome. What foul stories have you heard there? What plague have you brought back with you, perhaps on these flowers in my arms? My son has not yet dared to kiss me. Why?"

Their faces blushed dark in the uncertain light. But Cæsarion exclaimed:

"We drank, each of us, two cups of beer, and listened to sailormen's tales. There were no acrobats where we were, and the waitress who served us had dirty fingernails. We had something better to do than look at her! A sea captain told us how he was with you, sir, at Brundisium, and fought Libo with you, and set out with you to bring aid to my father in Macedonia. And he told us about the enemy's pursuit, and how you and he were in a frightful storm of water, and how the gods changed the wind at the last possible moment, so that you were saved, while the enemy's ships were wrecked."

"My boy is already growing subtle," the mother said to herself. "He has known how to set the potential ally into motion. Now we shall have it all! Hark."

Antony, in fact, had snapped at the bait.

"Do I remember it!" he cried heartily. "We were ready to go on the rocks—eight hundred horse and twenty thousand foot—when the gale shifted by a miracle. Who's your sea captain, lad? Do I know the rascal?"

"He knows you well enough, Father," Antyllus proudly replied. "He says there has been none like you since our ancestor Hercules."

Antony, rolling forward, threw an arm around the neck of each boy. Thus, towering between them he faced Cleopatra, warmed by that victorious memory, moved by such praise as he no longer received every evening in the palace. She stood looking at him inscrutably, patiently, biting her lip, with an air of smiling not on her face but maybe in her mind.

"Come, Cleo, after all, what harm have they done! They sat down with men who taught them bravery and stedfastness—"

"Must they go to Eleusis to learn it?" the brave and stedfast Queen rejoined wearily. She shrugged her shoulders, and now a faint irony curved her delicate lips. "Brave as you are yourself, it's not you who should have been present at this interview. Well, while you are asking Antyllus how he came by that smear of rouge under his ear, I will have a word with my Cæsarion."

Gathering the half-wilted flowers into one arm, she drew her son behind the lotus-tipped pillars.

For a while they walked silently from one patch of light to another, past the dim wall paintings in which Isis and the infant Horus were always reappearing, like a motive for her thoughts.

At last she murmured:

"Never lie to me, dear. Bring your boredoms and your temptations to me for still a little while. I have never yet betrayed your trust, have I?"

"No, Mother," he faltered.

"Nothing must harm you; nothing must degrade you; your life and honor are far too precious for that. What do I live and work for, except your future? When you are a man, and I have made you king—yes, even over the Romans—I shall trouble you no longer with my discipline. Till then try to be a good boy, and make me happy."

They faced each other in the rays from a circle of candles on a stand.

How like he was to the one who had departed into the shades—the very image of her first love as he must have been in his youth! The same brow and nose, the same eagle's gaze; but she had never seen tears in the father's eyes. He had already become too weary for tears when she, as a lonely child-woman who sees a smile at last, had flung herself into his arms.

The mother and the son retraced their steps behind the painted pillars. Cæsarion blurted out:

"It is true that there weren't any acrobats; but we did meet two girls in a magician's tent and kissed them while the fellow was doing his tricks. Then we bought them honey cakes and promised to see them tomorrow."

"But tomorrow you will read in Homer about Circe the Enchantress."

"I know; who turned men into swine. Yet Antyllus and I didn't do anything swinish. We wouldn't have thought of kissing them except that the tent was dark, and their eyes were large and shiny in the darkness. Out in the sunlight they looked quite different. The one named Phannion was thirteen years old. The other, who called herself Myromeris, was twelve." He hesitated, then ventured, "Mother, if I wash my lips well, will you let me kiss you good night?"

"No, dear, you may kiss me now," she said. "The truth has washed those other kisses away."

The two whom Rome called "the shameful pair"— those whom Egypt knew as "Royal Wife and Husband"—sat down in her study, where the walls were of softly painted stucco, the floor of glass mosaic, the furniture ivory, the rugs and hangings Persian.

Lamps of gold, representing sirens and harpies, shed their light upon a long table covered with countless papers; rolls of them, standing up in precious boxes, piles of them spread out under jeweled paper weights, others in pigeonhole cases, tagged with different colored labels.

Mardion, the eunuch, had been at work in the corner. Now he stood waiting to be questioned or to give advice, his plump hands folded on his girdle, his round face like a mask of wax covered all over with infinitesimal wrinkles.

Cleopatra explained to Antony:

"These letters came in today. Things are moving more quickly. At this rate you ought to have the whole fleet and army collected at Ephesus by the middle of winter."

She motioned to Mardion, who handed her a memorandum.

"Here is the list to date. We shall surely have Tarcondimotus of Upper Cilicia, Bocchus of Mauretania, Archelus of Cappadocia, Mithradates of Commagene, as well as the King of Galatia and the two Kings of Thrace. Eighteen, perhaps nineteen, Roman legions, the Greek, Jewish, Armenian and Syrian levies, the German and Arabian cavalry, not to mention the tribes that I shall call in from the desert. Tell him, Mardion, in round numbers, what it will cost as it stands."

The eunuch promptly replied:

"Twenty thousand talents, at the outside, should cover all expenses for half a year. Remember that Syria, Pontus and Armenia will send in their own supplies and a good deal more."

"It will still empty the treasury," the Queen reflected.

"There will be other treasuries," Mardion murmured, with a smile. "Is there not, sir, for example, one at Rome?"

Neither was listening to him. Antony had closed his aching eyes. Cleopatra was meditating on this amazing gamble.

It was win all or lose all now—the rule of the world or irretrievable failure. She who burned the lamps every night, when all others were sleeping or drinking, had calculated everything precisely, except the spirit of the man that sat fidgeting beside her. Could he hold together such a host with those trembling hands of his? Mars had indeed been transformed into Bacchus. Could he be changed back into Mars during this next half year?

At a smothered moan from Antony, she demanded: "What in the world are you gurgling about?"

"My mouth," he declared, "is no better off than the mouth of a salted herring."

"Bring him some water, Mardion."

The hero of a score of battlefields looked alarmed "No, no. Nothing at all, if it isn't to be a hair of the dog that bit me."

Involuntarily the Queen made a movement of disdain.

"You see," the sufferer explained, with a piteous look on his massive and mottled face, "when I cannot sleep it off, I have to walk it off. It's always been so, from the days when I first began it. How can I think of legions, kings and corn when my stomach feels as if it were at sea? I can't even read what is written here, for the wiggles before my eyes. Have pity, Cleo! Tomorrow, when I am better. Tonight let us take a nice long walk together. I'm sure you'll sleep sounder for it."

"Where, may I ask?"

"Why not in the city, as we used to do? Have you forgotten how we enjoyed knocking on the doors and running away, asking ridiculous questions of the passersby or else pretending that I was abducting you? What fun you were in those times! As for me, I still have a bit of boy in my heart."

"I admit it," she said.

"No, dearest, sheathe your claws; come out with me. How long since you've been in Rhacotis?"

"Ah, years," she admitted, and suddenly glanced down at the backs of her hands. She stood up, saying to Mardion:

"Tell the captain of the watch to have a file of Germans at the southern stairs in half an hour, armed, but in civil dress—"

"Pish!" Antony protested. "A guard for a walk in

Rhacotis, and with me there to protect you? Where is that old gay recklessness of yours?"

"Very well," she consented, "I won't offend your pride in your arms, big baby. Run along and put on some suitable clothes. And don't come back smelling of cardamom seeds, or I shall stay behind."

He lifted her high in his gladiator's grip, then, letting her down, kissed her on both cheeks. He laughed:

"Who knows but we may see something new and be jolly together once more?"

The sky was like a tent of deep purple spangled all over. There was no mist. A breeze was cooling the city.

Behind them to the east the two adventurers had left the region of great public buildings and temples. At the square before the causeway leading to Pharos Island they turned south toward the district called Rhacotis. Before them, high in the glittering sky, they saw the fire baskets flaring in the porches of the Serapeum, the temple that dominated the quarter of the Egyptians. But those lofty beacons disappeared as they entered the narrow streets, where the blood of all races was intermingled or else about to be blended.

In a maze of alleys, splashed with the gleam of lanterns, they heard a babbling in Egyptian, Cretan, Libyan, Latin, Ethiopian, Syrian, Phœnician, Gaulish and Persian. The Queen, who knew nearly all these languages, began to be amused.

"Not so fast," she objected. "My feet are no longer used to such hard going."

"They have trod harder roads than this, however," he returned gently.

And both thought of the long struggle that had begun in her girlhood—camps and battles in the sand, sieges withstood and undertaken, rough voyages toward precarious new wars, and that last journey of hers, when she had come to his aid on the coast of Phœnicia, to find him wandering on the lonely shore, haggard, shaken from his defeat by the Parthians, who had sowed in his soul the first seeds of self-dissatisfaction.

"There's one more path," he reminded her, "that you'll not linger on."

"Yes, the stairs to the Capitol," she assented, with an access of strength. But he made her walk slowly, his arm about her shoulder.

He had put on a cloak borrowed from a slave, and a felt hat with the brim pulled down over his eyes. Cleopatra, her body wrapped closely in yellow stuff, her head and face veiled with blue, resembled one of those graceful shrouded figures made famous long ago by the artists of Tanagra. Men told one another, looking askance at her slender silhouette:

"It is a beautiful Grecian whose Roman lover is bringing her to watch the dancers."

Then, openly, even pointing their fingers at her, they admired her lovely carriage, her tiny feet, shod in yellow boots with soles of milky vellum, her whole aspect of antique elegance and grace, which qualities escaped like an irrepressible fragrance from the folds of her disguise. A ragamuffin laid a spray of iris on the cobblestones for her to step on, then followed her begging.

"You see," Antony pointed out, "in order to pass unnoticed you must cease to be yourself."

"They watch you as much as me. They think you're a myrmillo who has killed a thousand netmen."

Unconsciously he straightened himself, drawing in his abdomen and throwing out his chest.

There were glowing cookshops still open to the street. Bushes and placards hung at the doors of winerooms. From the outbuilt upper stories, from balconies of latticework and open loggias, came a twanging of harps, the quavering songs of women, oaths, a rhythmic clapping of hands and laughter. In the air hung the odors of frying fish, decaying vegetables, rank perfumes and sewage.

The Queen's eyes began to dance.

"Let's take the hint," she said, "and see the dancers—or rather, those who watch them. I can hear the drums."

At once half a dozen loafers were ready to show them the way. A violent squabble broke out among the guides. As if about to do murder, each bellowed in the others' faces the name of this dance house or that, of certain dancing girls, their fame and their special attractions. Eyes glared; mouths were distorted; the howls of argument drowned out all other noises. Cleopatra, catching Antony by the hand, took to her heels.

Alone in an alleyway hardly wider than a fissure between two houses, with a mass of dyer's rags hanging overhead, she sank into his embrace, panting and laughing.

"What simpletons!" she gasped. "They don't know yet that they've lost us."

Her eyes shone at him gayly in the faint light of the stars that reached them through the masses of dangling rags. His mirth died away; holding her fast with one hand, he unveiled her face, which appeared once more, in this ignoble gloom, like the happy face of a girl. And suddenly his lips covered her sweet cheeks with kisses, and her eyelids, which had languorously closed themselves, and her lips, half parted in wonder at this moment of illusion.

"Little Cleo—great Cleo," he stammered, "dear wife, faithful companion, unalterable sweetheart! If I have sometimes doubted your future loyalty, it was because I saw myself becoming unworthy of it. But you must not cast me off. I will redeem myself. Tell me that you'll stick to me till the end."

Held up in his straining grasp, she dreamed for a moment, then quoted, in her unique and all-enchanting voice the words of Andromache to Hector, from the Iliad:

"'It were better for me to go down to the grave if I lose thee; for never will any comfort be mine when once thou hast met thy fate, but only sorrow. Thou art to me father and mother, yes, and brother, too, even as thou art my goodly husband.'"

His strength began to hurt her; but she did not complain.

"These are the sudden events," he said, "that come to us as the unexpected gifts from the divinities round us. Lie still in my arms for one more moment, dearest. Why should there be such magic in this dirty alleyway, with melon rinds underfoot, and a festoon of shirt tails flapping overhead? But when I hold you here I seem to hold all the treasure of my life, all the hope, all the joys and sorrows done with and to come."

He released her at last. Silently she wrapped her

face in the head veil, so that he saw, once more,
only her humid eyes.

In a din of drums and flageolets, stooping their
heads to avoid the smoke-blacked lintel, they descended
into the dance house.

Round the vaulted room, flambeaux stuck out from
sockets on the walls. In this shifting illumination
one saw the dancers hemmed in by tables covered
with wine cups and plates. They were brown women
of the desert, crowned with miters of tinsel and
feathers. Their painted eyes were closed as if they
were asleep, while their torsos, bare to the waist,
smeared with red, blue and yellow pigments, undulated to the clashing of the little cymbals attached to
their fingers like castanets. There were four of them
dancing. Each faced a different wall; each seemed
a reflection of the others, perceived in invisible mirrors. At intervals a roar of admiration came from
the spectators, whose lips remained parted and whose
foreheads were covered with drops.

"This way, master! This way, mistress!" the Egyptian keeper of the dance house whispered, understanding that these were persons of note.

He led them to a niche in the wall out of the gleam
of the torches, furnished with a table and two benches.
While wiping off the board, the man chattered obse-
quiously:

"What shall it be, beloved of the gods? I have
wine of the country, wine of mulberries and pome-
granates, Greek wine flavored with salt water and
gypsum. If you wish to perfume yourselves afresh,
I have also a bit of bakkaris and nard."

At this statement Cleopatra laughed behind her veil, whereupon Antony had the courage to say:

"Never mind the perfumes; bring us some of the good Greek."

She gave him a sidelong glance, but made no comment.

The dancers sat down on their mats, impassive, like idols that nothing but the conjuration of wild music could bring to life. The spectators surged on their benches. On all sides were tousled heads, woolly heads, bald heads, frizzled heads—Phrygian caps, sailors' hats and here and there a helmet. But when they had seethed and rattled their cups for a time a new shout was taken up, to swell into a chorus:

"Taui! Let us have Taui!"

The drums resumed their thumping. A new girl stood up alone, advanced and let a slow, homicidal smile dawn on her swarthy countenance, framed with chains of turquoise and silver. She began to quiver all over as tho an icy breeze were blowing in at the door. But Antony, having drained his second cup at a breath, watched a blind old man make his way amid the tables, led by a sickly-looking half-caste boy of ten, who was naked except for a string tied round his waist.

"Look, Cleo," he prompted her.

The spectators were cursing the blind man as he blocked their view. His face remained humble at their insults. Shuffling forward, stumbling over legs, he continued to raise his sightless eyes toward the ceiling and shake some coppers in an earthen dish. His tattered tunic was ready to fall apart.

"Yes," the Queen assented, "it is a Roman."

"A Roman soldier, if I know the breed," Antony growled.

The boy, catching sight of them, led the blind man to their table.

Isolated from the uproar by his infirmity, the beggar stood before them, staring over their heads, a film of tears always brimming those empty sockets. He was filthy, giving out as strong an odor as a flock of goats; his grizzled beard hung down over his chest; but on his extended arm were sword wounds half lost in the shriveled muscles. A profound placidity and harmlessness filled the beaked visage that had been young and fierce. The old voice went, in barbarous Greek jargon:

"You see, sirs, that I am blind. I haven't eaten today. I've taken only two coppers. If you refuse me, it's the gods who've refused me."

He started, for Antony had taken him by the wrist.

"Sit here beside me, old fellow."

"What do you ask?" the beggar mumbled in consternation, his countenance altered by fear of the unknown. "Are you a Roman, then?" Dragged down upon the bench, he shrank away when he felt a hand on his shoulder. "What game are you playing on me?" he lamented. "Have I offended you? Then pardon me and let me go."

"No," said Antony, patting the old man's cheek, "this time you have come into good hands instead of bad. Listen to me."

He whispered in the other's ear. The beggar indignantly tried to free himself. Antony persisted. Then the blind man, becoming as still as death, sat with his jaw hanging. Finally he began to tremble harder than the dancer.

Cleopatra, her elbows on the table, her chin in her hand, watched them as one might watch a play.

The dancing girls were all resting and repainting their eyes. A group of Ionian sailors were bawling out a song. The dark smoke of the torches hung like a pall in midair.

"I was there," the blind man quavered, his withered fingers curling round a wine cup. "I saw you there too! In beautiful armor, not deigning to put off your scarlet cloak, you were the first over the ramparts. When you disappeared we all thought you had met your end. Again, after the sack of Lissus, I watched you come among us while we were eating. You laughed and bore the salty jokes of the soldiers, giving hot ones in return. We loved you because you were not too haughty to sit down at our tables, as you are not too haughty, even now, to make me sit down at yours. And before the last battle at Pharsalia I was with you on the left wing. You walked along our lines at the head of your officers, so splendid that the men round me swore they would go on fighting for you with their throats ripped open."

Antony hugged the beggar.

"Old wolf! Were you Cæsar's man before that?"

"Yes, in Gaul, with the Tenth. Eh! the good days. sometimes, in my cellar, I recall them one by one. A glamor of brass rises before my eyes; I see the Eagles surrounded by drawn swords. I hear the trumpets, the whir of the javelins, and the legion shouting 'Alala!' like one man. We went into their cities singing, covered with foreign jewelry, snatching, with our arms still red to the elbow, at some squealing girl who soon became so fond of us that she wept when we departed. I gained a lot of booty for myself, but lost it all, somehow. I was strong; then I became old and finally blind. Such is the life of man. But henceforth I shall remember that I sat with you, your arm embracing me."

"Is this loyalty?" Antony asked the Queen, after rubbing his eyes.

She laid a finger against her lips.

"Who is with you?" the blind man inquired, timid again.

"A lady of this country."

"Ah, yes; you are not yet old. And may your youth be eternal." The beggar ruminated, then asked in hushed tones: "Tell me, sir, do you think that you could give me a good death? I know you're going to war with that rat Octavianus. If only I could be there, sword in hand, in the first line of the legions! Not to fight, of course, but to strike just one blow into the air as we come together, and then receive the end fitting for a soldier. The second-file man could close up over me in a jiffy— But I speak like a fool. Why should you go to that trouble? It was because it's hard, after what I have seen, to end alone in a gutter."

Antony, pulling a ring from his thumb, called the sickly boy to him.

"Lead your old friend to the Royal Palace, kiddie. Show the ring to the men at the gates. Say that this Roman soldier is to be taken in and cared for. Forward, veteran! No need of asking for coppers on the way."

The drums began a frenzied tumult. The four dancers, who all resembled the same idol, leaped to their feet. One bore a curved Egyptian sword, an-

ether a cage containing a black dove, the third a
whip, the last a vase full of fire. As they began,
Cleopatra and Antony issued into the street.

They walked in silence. The lamps became less frequent, the shadows deeper. The doors on either side
were shut and barred.

"Let us go home," said the Queen. "It is late. We
shall see nothing more."

Rousing himself, he mused:

"Back there is something more valuable to us than
the cavalry of Bocchus of Mauretania, or all the
spearmen of the two Kings of Thrace. The old legion-
aries, remembering me with warm affection, have made
me a myth for the young ones and the recruits, almost
as if I were already a hero of tradition. This is
worth while, Cleo. Octavianus is the object of no
such feeling."

"Live, then," Cleopatra rejoined, "so that nothing
can dim the luster of that fame."

He said no more, and they turned back towards
the lights. They became aware that a thin girl in
gauze was walking beside them, a double flute in her
hand. She was coughing and pleading faintly in Greek:

"Let me go with you, illustrious ones. Let me
play my flutes for you. I have no money with which
to buy even a dish of chickpeas; yet nobody plays
more sweetly than Acalanthis. It is because my face
has been disfigured that they won't have me; but you
needn't look at my face. You will look at each other,
and hear only the music."

They stopped under a lamp set before a shrine of
Anubis The flute player's paper-white countenance
was revealed. The cheeks and brows were scarred

all over with slashes, jagged, methodically criss-crossed and hardly healed.

"Who is to blame for it?" Antony inquired after a pause.

"Lykas the Cretan did it," mourned the girl. "Oh, now that you have seen me you will not have me! Nobody will have me! And I am still young."

Hiding her face in her hands, she began to wail hardly louder than a kitten, between fits of coughing, standing before the two strangers struck silent by her hideousness, in the flicker of light from the shrine of the dog-headed god.

"And where is Lykas the Cretan now?" Antony persisted, joggling her elbow.

"Yonder, sir, I suppose, in Fish-Sauce Street, unless he has gone to sea."

"Are you his slave?"

"No, my lord; I was born free."

"If you know the way lead me to him."

"Marcus!" the Queen protested, laying her hand on his.

But now he was firm, and his firmness disquieted her. She knew his Roman callousness to suffering—perhaps a greater callousness than that of her own Macedonians—and how war in many lands, with all sorts of ferocious allies, had made him especially indifferent to mutilation. But she was also aware of his peculiar sympathy for little creatures like this one: musicians and tumblers, pantomimists and singers, who in other days had surrounded him on his journeys, telling him their obscure sorrow and longings, and feeling his big fingers consolingly pinch their chins.

Would there be a scuffle? She had never seen Antony in a fight. Maybe it was because she had not that the Queen—once on a time so reckless, so curious, so sure of her destiny—let her hand fall to her side.

The flute player, with an obeisance, took Antony by the cloak to lead him forward. Cleopatra followed them.

By the light of a tallow-dipped bulrush, they climbed a ladder staircase to the second platform. They heard a woman laugh behind a door.

Of a sudden the Queen felt that they were in a trap, midway of this black shaft like a chute in a mine, cut off from the city, before the door that concealed at least more than one person. Unhesitatingly, with her perfumed fingers, she turned the scarred face of their guide toward the little flame. The eyes were terrified but honest. Nevertheless, Cleopatra urged:

"This is a bad place, Marcus. You are mad to go on."

"Pah!" he said greatly. "A Cretan!"

He drove his heel against the latch. The door flew open; he strode into the room. He saw before him, round a table on which some earthenware lamps were burning, six men and three girls. He said to himself at once, "These fellows look no better than so many pirates." He realized the fix into which he had got his Queen.

But she, motionless on the platform, was watching, not them, but him.

They may well have been astounded by the apparition of him—a huge, broad figure, a Roman face with set jaws, blazing eyes half-hidden under a hat brim. They rose slowly to their feet like one piece of mechanism that he had set into motion. The girls, scenting death, scurried into the corners.

The faces of the men were dark and savage. Some were bearded under their chins. One wore a red cap with lappets. Two, bare to the waist, showed on their bodies the seams and burns of sea fights. They eyed the intruder like beasts of prey confronted in their lairs, intent, implacable, ominously still. On the table, amid the lamps, were a checkerboard, wine cups and a basket of figs.

"Go, Cleo," Antony whispered out of the side of his mouth.

The flute player was already gone. The veiled figure of the Queen remained in the gloom of the platform.

"Which of you is Lykas?"

A man shorter but broader than Antony with a gaunt, deadly visage, a broken nose and sunken eyes, answered harshly:

"I am Lykas. What do you want with me?"

"To take the skin off your back," Antony said. "Has one of you got a whip?"

The Cretan sprang through the air—a knife had appeared in his fist. The two bodies met with a thud, welded themselves together, then twisted into unbelievable contortions. The quick stamp of feet was like a succession of blows. Through rents in their garments the straining muscles bulged out. But the eye could not follow those movements. There was a grunt and a crack. The Cretan slipped to the floor with a broken neck.

Antony, stooping to pick up the knife, was forced to dodge away. The others had hurled themselves upon him silently. He leaped over the table, caught up a stool, gave a deep shout of joy. His eyes were dancing; his face was transfigured. Cleopatra watched him now as one watches a stranger, while past her, unheeded, one by one, the girls darted from the room and clattered down the ladder.

"Evoël" Antony cried, laughing happily.

He was here—he was there. As the others fell, he kicked at their heads while aiming a fresh blow. The stool had become a single leg, with which he sent knives flying. But round him the faces of his enemies, convulsed and streaked with blood, kept rising and closing in. Then, all at once, three men managed to catch him round the body; he slipped, and one who had crawled behind him smashed at his skull with a jug.

Antony went down like a falling tower.

Four staggered to their feet. When they had regained their breath, and found a knife or two, they came to cut his throat. Their way to him was blocked by a woman who had stripped a blue veil from her face, which was as white as the winter moon. And they remained awestricken before that countenance.

"You have already done enough to merit death," she warned them icily. "Do no more, lest you merit worse."

As she spoke, the room was full of hooded men with drawn swords, blond faces congested by anger, beards like spun gold or copper.

They were the Germans that Antony had scorned.

When they had lifted him up on the table, and she had assured herself that he was merely stunned, silence fell in the sooty room. The Queen considered for a moment.

The great Marcus Antonius, the descendant of Hercules, the hero who was going to possess the earth, had been laid low by hoodlums. No doubt the silence of these Northern mercenaries could be counted on; but those ruffians, released, would go boasting over the seas, "It was I who broke the head of the man who wants to break the head of Octavianus." It would fly everywhere, that shameful story. It would be told in the Senate House at Rome. The soldiers of Octavianus would make a song about it. Above all, her own army, her fleet, the allied kings who were putting their trust in this man, the Romans still to be won to him from his rival!

She turned to the German captain.

"Can you swear your men to keep this to themselves?"

"I and my men will die before we speak," the merce   replied, blushing a bright red. "If desired I will swea them now, by the gods of our own country."

"At your leisure, captain. As for these prisoners, I will be merciful. Those who live are to have this choice: they may die tonight by the sword, or they may go to the galleys with their tongues cut out. Let all the doors of this house be closed, and the street cleared, when we leave. But first take these scoundrels away. I have smelled enough blood and sweat for a little while."

When he saw the southern façade of the palace rising before him in the light of its lanterns, Antony freed himself from the two German soldiers who had been supporting him. He pulled off and threw away the bandage from his head, put on the broad-brimmed hat, squared his shoulders under the cloak that the captain had given him.

"Remember," the Queen remarked in an undertone, "if you tell your Romans about this I'll never speak to you again as long as I live."

"I shall tell them that I caught a loose roof tile on my pate," he muttered.

"Does it still hurt, you frantic infant?"

"I am not whimpering, am I? But it annoys me that, with the best intentions in the world, I've merely exchanged one headache for another."

"Yes, merely a headache, as it happens. But tell me, Marcus, what you think would have befallen me if the Germans hadn't arrived, with you on your back inviting flies into your mouth?"

"Indeed, I'm a most lamentable escort," the culprit acknowledged. "But how in Hades was I to know that there were so many of them? I had kicked in the door, you see: I was in that embarrassment.

"True, at another moment I might simply have passed the time of night with them, telling them I had made a mistake in the house, and asking them to direct me to some imaginary person with a funny name. But you were there watching me, Cleo. What would you really have thought of Antony if he had retreated before six mangy sailors? As it was, I'd have done for them all, and showed you the stuff I'm made of, if I hadn't slipped on something."

"May Aphrodite pity me!" she sighed. "All these years of trying; yet I'll never make you over."

"As if I didn't know already," he assented humbly, "that you are the star of the world, and I the muddy pond in which you try in vain to reflect yourself."

Down the palace steps came running a flood of torch bearers, to light them up. The guard of the night was turning out on the terrace with a rattle. In the vestibule, Mardion, the eunuch—who had made

the Germans follow them after all—showed a sly
look of satisfaction. Quickly leaving a group of
ladies-in-waiting, some Romans, already half-tipsy,
wearing wreaths of roses, came forward to greet
the truants. Smiling and bowing low, they exclaimed:

"Hail to the New Isis and the New Dionysus, returning in triumph after rejoicing their people!"

"Yes," the Queen said dryly, "we have indeed rejoiced them. Excuse me, gentlemen, if I leave you
alone to your own pleasures. I have had a sur-
feit of mine and am off to bed."

She touched Antony's hand, turned on her heel and
moved away, a diminutive figure in the midst of the
lofty hall, which was like the hall of a giant's mausoleum, with its gold-encrusted ceiling far overhead, its
columns springing up as if into a remote and glim-
mering heaven, its wall-niches, as large as town gates,
adorned with colossal statues of the unhappy Ptolemies.

The eunuch followed her noiselessly from apartment to apartment, where the guards came to attention and slaves kept kneeling down.

"Go away, Mardion," she uttered at last. "I shall
not work tonight."

She went on alone more solitary, as it seemed to
her, than in many a long day. Lonelier than when,
as a girl and a fugitive in Syria, with every one
against her except the unknown Cæsar, she had drawn
out of her own character the strength to win from
her enemies this power, this wealth, this splendor,
this hatred of Rome and this undying fame. Her
little feet were sore; weariness dragged at her limbs;
depression stole into her mind. Yet she walked on with
that inimitable grace of hers, buoyant, fresh to the eye,

like a maiden returning from a promenade in a garden. She entered the children's apartment.

They were slumbering in their small beds beside the nurses' couches. She leaned over first one, then another, changing the position of a chubby arm, making a curly head more at ease on its pillow. Then, after standing there for a while, she forced her weary feet to bear her onward.

"Cleopatra is no longer young, no longer young," she breathed to the moving likenesses of herself, reflected on each side in polished marble.

She knew that the brown and yellow slaves of the dressing-room were waiting for her yonder, with their cosmetic boxes and unguent vials, prepared to aid her once more, before her sleep, in the struggle against Time. But they would not be able to draw out, with their flexible fingers, the age that was in her brain, or the disillusionment and uneasiness that were beginning to enervate her spirit like an insidious poison.

She passed a guarded vestibule and entered the ante-chamber of Cæsarion's rooms. An armed slave, who had been dozing on a threshold against a flowery curtain, jumped up, altho the Queen had made no sound.

"Is he asleep?"

"Sound asleep, Magnificence."

So she contented herself with pressing her cheek for a moment against the flowery curtain, as if it had been the cheek of her son Cæsarion, her hope and prayer, her reason, nowadays, for everything.

THE BARN AT GIRALDON'S

By Bernice Brown

Céleste had always been a plain-looking girl and not very bright. It is difficult to tell about some peasants whether they are mentally deficient or driven by their surroundings into an inarticulateness that takes on the nature of hopeless stupidity. Céleste, perhaps, had not been heavily endowed to begin with. But neither had life given her much to lift her above the fields and the beasts that she tended.

She was large-boned and square-browed. Her hands were big, and her feet and her shoulders at seventeen had the muscular development and stoop of a man's. Céleste's schooling had been simple. The parish priest had taught her to read and write and cipher. She could chant off the catechism, tho Père Gaudet doubted at times whether she could identify the separate words. She could make change, slowly but always accurately, her heavy fingers apologetically fumbling the coins.

At an early age she was dismissed from work in the kitchen and dairy. She was both too slow and too unadapted. At fourteen she was working in the fields along with her father, her two brothers and Jacques, the hired laborer. Céleste seemed to belong to the soil as much as the tumbleweed and the earth smell and the ʼow fog of autumn. She was earth-colored too, her brown frock, her brown hands, the brown hair drawn straight away from her low forehead.

Père Gaudet used to look at her at times with pity. And she seemed contented.

"She will never marry," he thought. "True, she would labor well in her husband's vineyard, and his farm would prosper—there's no doubt of that. But even the most hard-headed of our fellows wants more than an extra pair of arms to push a plow."

Indeed, Céleste appeared to miss nothing out of life She was never sullen in her silence. She demanded nothing that was not given her. She went sometimes to the village frolics and sat quiet against the wall, joining only in the great round dances when some village lout, out of jest, put his arm around her waist and dragged her in. These she danced solemnly and clumsily, never noticing she was the butt of jokes heavy with peasant cruelty and coarseness.

"Gee" and "Haw" they called to her for the turns in the dance as though they were shouting to a yoke of oxen. Céleste did as she was bid, simply, like a child. There was something touching in her earnestness, but only Père Gaudet had eyes to see it.

"My good child," he said once, patting her stooped shoulder, "you are a blessing to your old father. I doubt not that you do more work than your brothers."

"Pierre is good with the calves," she said, "and Léon with the garden. But Léon has not the great patience for picking off the potato bugs that is necessary."

Père Gaudet smiled. "And you have, my daughter?"

"Yes," she said, "I have the great patience for everything."

"I have seen the new barn that you have begun," said the priest.

Her eyes brightened.

He looked at her. "Very fine, very prosperous. It will be the largest barn in the canton, I doubt not."

"It will be splendid," she said; "great stalls for the oxen and a fold beneath for the sheep and a great loft above for the hay. It will hold a blessed harvest and wooden tubes to push the hay down to the animals and great rafters as large as trees to hold up the center beam."

Père Gaudet might have laughed, but he had seen the eyes of zealots with that same look, and the eyes of artists. Poor Céleste, and to waste such devotion on a barn!

Jules Giraldon, Céleste's father, was a successful farmer. He owned his land, forty arpents, with a wood lot, a great pasture and a creek that never went dry, even in the hottest August, and broadened out into a pool where the cattle drowsed knee-deep above their reflections. There was a wheat field and a great potato field and a garden of carrots and cabbages.

Jules had got his land from his father and he from his. It had been in the family, in fact, for three long generations. Pierre would inherit it some day. Léon would go into the village into the saddler's trade. As Céleste said, he had not the great patience for farming. Céleste? No one knew.

Perhaps she would stay on after Pierre married and work for him in the fields and eat her bowl of porridge in the chimney corner and grow older and more bent and go on pitching the hay down to the beasts from the loft where the rafters were as great as trees. Perhaps Pierre would not be kind to her. Perhaps Pierre's wife would resent her great clumsiness; perhaps the children would jeer and throw clods of earth at her as she leaned over the potatoes or drove the oxen, barefooted, behind the plow through the wheat field.

But none of this happened, because the war came. They were all at work in the fields when the first bulletin for mobilization was published at the Mairie. Victor Dandet, a neighbor who had gone to town for a harrow, saw it and stopped by at the Giraldons' on his way back.

"Léon, Pierre," he called. They came, startled, to the edge of the field, for even at that distance his face looked strange. "I have seen it. You are called There is war."

"War," they echoed—"with the crops not yet in!"

They stood silent, all four of them, for Jules had joined them.

"Yes," said Dandet, "your names are posted, Léon's and Pierre's and the Cordet boys and all of them."

That night at supper they told Céleste, or rather they didn't tell her. They only talked as tho she knew. They would leave in the morning for Sarle, their mobilization base. They must get their things together now, say good-by. Both boys went off after supper, Léon with the wagon, Pierre on horseback. Each had a girl he must see. Of course the war wouldn't last long. They might be gone only a few weeks. They might never even get any further than Sarle. It must be all a joke. And yet they were still too dumfounded to joke about it.

When they returned that evening Céleste was waiting outside. Pierre came home first. His face was grave. Marie's father had been sure it would be a long war. He had lived through the Franco-Prussian one. Besides, he could read the newspapers, and he knew about the Russians on the front in Siberia. This would be no child's play. Marie had kissed Pierre too in a way that made him feel her lips carried the terror of long separation.

Marie and Pierre were betrothed. It was a casual everyday betrothal, with much of sense and little of romance about it. Now it became a consecration Under the shadow of his going their relationship became a blessed one, something quite above the mundane. For the first time Pierre loved her, and he, in turn, became to her something precious, above value.

Even Céleste was not the lump she had always been For the first time Pierre looked at his sister as a person

"Where are my new boots?" he said.

"I cleaned them; they are on your bureau with your shirts and razor and the new soap and the relic of St Anthony." She put her hand on the bridle of his horse

He started to go indoors, then he stopped.

"I'll put away your horse." She looked up at him and smiled timidly. "When you come back there will be the new barn ready."

Céleste didn't mourn when the boys went, nor did she seem to grieve for them. She had no time to She was up at four now, in the field, gone all day, and at night, when the moon was full, she worked carrying stones to her barn and mixing her mortar. Heaven knew she was strong! She was like nothing human. All the women worked, of course, even Marie, whose father was the richest man in the village. But Céleste worked Sunday after Mass and clear through until evening. Père Gaudet demurred once.

"You must be careful, my daughter," he said. "It is not fit that you should overdo. It is not pleasing even to God. who watches all things."

She met his eyes, amazed. "But I promised God that I would finish."

"Don't be a fool, Céleste," he said. "The dear God asks us only to do our duty. It angers Him when we behave with rashness or with stubbornness."

Céleste only shook her head. "He understands. I have told Him. He has sent me as a sign the clear nights that are like the midday without its spears of heat."

Père Gaudet stopped. What was the use of words? She was more right than he was, more sure of herself.

In spring the British troops came nearer, and an Australian outfit was billeted in the village next but one. They could hear the rumble of artillery carriages now in the distance, and lorries and automobiles had begun to rut the roads in all directions around the farm. Céleste was undisturbed. What was it to her if the war were far or near? There was work to do. She must break up her land, get in her crops, drive her animals to pasture, bring them back at night. It had been a cold, snowy winter, and the work on the barn had progressed very slowly. With the warm, longer days now she would make up for the time lost.

Then came news of Léon. Brief, pathetic. In a month his citation was sent home and a letter from his major. Killed in action. That was all. Marie came over one Sunday to extend her sympathy. Céleste was out at the barn, but Marie went out there. Marie was dressed as she had been at Mass that morning, very pretty in a soft gray piqué with a little bunch of anemones tucked in her belt. She was sorry because of Léon, very sorry. But, after all, it had not been her

man. Pierre was still there. Perhaps the war would
end before Pierre was caught.

"You must not work so hard," said Marie at last.
"Even Père Gaudet says so. You will be an old woman
soon. And you are not yet twenty."

"I am strong."

Marie went away. She was sorry about Léon, but
she was sorry about Céleste too. Still, her heart was
not bowed down as long as Pierre lived, and she had
had a letter from him only yesterday.

In August a boy stopped at the farm to borrow a
wrench with which to fix his motorcycle. He had on
a uniform Céleste had never seen before, and he stood
very straight and tall and handsome. His hat tilted at
a desperate angle, and there was a look in his eyes that
was both furtive and daring.

Céleste fetched him a wrench, and he thanked her
and smiled and joked in abominable French that she
only half understood.

"I'm an Anzac," he said, "and I'm stationed next
door at Marte. We've a big place there, a dump.
Ever see it?"

Céleste shook her head.

"Well, you ought to. Take you over there some
day. It's a great place." He smiled again and looked
at her. No one had ever looked at her that way
before. "Want to go?"

Céleste nodded.

"Next Sunday, then, I'll come by, in a side car. I'm
the major's orderly. It's against the rules, but I can
take you as far as Loche. Then we can walk." Again
he smiled. "Get tired walking?"

This time Céleste smiled. She tired walking! She
even laughed and showed her white teeth.

"You're a great one," he said. "Little cabbage." He laughed too. "That's what the Frogs say. It's a compliment." He gave her back the wrench. "All right. Next Sunday I'll be over."

Céleste could not believe this had happened to her. Next Sunday! After Mass she always changed her clothes and went to work on the barn. Sunday was the day she got most done. Now, to waste a Sunday! To keep on her best clothes all day, her brown alpaca with the white cuffs and collar—it was unheard of.

Perhaps he wouldn't come. Perhaps he was only joking. He was so young and handsome. How could he have noticed her? Perhaps Sunday it would rain. Who could tell? Anything might happen. Céleste crossed herself and went back to the garden. She must finish the last row before sunset.

Sunday came at last, and Céleste went to Mass, as always. She wore her brown dress and bonnet and her black shoes, which she wiped off with her handkerchief before entering the chapel. It was a warm day that bade fair to be hot before noontime. All through Mass Céleste had a hard time fixing her mind on the service. There was a queer tightening in her throat she had never felt before, and her whole body felt lighter. She could not imagine to-day feeling tired, ever feeling tired.

Père Gaudet prayed for the men in danger, for all those in pain or bereavement. Céleste listened, but her heart kept on beating, beating scandalously, for happiness. She was ashamed suddenly. Besides, suppose he shouldn't come?

But she did not change back into her working blouse before dinner, as she usually did. No one noticed. Old Jules seemed to have gone off into a sort of apathy these days, and the rest had never given Céleste a thought one way or the other. After the dishes were done Céleste walked out into the sunshine. It fell warm upon her shoulders like a mantle. There was a smell of honeysuckle in the air, and bugs drowsed in the bushes and above the long grass.

Céleste was happy. She had never noticed nature before. It had always been something to struggle with, something that oppressed one. She had never noticed the song of the cicada except that it meant drought or of the tomtit except that it meant rain. To-day she noticed, for her ears were attuned, listening.

Finally she heard it, the distant splutter of the motorcycle bumping over the rough road. Her hands flew up to her head and brushed smooth her coarse hair. It was the first time she had ever made that gesture. She was glad she had washed carefully the night before and that her linen was clean. She had such a splendid sense of well-being. It might be a sin to be happy, but she was.

"Cheerio," he said. "I didn't expect to find you waitin' like this. You're a great old one now, aren't you?" He put an arm carelessly around her shoulders and kissed her, a rough, undirected kiss that burned on her cheek bone.

"You came."

"Sure, I came." He laughed. "What'd you think I did with my Sundays, anyhow? What do you do?"

"I work."

He laughed.

"I build my barn. Look," she pointed, "you can see it, there beyond the larches. It is beautiful, is it not? It is beautiful, like a church."

He laughed again. "Like a church. You're a great
old one for fair, now." He looked at her. "You
built it?"

She nodded, her eyes glowing like a child's.

"So it's yours too, is it?"

Again she nodded.

"Go on, now. It's your father's or your brother's."

"No," she said. "It is mine."

"Well, well. Come along now." He gave her a push
toward the motorcycle. "Let's get along. Against the
rules, this. But we'll keep off the main road."

She settled herself in the dumpy side car, and he
threw a leg across the bar of the cycle. The thing gave
a great cough and a lurch and spluttered into flight.
Céleste clung hard to the sides, the wind whipping her
face and hair and her breath coming in sharp gasps.

Harry Darrows gave a laugh. "How'd yuh like it,
old girl? Fast enough?"

Céleste smiled and clung fast. She was in the acutest
misery, but she was radiant. "It is of a most terrific
noise," she shrieked.

"Sure," he said. "It's a good old bus." He laughed.
"Afraid?"

She shook her head. He knew she was, tho, and
he put it up as fast as it would go. Silly old thing!
She joggled around worse than the major. How funny
she looked with her head bobbing like that! Well, he'd
give her a little taste of what he could do. "Guess we
won't go over to my place to-day," he yelled. "Too
much goin' on the roads around there. Movin' a lot
of new junk in, you know. Nothin' but an old dump,
anyway. Like this?"

She nodded.

"Want me to go faster?"

She shook her head.

"Don't yuh?" he yelled. "Then here goes. Watch us." He was going already as fast as the motorcycle would travel, but he bent over the bars and stuck out his elbows and pretended that the speed had doubled.

Poor Céleste believed him. She was now not only in terror but also in pain. She was jerked about and buffeted as tho she were astride a wild horse. She was bruised and aching, and she knew the next hillock would catapult her out of the car. And yet she would have suffered torments a thousand times worse than these.

Finally he slowed up, stopped.

"Well, old girl," he said, "had enough, then?"

She smiled and tried to stand up, but she fell back, stiff and dizzy. He threw his arm around her waist and drew her roughly over the side of the car. She clung against him, their bodies heavy and warm together.

"Give us a kiss for that," he said.

Their lips met. It was a long kiss, hard and demanding. Céleste pushed him away from her finally, weak and dizzy.

"You, you," she said.

He caught her arms and drew her to him again, laughing. "When I kiss anybody they stay kissed, I tell you. Eh, old girl?"

Céleste laughed, but she wanted to cry, and she had not cried since childhood. She wanted to cry, and she was afraid, and she was happy. That was what was so hard to understand about all this. It didn't matter somehow, how much he hurt her.

"See," he said, "I brought you a present."

Céleste looked at him.

"Let's set down in the grass over there and I'll show you."

They sat down, and he took from his pocket a handful of chocolates, wrapped in tinfoil, in strange shapes. "They're the major's," he said. "His girl sends 'em to him in a box this big"—he made a sign—"and I'll bet they cost five guineas. The major wouldn't miss these. Open your mouth," he said and he popped a great square into it.

Céleste closed her eyes and started to chew. What a funny taste! The chocolate was bitter, and inside was a funny liquid. He watched her face.

"See," he laughed, "they're filled with cognac, only it costs more. Like 'em, eh?"

She tried to smile. "They're funny," she said.

Harry Darrows ate one. "Not too bad," he said. "Well, here's something else, then." From his other pocket he drew out some broken sticks of candy, white striped with red, the sort children bought in the village. "And I've got this too." It was a locket, cheap and ugly and hung on a chain of blue beads. "I bought this at the store for you yesterday, at a big store. They had a whole lot of them on a table. But this was the only one that had blue beads." He screwed around to watch her. "Like it?"

She looked at him. But after a moment she couldn't see him; she couldn't see anything. What did it matter if he had stolen the locket, slid his hand along when no one was watching? What did it matter if the thing were tarnished and the beads glass? To her the locket was gold and the beads turquoise. It was an emperor's ransom. Overhead the birds sang and the

wind brushed the grasses and the sky was as blue as
the beads of the chain around her neck.

What did it matter if there came to them, even in
their peace, the distant tremble of guns? What did it
matter if she had one brother dead and another in
peril? What did it matter that her father was old and
on her alone devolved the heart-breaking labor of the
farm—that her barn was not finished yet, and she must
have it ready for the harvest? Céleste was not ashamed
of the selfishness of her joy. Youth had come to her,
and spring, and all the more stranglingly because it
was late and the winter had been long.

"Will you ever have to fight, my little one?" she
asked finally.

He shook his head. "Not as long as I'm detailed to
Major Hopkins. He's an old fellow," he went on, "and
they've put him in charge of the dump."

"Dump?" she queried.

"Sure." He laughed. "All the old stuff they can't
throw away and is no good to anybody."

"Oh," she said. Her French thrift understood the
business of salvaging.

"Sure," he said, "blankets and saddles and harness
and guns and rope and wire and automobile tires and
Holy Mother knows what ragtag and bobtail. All out
in the rain together. But we make lists of it, fine lists
on the typewriter. And the major pokes around and
goes over the lists and inspectors come and they never
move it away and it gets rained on some more. What
a piece o' cheese. Here, kiss me."

Then, after a long time, "But it must be of use to
someone." She looked at him gravely. "It could be
sold."

"Sure," he said, "but it isn't. It just rots there."
He yawned. "What the heck do I care? There's no
sense of any of this business, anyway."

That had never occurred to her. "No," she said,
"but the war is here."

The sound of lorries carrying troops up to the front
rumbled into their silence. Her arm tightened around
him. He was safe, and he was hers. Again she wanted
to cry. "It is late," she said. "I have the animals to
tend to."

"Lord," he said, "what a funny old thing you are,
anyway! Forget the animals."

She shook her head. "No, I must go now."

Harry Darrows looked at his watch. It was late,
later than he thought, and he had to report to the
major at six.

"All right, old girl, if you want to be an old killjoy."

Céleste didn't understand him, but they kissed, and
she scrambled into the side car, and again the fearsome
journey started. But this time it was racing not just
for the joy of teasing her, of seeing her head bob and
her hands clutch at the sides of the car. This time
it was because he was late and he was afraid of the
major, who had a very businesslike way of promptness
about him. At the crossroads Darrows stopped.

"Hop out, old girl," he said. "You've got to hoof
it the rest of the way. It wouldn't do to keep old
Fiddlesticks waiting."

Céleste got out as she was ordered.

"Next Sunday," he said. "Here, kiss me."

He left her standing there, powdered with the dust
of his tumultuous departure. Long she stared after
him until he became just a whirlwind of sand against
the line of the horizon. Seven days until another

Sunday. Seven years! And yet Sunday would come at last.

Céleste sat down and took off her shiny shoes. She had ten kilometers to go, and it would not do to run the risk of scratching them. Besides, they hurt her feet. But they were beautiful. Again she polished them off with her handkerchief, blew on them and polished them again. Then she wiped her brow, stood up and started homeward.

All week long Céleste did the work of a regiment, and her muscles sang, even at the close of the day of labor. There seemed born in her an inexhaustible spring of energy. Each morning she woke at four, as wide-awake as tho it were seven. The birds sang outside her window, and a corner of light slanted over the gray wall and touched the face of her birthday saint.

"Good morning, blessed one," she said. "It is a new day and there are only three more days left now." Then she got up and washed in the little basin and combed her hair and put on the sweated blouse and the sabots. Downstairs she drank her coffee and munched her end of bread. Then she gave her orders to old Jacques.

"Finish the cabbage patch this morning. Then the cow shed must be cleaned out. We will soon have enough to fertilize the last end of the wheat field. That is good."

Then came the milking and the driving of the cows out to pasture; then the cultivating in the potato patch; then the snack at noonday. Then the cultivating again, back-breaking work, for the bugs must all be removed by hand from the leaves; then the cattle again and the milking, and supper, and then the new barn.

She was proud of her barn. Next week Jacques
would help her. It would be roofed over by that time,
tight and secure, proof against all the buffets of winter.
When the hay crop was cut she would store it there,
a billowy, fragrant mass. Old Jacques would pitch it
up to her in the loft, and she would scatter it about,
building it up finally into a mountain that would touch
the highest rafters. Oh, Pierre would be proud of her
when he came back. Yes, the barn had been finished.

Sunday came and with it her lover. This time he
brought her some colored post cards and a bridle, in
excellent condition.

Céleste admired all the gifts; the post cards she
turned over and over, wondering at the strange buildings, laughing at the goats harnessed to the carts. Then
she admired the bridle.

"Where did you buy it?" she asked finally. "It is
of excellent leather and well made too. And hardly
at all worn."

"I polished it all up fine," he said, "with the major's
shoe polish. He has more than he can use."

"But the bridle?"

He drew her against him. "I went to Paris for the
bridle."

"Foolish one."

"Sure, or maybe it was Dublin." He laughed again
and pinched her ear.

She was too happy to care that he didn't answer.
After all, what did it matter where he got it? He had
brought it to her, and she loved him.

"Next time," he said, "I'll bring you something very
fine. You have but seven days to wait to see."

He did bring her many things too: a new saddle,

halter, a fine rope, a compass. They laughed a great
deal about the compass.

"That's to keep you from getting lost on the great
farm," he said, "in the cabbage patch."

Then she took him to see her barn. It was empty
yet and smelling sweet of the lumber. Darrows thought
it was very fine.

"It's so big," he said, "it would hold a thousand
saddles, with a few automobile tires thrown in."

Céleste laughed. The idea of anybody's wanting a
thousand saddles or a few automobile tires. But he
was a funny one. He loved to tease her, and she loved
to have him. Indeed, anything he might do would be
perfect. She loved him with complete disregard of
everything except the consciousness of her love.

"What would you say," he said finally, "to lettin' me
put a few things in your hay loft? We—we've got
some things at the dump we'd like to get rid of—that
is, for the present. They'd be out of the rain here, and
nobody'd know anything about it. See?" He stopped.
Her eyes loved him too much to deny him. "What'd
you say to my bringin' them over some dark night
now?"

Céleste stared at him. It was nonsense, but, then,
he had asked it of her. If he had asked for her right
hand, she would not have denied him. Besides, it was
her barn. She had built it. It was hers, beautiful and
solid and fine.

"What about it, old girl?"

"If you want it."

Darrows came in the rain one night in a lorry.
There were two others with him, and they looked very
strange as they moved about in the light of the lantern
she held for them. Céleste didn't like the other two

chaps, but they did exactly as Darrows directed them. Darrows spoke in a harsh, rough voice, and they worked very fast; then they hurried off, Darrows only crushing Céleste once hard against him, his clothes wet and his face wet and the hurt of his lips for a long time afterward against hers.

Next day she went out to look over the place. What strange things they had brought, many in unopened crates that bore a military address! No one had heard the lorry come in or depart. No one came up in the loft yet, for the haying had not started. They would not leave the things there long. He had promised.

But Céleste was uneasy. Nor had she liked the look of his face while he worked there. He was hurried and furtive and the laughter was gone. His kiss too had been different. Not that he had been always gentle, far from that, but this time it had been so hard and so brief and his arms had pushed her away from him afterwards. If they had pushed her in front of the oncoming lorry, she believed, it wouldn't have mattered to him much. And yet she loved him. She belonged to him, and he could do with her now as he would.

There were two more night adventures. The last time old Jacques heard the noise and came out and Céleste had to drive him back, scolding and threatening and bribing him to keep silent.

"In a week we'll move 'em on," Darrows said.

But they didn't. Soon the haying would commence. Soon Pierre would come back for his furlough. It didn't matter. Céleste loved her barn because now it could serve her lover. As long as no harm came to either it was all right. No; as long as nothing happened to her lover, what did anything in the world matter?

But the week passed, and Darrows did not come. Another week limped by. Céleste's longing passed from a dull ache into anxiety. Had anything happened to him? Had he been sent away? Was he in danger? She woke at four still, but with a threatening dread in her heart. She worked as hard as ever, but grimly, glad of the pressing moment because it took her a little way from her anxiety. She must begin the haying soon. That would keep her busy. But where would she store her hay? They had disposed of the old shed, for she had planned to use the new barn. Should she put it in, anyway, and bury all the things Darrows had stored there? Then for two days it rained, and that made the haying impossible, of course. He would surely come before the cutting, or at least she would hear from him.

Two days passed. They cut the field and stacked the hay in great mounds under the sky. The weather had cleared. It would stay fair now for some days, she felt. Meanwhile it was all right to leave the hay out of doors. Old Jacques fidgeted and demanded that the storing be begun, but Céleste put him off. She made excuses, insisted that they repair first the roof of the cow shed, repair the gate to the pasture, start tiling out the slew. Jacques scolded. Had she lost her wits? Now was the time to get the hay safely under shelter. He wasn't so old but that he still knew a thing or two.

Then one night there came a sound at her window. A pebble had been tossed against the pane. Céleste leaped up and looked out. There he stood, a black figure in the moonlight.

"Céleste," he called, "come down."

She wrapped a blanket around her coarse nightdress and, barefoot, fled down the stairs and out the door.

"My dear one!"

He was pacing up and down; he seemed at first scarcely to notice her.

She came close, drew him to her, timidly. He looked down at her.

"I may have to go away. Quick, you know. No warning. Never can tell. Orders." He stopped. "The things there"—he jerked his head toward the barn— "nobody knows about it but you?" His voice was sharp.

"Nobody."

Again he looked at her hard. "Well, nobody must. See? Nobody. They're not there. See? You don't know anything about them."

"No," she answered.

"Understand me?" He seized her shoulders.

"I understand. Nobody knows. Nobody must know." She waited a moment. "Tell me, what is wrong?"

He flung away from her. "Nothing. Only Sappers is a fool. He can't keep his mouth shut. Babbled around all over the place. The old boy got his wind up. Old Fiddlesticks."

"You mean the major?"

He nodded. "Sure, the major. See?"

Again she nodded.

"I've got to go now," he caught her to him. "Good-by old, girl."

A terrible sound came from her lips, like an animal,

like a wild thing, caught and hurt, hurt so that the life blood was gushing out in fountains. It was no word— only a sound, a strangle, a sob, a cry for mercy. Men on the battle field died with that sob sending up a challenge to their Maker, women in childbirth.

Darrows patted her shoulder. He felt uncomfortable, suddenly ashamed. "It's all right," he said, "old girl. I'll come back. I promise."

She stared after him as he ran off into the darkness, stared and stared. It seemed as tho she had been struck to wood.

He would not come back. She knew it. He had gone. That sound of his boots on the gravel was the last she would hear of him; the last she would feel was the clutch of his hands on her shoulders.

Next morning she shouted at old Jacques, who was on his way to finish the cow shed.

"Not there, you fool," she said. "To the haying. Is it not time the hay were put in? What do you think we have the sunshine for? You have indeed no wits about you, you dullard."

Old Jacques stood aghast. Was she crazy? Had he not for days urged the haying? Had she not been the one to send him off on wild-goose chases?

All day they worked in the field, piling the hay on the wagon. Then Céleste mounted the loft and Jacques pitched the hay up to her and she scattered it about, covering, forkful by forkful, all the crates and boxes and bundles, all the blankets and saddles and automobile tires and ropes. There they were hid, every one, under the fragrant, billowy mass of hay. They were safe.

On the way back to the house she met two officers. It was twilight now, but she recognized them, one a major, trim and gray-haired and grizzled, one a captain. They saluted.

"Mademoiselle." It was the major. "We have a favor to request." He stopped. Her straight gaze was disconcerting. "We have reason to believe certain goods belonging to the Australian Expeditionary Force have—found their way to your place here." Why did that girl look at him like that? "We are grieved and distressed, but it has become necessary that a search be made—a thorough search of your house and your barns and your properties. You understand?"

She nodded.

He turned to the captain. "Shall we search the house first?"

The captain made a sign. "I don't think it's necessary. Not the house." He looked down the lane. "You've a fine barn there, a big barn. We will do the barn first." He whistled, and two soldiers appeared from the roadside.

"The barn," he said.

Céleste did not take her eyes from them. Then she spoke, very calmly:

"Sir, it is dark now in the barn. I have just come from there. I will fetch a lantern."

"Good." They were embarrassed at her dignity. "I'm sorry," said the major.

She did not look at him. In a minute she returned from the kitchen, the lantern burning in a yellow flame at her side. "I will direct you," she said.

They followed. She led them through the stalls downstairs where the cattle were kept and the horses, through the room where the harness was and the wagon and the Sunday gig.

"Above is the loft," she said; she stood with one foot on the stairway. "I will lead."

"Let the sergeant go with her," said the major.

The sergeant stamped up after her, his boots heavy on the shallow stairs.

"See," she said. She held the lantern high above her head. The place was a tumbled ocean of grasses.

"Tramp around," called the captain from below stairs. "See there's nothing hid under the hay."

The sergeant took a step forward, when there came a scream from the woman. She had dropped her lantern in the hay, and in her effort to put out the blazing grasses she kept throwing them at the sergeant with her pitchfork.

"Stop!" he yelled. "You're crazy!"

On the roaring pile she kept tossing new fuel. She worked now like a demon. The soldier could not come near her. With her pitchfork she could have kept a regiment at bay. Not for nothing had she worked from early morn till evening. Not for nothing were her arms like iron and her hands as strong as grappling hooks.

"Stop," he yelled; "you're just making it worse Fire," he called, "fire!"

There were voices below, sharp commands, confusion.

"Stop!" he yelled.

He tried to touch her, to pull her away. The smoke was rising now in clouds, and the heat was terrific. He was gasping, blinded. He put up his arms to shield his face from the blaze and lunged toward her. Was she a devil, this woman, that she could stand heat like this, that she could wade into the fire as tho it did not touch her? The whole place was ablaze now, thundering, crashing. He caught her blouse and dragged her back, stumbling.

Dumbly she let him drag her down the stairs outside where the others were waiting, cursing, shouting foolish commands to each other.

"She upset the lantern," said the soldier, "then she just went crazy."

Céleste knew they were carrying her into the house She knew her father was there and old Jacques and that they were patting her and praying. It was an agony to move, it was hard to breathe even; then at last it became peaceful. From a long way off she could hear their voices.

"Her barn," said old Jacques. "She built it, and to think she should be the one to destroy it! The dear God has saved her from knowing that to-morrow morning there will be nothing but the stones out of the earth that she built it of."

"Nothing but the stones that she built it of," Céleste sighed. The major and the captain would come back, but there would be nothing—nothing but the stones she had built it of. She was tired. Now the dear God would let her rest.

A BAL MASQUE

By Alexandre Dumas

I said that I was in to no one; one of my friends
forced admission.

My servant announced Mr. Anthony R——. Behind Joseph's livery I saw the corner of a black redingote[1], it is probable that the wearer of the redingote,
from his side, saw a flap of my dressing gown; impossible to conceal myself.

"Very well! Let him enter," I said out loud. "Let
him go to the devil," I said to myself.

While working it is only the woman you love who
can disturb you with impunity, for she is always at
bottom interested in what you are doing.

I went up to him, therefore, with the half-bored
face of an author interrupted in one of those moments
of sorest self-mistrust, while I found him so pale and
haggard that the first words I addressed to him were
these:

"What is the matter? What has happened to you?"

"Oh! Let me take breath," said he. "I'm going to
tell you all about it, besides, it's a dream perhaps, or
perhaps I am mad."

He threw himself into an armchair, and let his head
drop between his hands.

---

[1] Redingote is a French corruption of the English word "riding
coat" and means generally a long, plain double-breasted street coat.

(Translated by R. W. Howes, 3d; copyright, 1907, by P. F
Collier & Son Co.)

I looked at him in astonishment; his hair was dripping with rain; his shoes, his knees, and the bottom of his trousers were covered with mud. I went to the window; I saw at the door his servant and his cabriolet; I could make nothing out of it all.

He saw my surprize.

"I have been to the cemetery of Père-Lachaise," said he.

"At ten o'clock in the morning?"

"I was there at seven—cursed bal masqué!"

I could not imagine what a bal masqué and Père-Lachaise had to do with one another. I resigned myself, and turning my back to the mantelpiece began to roll a cigaret for him between my fingers with the phlegm and the patience of a Spaniard.

While he was coming to the point I hinted to Anthony that I, for my part, was commonly very susceptible to attentions of that kind.

He made me a sign of thanks, but pushed my hand away.

Finally I bent over to light the cigaret for myself; Anthony stopped me.

"Alexandre," he said to me, "Listen, I beg of you."

"But you have been here already a quarter of an hour and have not told me anything." ,

I got up, placed my cigaret on the mantelpiece and crossed my arms like a man resigned; only I began to believe, as he did, that he was fast becoming mad.

"You remember the ball at the Opéra, where I met you?" he said to me after a moment's silence.

"The last one where there were at least two hundred people?"

"The very same. I left you with the intention of

abandoning myself to one of those varieties of which they spoke to me as being a curiosity even in the midst of our curious times; you wished to dissuade me from going; a fatality drove me on. Oh! you, why did you not see it all, you who have the knack of observation? Why were not Hoffman or Callot there to paint the picture as the fantastic, burlesque thing kept unrolling itself beneath my eyes? Unsatisfied and in melancholy mood I walked away, about to quit the Opéra; I came to a hall that was overflowing and in high spirits: corridors, boxes, parterre. Everything was obstructed. I made a tour of the room; twenty masks called me by name and told me theirs. These were all leaders—aristocrats and merchants—in the undignified disguise of pierrots, of postilions, of merry-andrews, or of fishwives. They were all young people of family, of culture, of talent; and there, forgetful of family, talent, breeding, they were resurrecting in the midst of our sedate and serious times a soirée of the Regency. They had told me about it, and yet I could not have believed it!— I mounted a few steps and leaning against a pillar, half hidden by it, I fixed my eyes on that sea of human beings surging beneath me. Their dominoes, of all colors, their motley costumes, their grotesque disguises formed a spectacle resembling nothing human. The music began to play. Oh, it was then these gargoyle creatures stirred themselves to the sound of that orchestra whose harmony reached me only in the midst of cries, of laughs, of hootings; they hung on to each other by their hands, by their arms, by their necks; a long coil formed itself, beginning with a circular motion, the dancers, men and women, stamping with their feet, made the dust break forth with a noise, the atoms of which were rendered visible by the wan light of the lusters; turning at ever-increasing speed with bizarre postures, with unseemly gestures, with cries full of abandonment; turning always faster and still faster, swaying and swinging like drunken men, yelling like lost women, with more delirium than delight, with more passion than pleasure; resembling a coil of the damned doing infernal penance under the scourge of demons! All this passed beneath my eyes, at my feet. I felt the wind of their whirling past; as they rushed by each one whom I knew flung a word at me that made me blush. All this noise, all this humming, all this coufusion, all this music went on in my brain as well as in the room! I soon came to the point of no longer knowing whether that which I had before my eyes was a dream or reality; I came to the point of asking myself whether it was not I who was mad and they who were sane; I was seized with a weird temptation to throw myself into the midst of this pandemonium, like Faust through the Witches' Sabbath, and I felt that I too, would then have cries, postures, laughs like theirs. Oh! from that to madness there is but one step. I was appalled; I flung myself out of the room, followed even to the street door by shrieks that were like those cries of passion that come out the caverns of the fallow deer.

"I stopped a moment under the portico to collect myself; I did not wish to venture into the street; with such confusion still in my soul I might not be able to find my way; I might, perhaps, be thrown under the wheels of some carriage I had not seen coming. I was as a drunken man might be who begins to recover sufficient reason in his clouded brain to recognize his condition, and who, feeling the will return but not

the power, with fixed eyes and staring, leans motion·
less against some street post or some tree on the public
promenade.

"At that moment a carriage stopped before the door,
a woman alighted or rather shot herself from the door·
way.

"She entered beneath the peristyle, turning her head
from right to the left like one who had lost her way;
she was dressed in a black domino, had her face cov·
ered by a velvet mask. She presented herself at the
door.

" 'Your ticket,' said the door-keeper.

" 'My ticket?' she replied. 'I have none.'

" 'Then get one at the box-office.'

"The domino came back under the peristyle, fumbled
nervously about in all her pockets.

" 'No money!' she cried. 'Ah! this ring—a ticket
of admission for this ring,' she said.

" 'Impossible,' replied the woman who was distribut·
ing the cards; 'we do not make bargains of that kind.'

"And she pushed away the brilliant, which fell to
the ground and rolled to my side.

"The domino remained still without moving, for·
getting the ring, sunk in thought.

"I picked up the ring and handed it to her.

"Through her mask I saw her eyes fixed on mine.

" 'You must help me to get in,' she said to me;
'You must, for pity's sake.'

" 'But I am going out, madame,' I said to her.

" 'Then give me six francs for this ring, and you
will render me a service for which I shall bless you
my life long.'

"I replaced the ring on her finger; I went to the
box-office, I took two tickets. We reentered together

"As we arrived within the corridor I felt that she was tottering. Then with her second hand she made a kind of ring around my arm.

" 'Are you in pain?' I asked her.

" 'No, no, it is nothing,' she replied, 'a dizziness, that is all—'

"She hurried me into the hall.

"We reentered into that giddy Charenton.[2]

"Three times we made the tour, breaking our way with great difficulty through the waves of masks that were hurling themselves one upon the other; she trembling at every unseemly word that came to her ear; I blushing to be seen giving my arm to a woman who would thus put herself in the way of such words; then we returned to the end of the hall.

"She fell upon a sofa. I remained standing in front of her, my hand leaning on the back of her seat.

" 'Oh! this must seem to you very bizarre,' she said, 'but not more so than to me, I swear to you. I have not the slightest idea of all this' (she looked at the ball), 'for even in my dreams I could not imagine such things. But they wrote me, you see, that he would be here with a woman, and what sort of a woman should it be who could come to a place like this?'

"I made a gesture of surprise; she understood.

" 'But I am here, you wish to ask, do you not? Oh! but for me that is another thing: I, I am looking for him; I, I am his wife. As for these people, it is madness and dissipation that drives them hither. But I, I, it is jealousy infernal! I have been everywhere looking for him; I have been all night in

2 Charenton Saint Maurice, the lunatic asylum near Paris, commonly designated as Charenton.

a cemetery; I have been at Gréve[a], on the day of an
execution; and yet, I swear to you, as a young girl I
have never once gone into the street without my
mother; as a wife I have never taken one step out of
doors without being followed by a lackey; and yet
here I am, the same as all these women who are so
familiar with the way; here I am giving my arm to a
man whom I do not know, blushing under my mask
at the opinion he ought to have of me! I know all
this!—Have you ever been jealous, monsieur?'

"'Unhappily,' I replied to her.

"'Then you will forgive me, for you understand.
You know that voice that cries out to you "Do!" as
in the ear of a madame; you have felt that arm that
pushes one into shame and crime, like the arm of fate.
You know that at such moment one is capable of
everything, if one can only get vengeance.'

"I was about to reply; all at once she rose, her eyes
fastened on two dominoes that were passing in front
of us at that moment.

"'Silence!' she said.

"And she hurried me on following in their footsteps.
I was thrown into the middle of an intrigue of which
I understood nothing; I could feel all the threads
vibrating, but could take hold of none of them by the
end; but this poor wife seemed so troubled that she
became interesting. I obeyed like a child, so imperious
is real feeling, and we set ourselves to follow the two
masks, one of which was evidently a man, the other a
woman. They spoke in a low voice; the sounds
reached our ears with difficulty.

[a] The name of a public square in Paris where executions
formerly took place.

" 'It is he!' she murmured; 'it is his voice; yes, yes, that is his figure—'

"The latter of the two dominoes began to laugh.

" 'That is his laugh,' said she; 'it is he, monsieur, it is he! The letter said true, O, mon Dieu, mon Dieu!'

"In the meanwhile the two masks kept on, and we followed them always. They went out of the hall, and we went out after them; they took the stairs leading to the boxes, and we ascended in their footsteps; they did not stop till they came to the boxes in the center; we were like their two shadows. A little closed box was opened; they entered it; the door again closed upon them.

"The poor creature I was supporting on my arm frightened me by her excitement. I could not see her face, but crushed against me as she was, I could feel her heart beating, her body shivering, her limbs trembling. There was something uncanny in the way there came to me such knowledge of unheard-of suffering, the spectacle of which I had before my very eyes, of whose victim I knew nothing, and of the cause of which I was completely ignorant. Nevertheless, for nothing in this world would I have abandoned that woman at such a moment.

"As she saw the two masks enter the box and the box close upon them, she stopped still a moment, motionless, and as if overwhelmed. Then she sprang forward to the door to listen. Placed as she was her slightest movement would betray her presence and ruin her; I dragged her back violently by the arm, I lifted the latch of the adjoining box, I drew her in after me, I lowered the grille and pulled the door to.

"'If you wish to listen,' I said to her, 'at least listen from here.'

"She fell upon one knee and flattened her ear against the partition, and I—I held myself erect on the opposite side, my arms crossed, my head bent and thoughtful.

"All that I had been able to observe of that woman seemed to me to indicate a type of beauty. The lower part of her face, which was not concealed by her mask, was youthful, velvety, and round; her lips were scarlet and delicate; her teeth, which the black velvet mask falling just above them made appear still whiter, were small, separated, and glistened; her hand was one to be modeled, her figure to be held between the fingers; her black hair, silky, escaped in profusion from beneath the hood of her domino, and the foot of a child, that played in and out under her skirt, looked as if it should have trouble in balancing her body, all lithe, all graceful, all airy as it was. Oh, what a marvelous piece of perfection must she be! Oh! he that should hold her in his arms, that should see every faculty of that spirit absorbed in loving him, that should feel the beating of her nervous palpitations, and that should be able to say: 'All of this, all of this, comes of love, of love for me, for me alone among all the millions of men, for me, angel predestined! Oh! that man!—that man!—'

"Such were my thoughts, when all at once I saw that woman rise, turn toward me, and say to me in a voice broken and fierce:

"'Monsieur, I am beautiful, I swear it; I am young, I am but nineteen. Until now I have been white as an angel of the Creation—ah, well—' she threw both arms about my neck, '—ah, well, I am yours—take me!—'

"At the same instant I felt her lips pressed close to mine, and the effect of a bite, rather than that of a kiss, ran shuddering and dismayed through my whole body; over my eyes passed a cloud of flame.

"Ten minutes later I was holding her in my arms, in a swoon, half dead and sobbing.

"Slowly she came to herself; through her mask I made out how haggard were her eyes; I saw the lower part of her pale face, I heard her teeth chatter one upon the other, as in the chill of a fever. I see it all once more.

"She remembered all that taken place, and fell at my feet.

"'If you have any compassion,' she said to me, sobbing, 'any pity, turn away your eyes from me, never seek to know me; let me go and forget me. I will remember for two!'

"At these words she rose again; quickly, like a thought that escapes us, she darted toward the door, opened it, and coming back again, 'Do not follow me, in heaven's name, Monsieur, do not follow me!' she said.

"The door pushed violently open, closed again between her and me, stole her from my sight, like an apparition. I have never seen her more!

"I have never seen her more! And ever since, ever since the six months that have glided by, I have sought her everywhere, at balls, at spectacles, at promenades. Every time I have seen from a distance a woman with lithe figure, with a foot like a child's, with black hair, I have followed her, I have drawn near to her, I have looked into her face, hoping that her blushes would betray her. Nowhere have I found her again, in no place have I seen her again—except at night, except in my dreams! Oh! there, there she reappears! there I feel her, I feel her embraces, her biting caresses so ardent, as if she had something of the devil in her; then the mask has fallen and a face most grotesque appeared to me at times blurred as if veiled in a cloud; sometimes brilliant, as if circled by an aureole; sometimes pale, with a skull white and naked, with eyes vanished from the orbits, with teeth chattering and few. In short, ever since that night, I have ceased to live; burning with mad passion for a woman I do not know, hoping always and always disappointed at my hopes. Jealous without the right to be so, without knowing of whom to be jealous, not daring to avow such madness, and all the time pursued, preyed upon, wasted away, consumed by her."

As he finished these words he tore a letter from his breast.

"Now that I have told you everything," he said to me, "take this letter and read it."

I took the letter and read:

"Have you perhaps forgotten a poor woman who has forgotten nothing and who dies because she can not forget?

"When you receive this letter I shall be no more. Then go to the cemetery of Père-Lachaise, tell the concierge to let you see among the newest graves one that bears on its stone the simple name 'Marie,' and when you are face to face with that grave, fall on your knees and pray."

"Ah, well!" continued Anthony, "I received that letter yesterday, and I went there this morning. The concierge conducted me to the grave, and I remained two hours on my knees there, praying and weeping. Do you understand? She was there, that woman. Her flaming spirit had stolen away; the body consumed by it had bowed, even to breaking, beneath the burden of jealousy and of remorse; she was there, under my feet, and she had lived, and she had died, for me unknown; unknown!—and taking a place in my life as she had taken one in the grave; unknown!—and burying in my heart a corpse, cold and lifeless, as she had buried one in the sepulcher—Oh! Do you know anything to equal it? Do you know any event so appalling? Therefore, now, no more hope. I will see her again never. I would dig up her grave that I might recover, perhaps, some traces wherewithal to reconstruct her face; and I love her always! Do you understand, Alexandre? I love her like a madman, and I would kill myself this instant in order to rejoin her, if she were not to remain unknown to me for eternity, as she was unknown to me in this world."

With these words he snatched the letter from my hands, kissed it over and over again, and began to weep like a little child.

I took him in my arms, and not knowing what to say to him, I wept with him.

RUTH

By Chester P. Crowell

Ruth had just won a medal of some kind awarded by a scientific society. She is a chemist. I do not understand such matters so Tom, her husband, tried to explain them to me during lunch at the club. He was fairly bursting with pride. He is a mechanical engineer and professional inventor, a genius, I am told. It was obvious that I ought to call on Ruth and offer congratulations. I did so and thus happened to see the queer room Tom calls her junk shop. Ruth's father refers to it as the joss house. Ruth and I went to school together.

I fell in love with Ruth at the age of nine and have never quite recovered. She posed as the Goddess of Liberty when her class graduated from high school. Ever since then I have been a bit maudlin on the subject of patriotism. And I do not greatly admire Bartholdi's statue in New York harbor. It is, perhaps, good enough as art, but I have seen the living goddess.

When I announced that I would call Tom said: "I want to hatch a little conspiracy with you. Try to get a peek at that junk shop of her's and then kid her about it."

"Why?" I asked.

"Because," he replied, "if the story ever gets out

it will hurt her professional standing. I wish she
would cut it out."

I was about to ask what this mysterious—and evidently offensive—room contained when Ruth's father
appeared. He is also a chemist, and biologist, something else I know very little about. Tom gave him a
summary of our conversation, concluding with an
appeal for him to join in the request just addressed
to me.

"By all means," he agreed. Then he said: "If
Ruth isn't careful she will be laughed at. Otherwise
I don't mind. There is no great harm in it." His
last sentence was not the truth. Ruth's father is a
generous, tolerant, kindly man. It would be like him
to say such a thing. But he didn't believe it. My
expression must have betrayed something; for a
moment later he added: "The basic principles of ac-
curate thinking are more important than anything
else in the world. Ruth is now a great scientist, but
if she is not careful—" He snapped his fingers. I
cannot adequately describe the effectiveness of that
gesture. It was as tho he had tossed a dead mouse
into a trash container. And all this time I knew nothing about the interior of that sinister room. But
on the following day when I called, Ruth said, very
earnestly: "Listen to me, my first sweetheart. There
is conspiracy in this house and it is directed against
your goddess. It is a very kindly conspiracy as you
will know when I tell you that the villains are my
husband and my father. Finer men never walked this
earth but they do not understand—and I cannot tell
them."

"Why not?" I interrupted.

"Because I am a woman."

"Then how are you to tell me?"

"It comes within the borders of a science you understand. Having heard the facts you can explain them to another man."

"This is interesting," I commented. "Shall I set it down that the learned Doctor Ruth Vaughan says no woman can lead a man into a new field where the scientific laws are strange to him?"

"Yes," she replied, "you may set that down as final. However, with one qualification. A woman may work by indirection and make the man think he is leading her."

"Is there any limitation in the other direction?" I asked, smiling.

"None," was her reply. "Women follow not only against their better judgment but against their positive knowledge; yes, even when they see the ears of a jackass flapping on the guide. They cannot help it." Ruth laughed and so did I, after this speech. "It will not be that way forever," she added. "We women of this generation are paying a terrific price. We are the martyrs. We see things with open eyes, we read, men share their store of facts with us, some women even think, but the ghostly hands of uncounted centuries pluck at our marching feet. Specters sneer at us in the night; they are the jealous wraiths of long departed female ancestors who were beasts of burden."

I lighted a cigaret. Ruth stared at the blazing logs in the fireplace. Finally, after glancing at her wrist watch, she said: "I am going to show you something, a room, a sanctuary, a madhouse—call it what you will and think what you please but do not laugh. We are going to spend an hour there. I want to tell you a story. After that—do as you please—but I think you will understand." She rose and I followed.

A shaft of late afternoon sunshine glistened upon the polished oak door before which Ruth stopped; its glass knob was a flashing jewel until she took hold of it. The door swung open and we looked into blackness pierced here and there by tiny dots of light like the eyes of cats in a dark cellar. Candles. The air was heavy with incense. We entered. She guided me to a chair that I could not see and then found another for herself; at the time it seemed that she merely disappeared. The first object that emerged out of the darkness was an enormous Alaskan totem pole reaching clear to the ceiling. Its malevolent green eyes contemplated me. I felt gooseflesh. Next I discerned a bronze Buddha, more than life size. The air seemed cold. My feet and hands were chilled. I must have been very nervous. Looking around uneasily I discovered some sort of an Egyptian monster with wings, claws, and the mouth of an animal looming just behind and above me. Its dead, stone eyes were like the sockets of a skull.

Very gradually my own eyes adjusted themselves to the dim light and I could see on the floor a geometric design done in fine sands of different colors. It was exotic but had a weird beauty.

"What is that?" I asked, pointing.

"An Indian medicine man in New Mexico sold me those sands," Ruth answered, "also the pattern. It is a pattern that brings good luck." I recollected just in time to keep from laughing. On a low table near me there was a pile of little cards.

"May I smoke?" I asked.

"Certainly," Ruth replied. I lighted a match and

looked at the cards. They were covered with Chinese
characters. Prayer papers, they are called. The
room was filled with queer things.

"This is a very strange place, isn't it?" Ruth asked.
Her voice was actually solemn.

"It is," I agreed, trying to speak casually.

"But not more strange than the world through which
a woman walks," she added. "I am going to tell you
a story." I waited perhaps fifteen seconds but it
seemed a long time.

"When I was a little girl and you used to look at
me so adoringly," she began, "I worshipped my father.
Any daughter would have done so. He was and is a
sort of demi-god, handsome, with the manners of a
prince, marvelous in his chosen profession, sure of
himself, a beautiful character. We worked together in
his laboratory and I did not realize at the time how
much he was teaching me. He has hypnotic power
with a woman. There are men like him. I have
seen others. Such a man can pour his mind into a
woman so that she conceives not only his thoughts
but his thought processes. He did that to me. It
seemed that we would always go on working together;
that chemists and biologists were the only important
humans. All others were aliens; even insects.

"Later on, however, I began to wonder in a vague
sort of way why we should devote our whole lives to
this work. You see, he lived in and for science,
alone. But I dared not ask him such questions. I
was afraid he would vote me a fool. He was so sure
of himself. But day by day I became less sure of
myself. Something was going on in me that I couldn't
express. One night we went to the theater together.
We were inseparable. After that I knew what was

troubling me. I wanted to love and to be loved. For months I lived on romances of my own creation. The fairy prince was always a young scientist, somewhat like my father. Really my father was a wonderful sweetheart, otherwise he could not have held me so long. He used to advise me, sometimes, never to marry but to live in an intellectual world where one could create his own beauty and happiness. He called it the unicellular life.

"And then I met Tom. The whole thing was mysterious and not of this earth. There was I, a romantic girl, dreaming of a handsome young scientist with charming manners—like my father—and in walked Tom! When he said he loved me I wasn't even astonished. I couldn't be certain that he was real— perhaps I had materialized him out of my dreams, somewhat as the fake mystics say they do. But that is only a part of the unreality. He thought I ought to go on with my work; that nothing should interrupt it. We spoke frankly of the possibility of children if we married and voted them out. He had his work to do and I had mine. We would be sweethearts all of our lives. Can you imagine a more perfect lover for the girl I then was? And to make it the more complete my father warmly approved of Tom.

"I soared into love. Why do people say they fall into love? The sensation is precisely opposite. One soars. It is levitation, elevation, one swirls upward dizzily into unimaginable vistas of beauty. I was so happy that the fluttering of my own heart made me gasp.

"Well, we were married. I went on with my work. He went on with his. At that time none of us had much money. The chemical industry didn't amount

to much in this country before the world war. And
Tom had not yet perfected his first invention. He
was on a salary. Father remained at home but Tom
and I lived in a little family hotel. Mother died, you
recall, when I was in high school. The plan was for
Tom and me to save our money so we could move
east and find employment with larger firms.

"One afternoon when I was on my way home with
my pay envelop, twenty-five dollars, I stopped in front
of a shop window to see a display of aluminum kitchen
ware. There was a sauce-pan I coveted. That window
fascinated me. All the things in it seemed beautiful.
There was an ice box. It was wonderful. I wanted all
of those things. A sort of madness seized me. I
stared as I have seen other women stare at jewels.
I cannot tell you how much or in just what way I
loved Tom. I wanted to cook for him. I recalled how
happy my mother was when she cooked. It was her
art. The table was always so beautiful. And her
face—you could almost see the halo. So I bought
that sauce-pan and hid it in my trunk.

"I continued to buy things, little odds and ends.
Eventually my trunk was full. I hid other things in
the closet, in the bureau drawers, everywhere. I became a silly magpie, always looking for a possible
hiding place. And then I began to look at houses.
On Sunday mornings I would read the advertizements
of furniture shops. I did all of this secretly and with
a feeling of guilt. During this time there was no
question in my mind about the course Tom and I
had planned. It was absolutely necessary for us to
find a larger field. I knew I had no right to fritter
away our money. But I could not resist. Sometimes
Tom would find one of my purchases. All of them

were not so cheap as sauce-pans. He knew I was
wasting money, and quite a lot of it. He would say:
'You ought not to do that, Ruth.' But I had got hold
of a habit-forming drug. I was in the grip of a
vice. I was helpless. No one need ever tell me about
the drug habit. I can understand how its victims
suffer. Sometimes I used to wish that Tom would
beat me; chain me to the bed, anything. My will
power was apparently gone; at any rate that is what
I told myself at the time. No woman's will power
is ever gone. As a matter of fact I was indulging
my will. We have that strange faculty of mind which
makes it possible to blot out all obstructing facts.
What we want we march toward. Reason in such
circumstances deters our will so we throw it overboard.
Women can do that easily. Even I who know it so
well that I laugh when I see another woman performing
still do the same thing without a blush. We are strange
creatures—even to ourselves.

"Next I wanted a child. And I felt just as strongly
about a child as about the furnishings for a house. It
seemed to me that I would die—that I would choke
to death if I could not have a baby. I used to visit
an old woman who told fortunes with tea leaves and
ask her if my children would be boys or girls. It
was pleasant to talk this nonsense and listen to her.
Another woman showed me how to read cards. It
is absurd, of course, but I would spread them out and
move them about, muttering a ridiculous incantation.
Finally there were three cards to be picked up and
it was very exciting if my wish card happened to
be among them. I wished for a baby every time.
But months passed and I was disappointed.

"One day I talked with a charming girl who had

recently married. She was a Roman Catholic and informed me quite frankly that she was going to make a novena for a child. Now you know none of us have any religion but immediately I asked that girl if I might go with her. Do you see how queer we are? I didn't believe in a novena but I was none the less on fire with impatience to go with that girl. Well, we went to the church. That was in January. Louise was born the following November. I know nothing about novenas. On that score I have nothing to say. But the child was born just the same.

"Now the facts I have related are important only as they serve to point out to you that shortly after the wedding I was an entirely different sort of person from the girl Tom married. And mark this: I did not will it so. Reason told me that Tom was right. I wanted to help him. This, my friend, is a man's world. To a woman it is all crazy. We women are still peering at it timorously, for there are dragons abroad.

"But I must get on with the story for we are coming to a dragon; and you, being a man, will like that. As soon as I was sure that there would be a baby I rented a house and bought the necessary furniture. Yes, I did that. Poor blind fool that I was, it seemed to me the baby would justify anything. I spent every cent we had. Tom always left the money in my care just as my father had done. Well, it was terrible! I told Tom that I had a surprize for him. That was on a Sunday morning. I had saved it until then so that we might have a whole day together in our new home. It was my intention to tell him, during the day, that we would eventually be parents. I lured him out of the hotel to go for a walk and then led him to the house.

"When I opened the front door he must have guessed what I had done. Naturally I had to produce the key from my purse. Anyway when I walked in he did not follow. I was chirping about this and that when suddenly I realized that he was not in the room. Tom rode out of town that night on a freight train and my little dream world went black. Naturally no one knew where he was. Weeks passed and we did not hear from him. I went home to my father. Nothing seemed more natural than that my father should be very angry with Tom. There are ways of tracing a man; I was afraid my father might find him and do something violent. Therefore I hastened to confess all my offenses, hoping this might reduce his wrath.

"But he wasn't angry. It was perfectly clear to him that I had violated the code of a man's world. I had broken my word and misappropriated money entrusted to my care. He could understand that perfectly. Any man can see it. When I had told him the whole story he said: 'Well, Ruth, you have now tried the wife business and I gather from your account of it that you struck out. Forget it. Let's go to work in the morning. I'm glad to have you back with me again. I've missed you.'

"And do you know what I did? I went to work on the following Monday morning. I told you my father has hypnotic power. He actually made me think this tragedy didn't greatly matter. Good Lord! He was glad to have me at home again. And because he was glad, he made me believe that I must necessarily be happy also. He does such things even now. He seems always to have a strangle hold on life and fate. Nothing rattles him. The world, just as it stands, is apparently comprehensible to him in its last

detail. He looks through the microscope and sees
order. He looks through the window of his study
and sees natural law ruling the universe. Lord, what
a man! There is no mystery in anything. I struck
out. A baseball term. To him my marriage was
merely an experiment. He makes thousands of tests
in the course of a year—he doesn't expect all of them
to succeed. Therefore why should I? And, yet, he
has a heart. He is kindness itself. But it is a man's
heart. I could never have opposed him as I opposed
Tom. And that interests me, too, because it is con-
trary to the usual experience of women, I believe.
More frequently they underestimate wonderful fathers
and later build myths about their husbands. They
can do nothing well at home when they are girls but
they learn soon enough to serve their husbands. In
my case father was the demi-god and Tom the human.

"But I tell this story too slowly. Some months
later Tom wrote a letter to my father. They have
always been the best of friends. He had sold the
patent rights of his first invention and the second was
nearly ready. He was now financially independent.
Would I like to come and live with him? You see
what this means? All was well in his man's world
and now the woman might enter. However, please
don't think I am speaking ill of Tom. He was very
right in all he did for this is a man's world. Tom
must meet its conditions or it will grind him to mince
meat. It will trample and rend his bones. I see all
that clearly enough. Well, I went to him and we have
lived happily ever since. We have a house, as you
see. Every day I cook. Not every meal. But still
I cook for the man I love. And I have my children.
Also my work. You came today to congratulate me

because I have won that award. Well, my dear first sweetheart, I am glad I won the award. I do not underestimate its importance nor the value of chemistry to the human race. But the victory was won in a world that is not quite mine. Therefore it is less important than the fact that Tom loves me and that Louise is beautiful. I try to be vain about my little medal but I am not. In the last analysis I am a chemist because my husband and father are proud of me as such. You could never guess what I was doing when the door bell rang and you were announced. I was standing in front of my mirror, holding the medal in my hand, and I said to myself: 'You female!' For that is what I am. And instead of winning honors in chemistry I wish I could do something to make the way a little easier for women. They are so often stepped upon and cruelly hurt by those who love them. But I have not the remotest idea what to do for them. Their troubles spring up within themselves. As this man's world in which we live opens its doors to receive women in new fields of endeavor it does not at the same time open its heart. Nor do the women always play according to the men's rules. Therefore things are becoming more and more jumbled.

"My little baby, my Louise, is going out into this world very soon. She is engaged to be married. And it frightens me. Therefore I do what all men have done when frightened—I try to turn to God. Chemistry cannot help me now. I do not know what to tell Louise. Does any mother know? Will any mother ever know? My dear friend, I am not religious. I have never been religious. Tom and my father are afraid that some crazy superstition is at work in my mind—that I am becoming a mystic.

I know what they think. I have lived in their man's
world so long that its reasoning is perfectly clear to
me. In chemistry there exists only cause and effect.
One must think in a straight line. Once you begin
looking for miracles in a chemical laboratory it is time
for a straight jacket. But I have two minds. In one
I am a woman; in the other a scientist. The two do not
merge and jumble as they would in a man. He has
only one mind. He cannot think on one plane as a
biologist and on another as a parent. But I can—for
I am a woman.

"If life were organized sanely I could say to the
bridegroom: 'Here is my Louise. She is composed
of so many parts water, so many parts lime, so many
parts sulfur. Therefore she is soluble in this, that
or the other. But I do not know what elements are
in her. Nor can anyone say what elements are in the
young man. And worst of all the elements will not
remain constant. Now stop and consider for a moment what it means to me as a scientist when the
world tells me that a young man and a young woman
are usually soluble in each other but not always. Good
Lord! If that were true in my laboratory I should
go crazy some day and jump out of the window. Do
you wonder that I turn to a silly totem pole? I
care not a jot what anyone thinks so long as these
things comfort me. There was a Japanese boy in the
laboratory where I worked after Tom ran away and he
brought me prayer cards to help me find my husband.
Well, I found him. Once I saw an Indian medicine
man cure his patient with these sands. Probably
it is all foolishness. But who knows? Anyway, I
am just as good a chemist as ever. Surely it does not
hurt me to come here and hope for my daughter's

nappiness. She will soon be sailing a sea that no man has yet charted. So I pray for her.

"We will go now. I make no request, but if you feel that it would be right, perhaps you may have an opportunity to say something to Tom and my father. Something that they will understand. I cannot. When they speak I know they are right, for they are men and I am a woman."

A MOTHER SITS BY THE FIRE

By F. Britten Austin

A clock struck six in thin, silvery notes, somewhere in the darkness of the fitfully illuminated room. Outside, a winter wind rattled the window panes. The sounds made no impression on her consciousness. She sat withdrawn from contact with the world, her eyes fixed on the glowing heart of the fire where she forgot she looked. She forgot where she was, lost the sense of time in a reverie where the past reenacted itself so vividly as to obscure the present. Only, like a part of herself, not needing the verification of a glance, was she conscious of the baby she had rocked to sleep in the cradle by the side of her chair, one hand still drooping pendent toward it. There was a brimming spring of happiness in her heart.

Her thoughts seemed to exteriorize themselves as they played, released from check, in front of her dreamy mind. She looked at them rather than thought them, saw them curiously vivid—flitting glimpses of that quiet, well-ordered household beyond the closed door that for a month she had had to trust to function without her direction—of that moment (how far back it seemed!—not just a month, surely!) when Rudolph's strong arm had supported her up the staircase and she had fought down the fluttering fear of the woman who knows her hour is come—of doctors and nurses—of memories she would not look at, already half-obliterated—of the doctor's face smiling at her from a cloud of pain that had suddenly broken: "You have your boy!"; she would hear his voice as long as she lived—of that inexpressible moment when she had first looked down at the little bundle close against her side, had seen the tiny little strange face, miraculously alive, miraculously owing its life to her! The fire went blurry through inexplicable tears.

There came another vision—Rudolph bending over the beribboned cradle, while she watched him from the bed, in a curious suspense for his first word of comment. He looked to her, spoke, sententious as ever: "Looks all right!" If only he could have been just a tiny bit enthusiastic! He had come across to her, looked in her eyes with that funny look of his. "And now you have got everything in the world you want, old lady!" Had she? She pondered Rudolph.

Were all married couples like that? she wondered. Sometimes they seemed so close together—and then they went poles asunder, unbridged gulfs between them. It was disconcerting. Her heart chilled as she realized how much of a stranger he was sometimes, a stranger she repelled with a little aversion she would not admit to herself. Was it her fault? It had not been like that when the baby was coming. They had been so closely knit that it seemed nothing could sever them. But since—it seemed a stranger who had kissed her that morning, told her she was still young and very, very beautiful, and she had broken from his arms at a murmur from the cradle. He ought to understand! She dismissed the thought of Rudolph, stifled a funny little uneasiness of conscience in herself.

Nothing should interfere with her enjoyment of this

hour. Only too rarely did nurse go out, leave her to undisturbed solitude with that gurgling baby who was her very, very own. She thrilled at the realization. In a few days now the duties of life would begin again for her. But for the moment she was free— free to steep herself in the quiet ecstasy of happy motherhood. He stirred; slept again. She stared into the fire, saw visions.

What would he be, this boy of hers? Clever, of course, like his father—big, strong, handsome—chivalrous to women. She saw men admiring him, giving him that blunt man's friendship that, womanlike, she could never get quite to understand. She saw him overtopping, outshining them all. She imagined careers for him—abandoned them one after another at the moment of success as insufficiently successful. But, whatever he was—however dazzingly distinguished from his fellows, he was still her boy—her boy who came to his mother with loving, grateful eyes, sharing his life with her, as happily proud of her as she was of him.

The bundle in the cradle stirred again. She looked down upon it with wet, shining eyes, slipped a finger into the tight clutch of that tiny hand.

"Oh, Peter, Peter!" She shook her head at him as tho to tease him, her voice a loving murmur. "Do you know why I called you Peter? It was very, very wicked of your wicked mother. I said to myself as I first looked at you, 'Thou art Peter, and on this rock I build my—happiness!' "

. . . .

The last of them had gone. The sudden quietness closed on her. As she turned from the door, a strange woman, in unrelieved black to her throat, moved in the wall mirror, caught her eyes. She stared at her for a moment before self-recognition dawned in her semi-paralyzed mind. She sat down abruptly in the shock of renewed realization, buried her face in her hands. Rudolph!—Rudolph!

Yet she could not weep. After a timeless lapse, where her soul reeled through blackness, her hands pressed convulsively tight upon the eyes that burned against her brain, she raised her head, her fingers hot and dry as she dropped them from her brow. She sat immobile, staring in front of her. The ghosts of hallucinations played over her fevered senses, brain echoes of familiar sounds that startled her with their unreal reality—the quick firm footfall of a man who springs up-stairs, her own name called cheerily from the door. She listened, in spite of herself. Where should have been those familiar tones, there was a void of sound. She would never hear them again.

She would never hear that step—that voice—again. Never again would she see that face which almost limned itself before her eyes and disappeared bafflingly before she could attain visualization. She had seen it for the last time before they carried out that wooden case. Rudolph!—Rudolph! She looked toward his photograph, unable to credit that a human being could disappear so utterly, her brain numbed in the presence of the mystery of death.

The door opened stealthily. A shock of short, fair curls, a pair of wondering blue eyes came cautiously through the gap at a level with the handle. She sat motionless, as tho under a mantle of ice that held her prisoned, staring with dry eyes into a futurity that was blank.

"Mummy!" There was a rush of little feet across

the room. A pair of warm little arms flung themselves impulsively round her neck. A little face came close against hers, cheek against cheek, snuggling to her. "Mummy! You do want me, don't you? Nursie said you didn't!"

She looked at him, and frozen fountains broke up in her. The ice vanished from the arms that clasped him instinctively.

"Peter! Peter boy!" Her voice came with the first sob of that emotion that had been frost-dammed in her. "I want you more—much more—that ever I did!"

"Mummy! *Darling* mummy!" He hugged and kissed her in happy reassurance.

There was a little silence while she held him close. He looked up at her.

"Mummy! When is Daddy going to be better?"

"Peter dear—Daddy is better—but he has gone—gone right away—with the angels." She swallowed.

She had expected a wild, convulsive outburst of grief. He looked at her in grave surprise.

"Daddy won't come back?" he asked.

She shook her head, scarcely able to speak.

"No, dear."

Her emotion touched him to a consolatory indignation.

"Mummy!" He threw himself close against her. "Mummy! I won't go away from you. I won't leave you—ever! Mummy darling, you've still got me!"

A flood came up in her—an immense gratitude. A vow registered itself, sacred for life. She crushed him to her passionately, pressed her lips speechlessly upon his curly head.

He looked up to her, protestingly.

"Mummy!—you're crying on me!"

She smiled at him.

* * * * * * * *

She looked out of the window of the little house in the half-built suburban road. A receding motor car swung round the corner, disappeared. She was trembling. The man's voice, pleasantly masculine in its persuasive appeal, still rang in her ears. She found herself looking at a memory of his strong face, his sympathetic eyes. How they had lit up when she had come into the room whither the little maidservant had shown him! And she had never suspected—Geoffrey Dane, Rudolph's friend!—his executor who for these seven long years had so loyally watched over her little capital without a hint that he was more than a friend to her! He was suddenly different.

Something stirred in the depths of her. She almost yielded to the impulse to look in the mirror, to see whether she was still as young and good-looking as, smiling at her self-deprecation, he had said she was. Could she be happy with him? The answer was an instinctive affirmative. She contemplated the strangeness of it; fitted, tentatively, the new name to herself —Mrs. Dane.

"I shall hope while you think it over," he said, as he departed. Yet she had given him little grounds for hope. What had withheld her? Rudolph? Rudolph was shadowy in her memory, needed a glance at his photograph to be questioned with any certitude. No reproach for disloyalty looked at her from the frame. He would probably have counselled her to accept. She turned again to the window, looked for Peter, already overdue from afternoon school.

Peter! That was the touchstone. Not for herself, but for Peter, she must decide. For her the world held only one reality—that twelve-year-old boy whose mere step outside the door made her heart beat faster. Other existences were but shadows, of significance only in so far as they ministered to him. He was a good boy, she told herself, even if he was a little wild. She was glad he was not precociously clever—those precocious boys never did anything when they grew up. There was nothing soft about him. Even while she winced under it, she admired the masterfulness of his spirit. No—that was not he coming round the corner. She wished he wouldn't be so late. One read of so many accidents!

Peter! . . . What would Peter say? More important, how would such a change affect Peter? Geoffrey Dane's words echoed in her, "I'll treat him as my own son." He was certainly a very wealthy man. But there might be later children of his own. . . . It wasn't safe to count on money like that. Besides, anyway, Peter would have Rudolph's money. She had to pinch to keep the capital intact, but it was and would be intact for him. Money could not determine this problem.

There was another thing. It had been lurking in the back of her mind. She pulled it out now, bravely, and looked at it. "In any case, the boy ought to go away to school, you know."

Geoffrey Dane had said it kindly enough, but the words had rung an alarm bell in her heart. Did he mean to separate them? . . . Part her from the boy to slip into his place? A blind antagonism had leaped up in her. He was apparently quite disinterested, however; concerned only with the boy's welfare. "It's not good for him to be brought up by a woman, particularly one who loves him perhaps too much!"

He had smiled at her. She could not love him too much—that was absurd!—but there was a truth in the first clause that would already have been familiar had she allowed herself to admit it. Peter needed discipline—a man's authority. But to send him away to the unknown hazards of a school!

The view from the window ceased to exist as she pondered the problem. She thrilled with a sudden solution. If—if she accepted, she could make a compromise. She would marry Geoffrey Dane on condition that she kept her boy! With a man to hold him in hand, he need not go to boarding school. If he was firm, Geoffrey Dane was justice itself, and always kind. It was the ideal influence. Peter never dared to be rude to her when Geoffrey Dane was present. She saw, suddenly, those sympathetic eyes looking at her as no man's eyes had looked at her since Rudolph died—and thrilled queerly with something that was more than gratitude. She slid off the burden of a responsibility that had grown too heavy for her—surrendered her tired self, in anticipation, to his arms. With him, life would be easy, happy. She smiled, unconsciously, as she had not smiled for years.

There he was! . . . Peter came round the corner, whistling jauntily, swinging his satchel, flinging it after a cat that fled from him. She hastened to warn the maid to prepare his tea.

She was in the dining room when he entered—he hated to see her looking out for him. He knew that she frowned at his muddy boots but affected a superb indifference.

"You are late, dear," she said, as she kissed him.

He slipped from her embrace, dropped himself to a seat at the table.

"I was playing with some other chaps," he said, in a tone which indicated this was the limit of concession toward apology.

The meal commenced. She watched him as he ate, hungrily. She must tell him. But how? A nervous flutter within her almost inhibited speech. She made the effort.

"Mr. Dane has been here this afternoon, Peter," she said, trying to keep her voice normal.

He did not look up from the jam to which he helped himself.

"That chap seems always to be loafing round here lately." His tone was that gruff ungraciousness which he knew hurt her. "Any one would think he was after you, Mother."

She was silent. He looked up, disconcertingly suspicious eyes on her.

"I say, Mother, that's not what he's after, is it?" he said sharply. "I don't want any rotten stepfather!" She could not answer. She bit her lip, her eyes filling with tears.

The sight of them touched the better nature in him. He jumped up from his chair, came round to her impulsively, put his arms around her neck.

"Sorry, Mother." What a big understanding boy he was! "But you don't surely mean you want to marry Mr. Dane?"

She looked up at him through her tears.

"Peter—Peter dear—I—oh, I don't know!"

He embraced her tightly, squeezed her resolution from her as he caressed her.

"Mother, don't be silly—you don't want to marry any one. What on earth for? We don't want any one else. I've got you—and you've got me. And that's all we want, isn't it?—just each other?"

She had a vision of a little curly-haired boy running to her in her grief, heard a childish voice: "Mummy darling, I won't leave you—ever!" A self-reproach came up in her; she smothered it for one last effort to be sure.

"Peter darling, don't you like Mr. Dane?"

"I can't stick him!" The answer was passionate in its vehemence.

It slammed a gate in her. She looked like a prisoner into those unrelenting young eyes above her.

"All right, Peter dear, I won't marry—any one."

"Promise?"

"I promise."

He contemplated her for a moment.

"There's no need to look so miserable about it, Mother. Can't you smile?"

She smiled.

He resumed his seat, reached for the bread-and butter.

Another thought flashed into her, almost made her heart stop. Her compromise had failed!

She steadied her voice before she spoke.

"Peter dear, would you like to go to boarding school?"

His face lit up.

"Rath—er!"

. . . .

He was so big, so authoritative, that a fear of him mingled with her love. As he sat there, puffing irritably at his pipe, she could not reconcile him with the thought that once she had held him in her lap. His angry words still rang in her ears.

"I know you'd like to make a milk sop of me, Mother—but it can't be done!"

Was she wrong to try and curb him, to try and guide him? For all the twenty-two years of which he was so conscious, he was still only a boy. She despaired at his resentment of her feeble effort to use an unaccustomed authority. Had she done right in sending him away from her to boarding school, to the University?

The first, yes; but the second——? Mr. Dane had disapproved of it, had prophesied the extravagances, the depletions of her capital that it made her tremble to remember. He had been ashamed to bring his college friends to the little house. Behind a closed door in her memory were long hours of lonely tears. She had no resentment. She gloried in these sacrifices if they had been for his good. But had they been? A cold fear gripped her heart as she watched his jaunty assumption of a man of the world.

She was frightened for him. Surely a University education ought to have facilitated his start in life! It was true he had not specialized, had no particular qualifications. But he ought to have made powerful friends. Her mind turned abruptly from this subject. She knew none of Peter's friends, imagined them only with dread from the hints that escaped him. If only he would not be so big in his ideas, would be content to make a beginning with whatever work he could find! At the same time she sympathized with the humiliation of his pride she herself had counselled. A secret resentment sharpened itself in her. Considering all things, Mr. Dane might well have offered him more than an ordinary junior clerkship in his office.

He looked at her. It was as if he read her thought.

"And if you think I'm going to quill-drive in old Dane's office, you're mistaken, Mother!"

She found her voice.

"What do you propose to do, then, Peter?"

He shrugged his shoulders.

"Oh, something will turn up! I'm sure to get a chance—a real chance—presently. That's, if you don't spoil it!"

She blanched under the stab.

"Peter dear—do I spoil your chances for you?"

It was as tho she bared her breast for him.

He shifted his glance uncomfortably, shielded himself under bad temper.

"You're spoiling this one. Just because of the miserable money!"

Mr. Dane's warning voice sounded in her ear like that of a watching spirit.

"It would mean selling more stock, Peter," she said, quietly.

He glared at her.

"Oh, of course, Mother—if you're always going to throw that old business in my face! You know perfectly well a man couldn't live in my college on my allowance!"

His eyes dropped under her steady look.

"Have I ever reminded you, Peter?" she said, gently. "I don't want to remember it. But I do want to understand what sort of a chance this is, if it is a chance."

"I don't say it's a chance now, but it's pretty sure to lead to one. A fellow like Jack Freeman hears of all sorts of good things—and I should be a fool to refuse this chance of a trip with him."

Her eyes probed him.

"Jack Freeman's father is a millionaire, Peter, I know—but is your friend likely to hear of good things for you in Paris?"

He flushed.

"Well, I don't say this is a business trip, Mother— it's just a jolly party. It gives me a chance to see a bit of the world, and it keeps me in the social set of useful people like Jack Freeman, Herman Morris, and the others."

"Herman Morris is going too?" Her tone was sharp with alarm.

"Yes." Obviously, he could have bitten off his tongue for this unlucky slip, but she noted, with a sudden gratitude, that still he could not lie to her. All through his boyhood, this had been her touchstone.

"Peter, after that chorus-girl case—would you like to introduce Herman Morris to your mother?"

She saw color heighten round his eyes.

"I'm not responsible for other people's morals, Mother—neither are you!"

A sudden, dreadful suspicion flashed into her. She rose, without knowing it, from her chair.

"Peter, tell me the truth. Will there be *only* men in this party to Paris?"

He did not answer.

She felt as tho she were going to faint. The room went round her in the instant before she mastered herself, found the support of a chair back.

"Peter—Peter——" Speech failed her.

He also rose, flamed out with that sudden anger of his.

"Look here, Mother—you don't seem to realize that I am a grown man. You can't treat me any longer like a child!"

Her eyes never left his face.

"And—and you would break into our capital for—for that?"

"I tell you—I'm not a boy. I'm a man—and I'm going to run my own life as I like! I know what I'm doing."

She summoned up all her courage, fought off the dizziness.

"And if I refuse—refuse to give you this money?"

He shrugged his shoulders.

"There are people who will lend it to me. It is better that you should understand, Mother. I am out of leading strings."

She clutched at one last hope.

"And if I ask you—beg of you—not to go?"

His answer was coldly brutal.

"I am sorry, Mother, but I have already promised."

"You are going—in any case?"

"In any case. I am of age. I claim my liberty, Mother."

She took a deep, trembling breath, difficult in the anguish that seemed like a cramp upon her heart, looked at this stranger—this stranger who was her Peter—in a despair that had no words. For this moment of repudiation she had sacrificed her entire life. The mockery of it smote her. She craved to fall dead, and the mercy was withheld. Peter!—her child Peter had gone like a dream from which one wakes. With an inarticulate cry, she went, seeing nothing, out of the room.

It was her bedroom to which she went like an automaton, obeying a blind instinct to be alone with her hurt. She fumbled with one hand out along the bed—and then suddenly she went down on her knees, her face between her hands. She prayed. She prayed as in all her life she had never prayed before. She had given him all this earthly existence of hers—what more could she give him? The thought flashed into her.

"O God, do with my soul as Thou wilt, but save him!"

Prayer ceased in her, but still she knelt with hands

over her face. Thought awoke suddenly, moved with an unexperienced swiftness and lucidity, leaping from an echo of his words still audible in her. He was a grown man! He was no longer a child. She had trusted him insufficiently—had thought to keep him in those leading strings he resented. A sudden resolve formed itself in her. She would trust him to the extreme of completeness! If she could not thus trust him, life were better ended for her. He claimed to be a man—she would give him his chance to prove it.

She rose to her feet, went to the writing desk in the corner of her room, sat down to it, took a sheet of paper and wrote.

"DEAR MR. DANE:

"*Will you please take this as authority to transfer to Peter all the securities you hold for me? I feel that now he is of man's age he should undertake a man's responsibility——*"

She looked round sharply in the sudden, instinctive knowledge of a presence at her back. It was Peter, looking over her shoulder.

"*—I have implicit trust in him.*" Her pen flew over the paper. She signed her name. Then she turned to Peter, handed him the letter speechlessly, trying to keep her hand still. He pushed it back.

"No, Mother," he said. She stared at him. There was a new tone in his voice. "I've had enough of your money." He spoke evidently with an effort, overcame a shamefacedness for which she loved him. "I want to tell you something. I've been thinking—and I've decided to go into Mr. Dane's office if he'll have me."

She sprang to her feet, was held, a little thing, in his big strong arms.

"Peter!"

"And, Mother"—he looked down into her eyes, checked, boyishly diffident of the words that meant so much to her—"I've not played the game to you, the best little mother in the world. Forgive me for making you unhappy."

"Peter! Peter darling!" she said, the tears streaming down her face, "it's the happiest moment of my life!"

. . . .

She smiled happily as, duster in hand, she went over the little house, the last touch given. It was a picture of domestic neatness, fresh and pretty with its new curtains against the sun. She wondered what Peter would say when he saw it; imagined herself in the hug of his arms, held there for the good-humored, affectionate reproach, "Mother, you work too hard!"

But he would be pleased. She was innocently excited at the surprize it would be for him. She had been wise to persuade him to go away alone for that month. He deserved a real holiday, free from the constraint her presence inevitably laid on him. He had had a hard time at the office. He was an important man there, now. Mr. Dane was pleased with him, had hinted, on one of those rare occasions when she saw her old friend, at a possible partnership in the future. Her mind leaped back years to a dreadful evening when Peter had hesitated at what she now saw to have been crossroads. She could scarcely identify that rebellious boy with the steady-eyed young man who had kissed her good-by. Eight years! He had made good from the start.

She thrilled with pride in him, reverted to that possible partnership. That would mean more money— Peter would probably want a larger, more fashionable house. She looked affectionately at the little home about her, imagined removal from it with regret. So much of her life had been passed there and, looking back, it seemed a happy life. She would be well satisfied to live there all her years—with Peter.

With Peter—but suppose (she forced herself to admit it as an academic possibility against the instinctive revolt of her mind) suppose Peter married! She saw herself fleeing as into the wilderness. She could not live alone in that house haunted by all their happy days together.

She banished the unworthy thought. Of course, she would be glad if he found a wife—*a good* wife. She stopped and contemplated, under pretext of dusting it, the photograph of him in her bedroom. Perhaps it would never happen. He was still her boy, bless him! the boy who had kept his childish promise had never left her. He had told her once that she was the only woman in the world who meant anything to him. She kissed the glass over his dear face.

There was his key in the lock! She hid the duster, glanced to see if she was tidy for him. What would he say to the clean, new-pin aspect of the house, to the new curtains? She could scarcely wait in anticipation of his surprize, of his first words of praise. She heard the maid tell him she was upstairs, heard his quick tread as he leaped up the staircase. He burst into the room, curiously boyish, his face all smiles.

"Hallo, Mother!"

"Peter dear!" She was in his arms. "You have enjoyed yourself?"

"Heaps!" He looked down at her. "Little Mother, I've something to show you downstairs."

A present, perhaps? Dear boy! She smiled at him.

"I had something to show you, too—upstairs and down, Peter." He looked puzzled. "Don't you notice anything?"

He glanced around him, shook his head.

"No. It all looks just the same." He saw disappointment in her face. "What is it, Mother? Sorry I'm dense!"

"Never mind, dear." She would let him discover for himself; it was only a pleasure deferred. One couldn't expect a man to notice domestic things at once.

"Well, come downstairs, then. I've got a surprize for you."

She let herself be led, with his arms around her, to the staircase; descended to the turn of the stairs. She stopped suddenly as tho a sword had gone through her. Standing in the hall was a girl, at first glance young and pretty under her summer hat.

She turned to him. "Peter!" But Peter had already leaped down the stairs, was leading the girl toward her. She forced herself to continue her descent. It was as tho the earth quaked and opened.

Peter was speaking.

"Forgive me for not writing to you about it, Mother. I wanted it to be a great surprize for you." He radiated a happiness that could see nothing beyond itself. "This is Ruth. I want you to love her—for she has promised to be my wife!"

She looked at the girl's face, met a pair of soft brown eyes.

"Mrs. Harcourt,"—the girl's voice was sympathetic, on a note that disarmed antagonism—"I told Peter he ought to have written to you." She called him Peter already! "Can you forgive me?"

Peter threw his arms round both of them, pulled them together. He laughed boyishly.

"Forgive? Nonsense! What has Mother to forgive? We're all going to be happy together—the three of us—happier than we've been in our lives, aren't we, Mother?"

She found herself holding the girl's hand as she looked into those brown eyes for discovery of the real woman behind that pretty face. Peter's happiness depended on that unknown. Suddenly she bent forward, took her in her arms with a kiss that sanctioned.

"Be good to him, dear," she said.

Peter looked down at her wet eyes, his enthusiasm dashed a little.

"You're pleased, Mother, aren't you?"

She achieved a heroic smile to reassure him.

"Yes, dear."

She led the girl into the drawing room, left them on the pretext of ordering the tea. Peter followed her out.

"You *are* pleased, Mother, aren't you?" He held her shoulders with his big strong hands as his eyes questioned her. "You'll love her when you know her. Don't think you're losing me. You'll often come and stay with us when we're married—and it'll be like old times again."

She turned a mute face up to him for his kiss.

"Go back to her, dear," she managed to say.

She invented pretexts to linger in that kitchen. Not for some minutes could she nerve herself for the ordeal of seeing them together—and then, suddenly, she could not stay away.

She went along to the drawing room. The door was half open. Peter's voice, a strange new tone in it, arrested her on the threshold. He held his affianced in his arms, looking up to him as he looked down to her.

"There's never been any real thing in my life till now, dearest," he said, as he bent down for the meeting of their lips.

On his face was a look his mother had never seen

She crept away into the next room, pretty with the new curtains, sank into a chair, sobbed suddenly as tho her heart would break.

. . . .

Her thoughts ran on. It seemed a long way back now, that pretty little house where Peter had grown up from babydom to manhood. It was lonely in this diminutive apartment whither she had removed the little furniture she had not given Peter for his home. He rarely visited her. Weeks passed without his seeing her while she sat and listened for that sharp ring at the bell which should announce his presence. She did not blame him. He worked hard at the office, and after business Ruth, of course, liked to have him. They almost never came together. Ruth pointed her temporary relinquishment by allowing him to come alone when he did come.

It was very lonely, and as she sat she wondered whether it had all been worth while. She looked back along a vista of sacrifice—of sacrifices of which Peter knew nothing, or had long ago forgotten. All her own life she had immolated for him, and at the end he thought (it was right that he should, of course!) only of another woman. Had she married Geoffrey Dane all those years ago—she remembered Peter's petulant, childish jealousy to which she had weakly surrendered —she might have been sitting now by a companionable fireside, and Peter, married probably in any case, would not have been more lost to her than he was. Tears of self-pity came into her eyes. There was a pointless irony in life, she thought.

A resentment stirred in her. They lived selfish lives, Peter and Ruth, without a child to cement their home. It was Ruth's fault, of course (pleasure-loving little thing!). If she could have a little grandchild to prattle round her! She almost hated Ruth for withholding it.

○   ○   •   •   •   •   •   •

Seven o'clock struck in thin, silvery notes from somewhere in the darkness. The fire had gone down. The winter wind rattled at the window panes. She bestirred herself, put on another log, switched on the light which revealed the dreary solitude of her room.

There was a sharp ring at the outer bell. Peter! Her heart leaped. She almost ran to the door, opened it. It was Peter but—she noted it with a little stab of disappointment—Ruth was with him.

Peter smiled at her, the affectionate old Peter!

"Ruth has something to tell you, Mother," he said as he kissed her after she had closed the door behind them.

The pretty young wife nodded brightly to her, her face somehow more sympathetic than usual. The two women went into the bedroom for the younger to remove her hat and suddenly the daughter-in-law bent and whispered in her ear.

The old lady gave a start of joy.

"Oh, my dear, my dear!" she cried, throwing her arms about her and kissing her in a sudden annihilation of all hostility. "I'm so glad! I'm glad for you. A woman can't know what happiness is"—she smiled in an ecstasy of transfigured memory—"until she is a mother."